THRONE OF MAGIC

HEIRESS OF MAGIC TRILOGY: BOOK 3

H. D. GORDON

For my family.

SURAH

Chaos ran unchecked through the streets.

Stacks of black smoke rose into the air, flames burning through the buildings below them.

Alarms sounded, many having been set off when the surge of magic returned to their world. The cries of mothers, children, and men alike could be heard even from where Surah Stormsong sat looking down at the madness below, high upon the balcony of her father's castle.

Her castle.

It was no longer her father's. It was *her* castle now. She wasn't sure she would ever get used to that.

And, really, if things continued in the trend they seemed to have adopted, she might not have to get used to it. She was smart enough to know when the foundation of things was being threatened. If Black Heart and the crazy Fae Queen had their way, a new regime was already on its way in.

Surah could feel his presence behind her even before his enormous head rested upon her shoulder, the soft fur there tickling her neck.

"There will be no change in regime, love," Samson told her, his deep voice sounding only in her mind.

Surah answered aloud, but found she did not recognize the sound of her own voice. It was as if something essential had been lost. She supposed it had.

"I am the last of the Stormsong line," she said, voice inflectionless. "Not another soul walking this earth shares the same blood as mine."

Samson moved around to the front of her, blocking the worst of the view below from her sight with his large, black-and-blue striped body. His amber cat eyes met the violet of hers and held firm.

"Yes," he agreed. *"You are the last of the Stormsong line, and rightful heir to the throne. You are the daughter of kings and scholars, the blood of the highest men. You have suffered, my dear heart, and lost more than most could stand. On your shoulders rests the fate of your people, a weight too much for most to bear. You are not most. You are Queen Surah Stormsong, and that is your city down there, and your people tearing it apart."*

Samson paused, licking her hand with his warm, rough tongue and nuzzling his head against the thick velvet of her cloak.

"So tell me, my queen," he continued, *"what do you intend to do about it?"*

Surah's head lifted, and the broken pieces of her heart seemed to shiver in her chest—not quite beating again, but warmed by the faith of her best friend. Yes, she had lost her family, her father, the faith of her people... and Charlie.

But she was indeed Queen Surah Stormsong, first of her name and rightful heir to the Sorcerer's throne, and whether they liked it or not, those were *her* people down there.

Surah stood, her chin lifting and shoulders squaring, and released a deep breath, thanking her giant tiger with a rub behind the ears, which Samson accepted happily.

"I'm going to get control of my kingdom," she said. "And then I'm going to lay my father to rest... After that, I suppose I have a Sorcerer and a Fae Queen to attend to."

"And what about Charlie Redmine? What are you going to do about him?"

Surah sighed and shook her head. If she spoke on that matter, she was afraid she just might cry. And there was no time for that. There was no room for weakness. War was upon them, and war called for warriors.

Samson's mouth opened wide in a yawn, and he stretched his lean body, running his tongue out over his face. He knew her well enough to know when not to push something.

"First things first, then", he told her, *"we need to pay the council a visit. We don't know what Theodine Gray has told them, and the death of both your father and your uncle will soon spread. We don't want the council members even entertaining unseating you. "*

Surah nodded, grateful for the change in subject and happy to feel something through the numbness that had befallen her, even if it was just a burning hatred for her late uncle, Gregory Brightstar, Head of the Royal Council.

Her heart wrenched when she thought about how she'd found her traitorous uncle standing over her father's dead body, and how she had taken her own daggers to her uncle for his treachery.

It had been righteous, the killing of Gregory Brightstar, but righteous or no, a king and the head of his council were now dead, and Gods only knew what Theodine Gray and the council members were planning on doing about it.

Everyone who shared her blood had died within this legacy, and she would be damned if they would take it from her.

"Let's go put some people in their places, Sam," she said.

The giant cat's mouth twitched in a way that Surah knew was his feline version of a smirk.

"I thought you'd never ask."

2

———

SURAH

*S*ure enough, they were holding a meeting without her.

Surah's violet eyes narrowed as the doors to the council chambers swung open with a flick of her wrist.

It felt good to have the magic back. For that, at least, she was thankful.

But she would not forget that the death of her father was the price paid for its return. And that those who had caused its disappearance in the first place needed to be dealt with.

Surah walked smoothly over to the head of the long, wooden table in the center of the room, Samson trailing at her side. A thick silence had fallen over the gathered, and all eyes swiveled her way.

Another flick of her wrist and the chair where her father had once presided over these meetings slid out from the table. The scrape it made against the hardwood floor was the only sound in the room.

Everyone present—including a very alert Theodine Gray, whom Surah did not fail to notice had taken her uncle's previously held seat—seemed to be holding their breath.

Surah met their eyes in turn and took a seat, the look on her face somehow both inscrutable and challenging.

Theo spoke first. "My lady," he said, "should you not be resting? You've been thro—"

Surah held up a hand, cutting him off. Something in her violet gaze had him shutting his mouth. "You will address me by my proper title, Hunter Gray—as your queen," she said, pausing to meet the gazes of everyone in the room. She was met with slightly wide eyes and silence. "And as queen, I'm not pleased to find my council meeting without me."

"It's true, then?" said Lord Nightborn, Head of the Treasury. "King Syrian is dead?"

Surah's voice was inflectionless as she spoke. "My father was murdered by Gregory Brightstar," she said. "And for his treachery, Lord Brightstar has paid his debt."

There were gasps all around, save for Theo, who was watching Surah very closely. He seemed to come to some kind of decision, giving a nod of agreement.

"I can confirm this," Theo said. "I was witness."

Surah hid her surprise at Theo's backing, thinking that maybe bringing things to order in her court would not be as difficult as she'd anticipated, but when Theo spoke next, her heart sank down in her chest and settled somewhere on the cold floor.

"Lord Brightstar met justice, but we mustn't forget the root of his treachery," Theo said. "There are those who oppose the kingdom, and who seek to see a new face upon the throne."

Surah did not miss the veiled challenge in Theo's eyes as he said this. Her jaw clenched, but her tone registered as even.

"And they've *got* a new face for their throne, Lord Gray," she said. She looked to the rest of the council, five members in all now, with the loss of her uncle—one from each of the six royal families. "I need to know that I have your loyalty," she told them. "If I've got opposition, tell me now, or accept me as your queen."

There was a moment of silence where Surah was sure time stopped along with the beating of her heart.

Then, slowly, one by one, the council members began to rise from the table. Now Surah's heart felt as though it was jammed up in her throat.

She realized she was holding her breath when each member took to their knees, kneeling before her.

Lady Nightborn and Lord Lancer—the mother of Merin Nightborn and the father of Cynthian Lancer, both of whom had been murdered by Black Heart when this whole mess had started—were the last to kneel.

Surah found she could breathe again when they, too, finally bent knee, though she did not miss the fact that they were merely following suit, and were obviously more than reluctant.

An enormous weight settled down on her shoulders as she recalled that beyond the stone walls of the castle, her kingdom was in a state of emergency.

"Please, rise," she said, and waited as the council members reclaimed their seats.

Again, it was Theo who spoke first. "We are at war," he said, opening the floodgates.

"You don't say," Lady Nightborn muttered.

"We can't afford a war," chimed Lord Goldday.

"We've been at war since my daughter was murdered," thundered Lord Lancer.

"The Fae are the ones we've got to deal with first," Theo said. "The Fae Queen has clearly aligned herself with Black Heart."

"Why would that mad fairy do such a thing? What could she want?" asked Lady Rain.

Lord Lancer scoffed. "Territory and power, of course. It's what the races have always gone to war over."

Lady Nightborn, who had only been listening since her first utterance, spoke out above the voices now. "Is anyone going to address the elephant standing in the middle of this table, or not?"

Silence fell once more, and Surah's shoulders tightened a fraction as Lady Nightborn turned toward her.

Lady Nightborn began, "I'm very sorry for the loss of your father, our king. Syrian was a great man, a man who truly believed in doing what was best for the people. I believe he passed that trait on to you, and I've loved you like family since you were a little girl."

Surah said nothing to this, only waited.

Lady Nightborn placed her hands on the table, leaning forward. "But what is your involvement with Black Heart's brother?" she asked. Her eyes scanned the rest of the party. "Does no one else find it suspicious that Lord Brightstar publicly accused her of treason, and now he has died at her hands?"

The first thing that popped into Surah's head to say was that she could see to it that her uncle wasn't the *only* one who died by her hands, but she bit this response back.

Threats rarely made good solutions in such situations, and she reminded herself that Lady Nightborn was a grieving mother. Grief was something Surah could more than relate to.

Samson's deep voice sounded in her head. He'd been so silent thus far she'd nearly forgotten he was there.

"*Grieving or no,*" he told her, "*remember there are places these people need to be put back into.*"

The enormous cat took to his feet, moving around to the back of Lady Nightborn's chair, making her shift uncomfortably.

Surah had to suppress a smile. Maybe she would hold off on threats, but she made no promises of her Great Tiger. He needed only to be near for one to feel the pressure.

"I'll ask once more," Surah began, meeting Lady Nightborn's eyes, "and then we'll be done with this... If there is anyone who doesn't wish to call me Queen, leave this room and don't return."

Lady Nightborn let out a small huff, but said nothing. Neither did anyone else present.

Surah nodded. "Good, then as such I will not be questioned on my personal affairs," she said. She turned to Theo, eager to be done with the subject of Charlie Redmine. "Hunter Gray, have all available hands on border patrol. We can't afford to have the Fae entering our Territory again."

"The magic protecting the Territory is back in place, my queen," Theo said. "Do you not think they would be of more use here in the city, protecting the castle and controlling the citizens?"

Surah shook her head. "We can't leave the rest of the kingdom unprotected. That's what Black Heart wants. He wants to show the common people that when it comes down to it, we don't care about their safety as much as ours, that we think our lives have more value than theirs."

There was a moment of silence where none of the royals spoke the two words that popped to the forefront of their minds. Surah could practically read them on their foreheads: *We do.*

For the first time, she wondered if Black Heart did not have a point in his madness. If her own council felt far superior to those they were supposed to serve, how could they be expected to do anything but put their own interests first?

"You are queen now," Samson told her. *"You may rebuild this world in any manner you see fit."*

"A queen is nothing if not the champion of her people," she replied silently.

"Then champion away."

"Extra Hunters are to be sent to every border station," Surah said, her tone allowing for no argument. She stood from the table, her chair sliding back with a loud scrape. Samson took to his feet as well, towering over those seated and making them shift uneasily in their seats.

"May I ask where you're going, my queen?" said Theo.

Surah's violet eyes were hard enough to make a lesser man shiver, but Head Hunter Theodine Gray was not a lesser man.

"Since I'm now queen, a new Keeper must be named, and there's also a city to be tamed. Do you have any more questions, Hunter Gray?"

The way he looked at her seemed to convey so much, and in the silent space between them, she could practically read the thoughts in his head. She wished she could take that last part back, because Theo had asked for her hand in marriage, and she had not given him an answer.

He had seen her and Charlie kiss, and had not spoken to her about the matter yet, either. He'd taken her side both publicly and before the council just now. He'd held her in his arms as she'd cried over her father's still-fresh body. Then, he'd taken her to her room and left her be until she'd just entered the council chambers.

Of course he had questions. Tons of questions, and for the first time ever, she thought that Theo just might deserve answers.

But he said nothing to this, and this only made her feel worse. She could practically feel Samson rolling his eyes beside her, but before she could stop herself, she spoke.

"Hunter Gray," she said, "Would you assist me in restoring order to the city?"

Surprise sparked behind Theo's eyes, but he only nodded, standing from his chair. When he approached her, she slipped her arm through his, giving him a smile that was not completely forced.

"Careful now, love," Sam told her. *"Let's not be brash."*

Surah ignored this, wondering why she had never noticed

how handsome Theo was when he smiled, and why he didn't do it more often.

"I would be honored to assist you," Theo said, and Surah couldn't tell if it was her grief, her fear, or her heartbreak, but there was a small part of her that wanted very much to believe him.

The rest of her was somewhere else completely. The rest of her was with the man who had somehow captured her heart and still refused to let go despite all the stars in the universe being crossed against them.

Black Heart wouldn't kill his brother for taking her side… Would he?

This was all it took for her to realize the answers to her questions. She could deny it to others all she wanted, but she could not lie to herself. She loved Charlie Redmine like the sun loved the day and the moon loved the night."

"Oh, Charlie," she thought. *"What am I supposed to do now?*

Of course, it was Samson who answered her.

"The best you can, my love," the giant cat told her. *"That's all anyone ever can do."*

3

———

CHARLIE

*H*e awoke to the bell-like giggling of children, his eyes peeling open slowly and reluctantly, as if the lids weighed ninety pounds.

Sitting up took considerable effort, but he was jolted into awareness when his vision cleared and he saw multiple sets of strange eyes staring back at him.

Charlie's head whipped around, taking in his surroundings. He was in some sort of cage made of thick and thorny green vines. The ground on which he sat was covered in velvety leaves as soft as bird feathers. The air smelled green, like summer rain and healthy vegetation. There was even a slightly sweet taste to it, as though invisible sugar hung in the atmosphere.

Enormous trees unlike any Charlie had ever seen towered around him, the canopies above made up of soft pastels, as if the leaves were composed of cotton candy. Morning light was just beginning to filter through the trees, a golden hue coloring the places it touched.

There were several Fae children surrounding him, their wide, slanted eyes blinking with mischief.

I'm in the Fae Forest, Charlie realized. Then amended: *I'm being held captive in the Fae Forest.*

"Good morning, little brother," said an unmistakable voice behind him.

The Fae children scattered, disappearing into the forest as if they could melt into the trees.

Charlie twisted around and met the eyes of his older brother, Michael—or as he was more commonly known, Black Heart. He hated the feeling that stirred in his chest when he looked at him. Charlie had to crane his neck all the way back as Michael stared down at him, because the cage he was in was not tall enough for him to stand up.

"What is this?" Charlie asked, gesturing to the thorny vines that surrounded him. He was helpless to keep the sharpness out of his voice. "What am I doing here, Michael?"

As always, Michael was indifferent in the eye of the storm, Charlie clearly paying the price for his brother's messes, as he seemed fated to continue doing.

"This is the Fae Forest," Michael answered. "And you're sitting in a cage on the floor of it."

Charlie's jaw clenched, making his brother smile. "I guess you figured that part out," Michael continued, hiking his dark cloak up and crouching down so that he and Charlie were eye-level. "In short, you're here because I just haven't the heart to kill you."

Charlie shook his head, eyes narrowed. "You haven't a heart at all, brother," he said.

This made the darkness that so filled Michael rear up behind his eyes, which were the same blue-green as Charlie's.

"How can you say that to me?" he snapped. "Tristell wants to kill you, and she's right that I should. You've done nothing but try to sabotage me every step of the way, and have scoffed at every lifeline I've tried to throw you."

Charlie stared at Michael in disbelief. All of a sudden, his anger bubbled up like hot liquid and spilled over.

"I hate you," he said.

There was a flash of a moment where Michael looked genuinely hurt.

Then, it was gone, overshadowed by the dark presence that had locked onto his soul, the one named Black Heart. He studied Charlie for a moment through the green confines of his cage, his face unreadable.

"Careful, Charlie-boy," Black Heart said. He looked at where Charlie's hands were still gripping the thorny vines, and a humorless half smile pulled up his lips. "You're bleeding. Those are Faevian Vines. They hate being touched by anything but Fae-born, so I'd keep my hands off them if I were you."

With that, Black Heart stood, staring down at his brother for a long moment without an ounce of pity behind his eyes. He turned on his heel and strode off into the forest, his dark cloak rippling behind him.

Charlie let out a defeated breath, peeling his grip free of the vines he'd been holding, the holes the thorns had made stinging like the devil now that he was not too distracted to notice. Looking down at his bloody hands, his heart felt as heavy as a boulder in his chest.

Time passed, and he could do nothing but let it. His cage was as unbreakable as he was sure his brother and that crazy Fae Queen knew it to be, and his heart was weary.

After an undeterminable amount of time, the Fae children returned to stare at Charlie, their slanted eyes looking in at him, chattering amongst each other in the strange language they had. They slunk out of the vegetation and trees the way the shadows slink out of the night.

Charlie could hardly see them, his mind with the woman he had fallen in love with despite his best efforts against it. The woman who had shown him mercy when he was but a boy. The woman from whom his brother was trying to steal a kingdom.

I may never see her again, he thought, and was crushed under a sadness that felt as heavy as a mountain.

Charlie closed his eyes and breathed. There was nothing else to be done. One way or another, it would all be over soon.

That much, he could feel in his bones.

And he was very much right.

4

SURAH

Theo held his peace until they were alone, for which Surah was grateful.

Of course, they weren't *entirely* alone; Samson sat near, his huge head resting on his paws, looking uninterested despite the fact that both Surah and Hunter Gray knew they had the cat's apt attention.

They were standing in the portal room, getting ready to go into town and attempt to bring order to things, when Theo pulled her to a gentle stop. Surah's heart skipped a beat, but her face only showed mild curiosity, as if the fate of their people did not depend on the choices they made here.

Theo stared at her for a moment, his silver eyes somehow deeper than Surah had ever seen them. She expected him to remind her of his marriage proposal, or to bring up Charlie and demand an explanation of their relationship.

Or perhaps to mention her uncle and her father, and the circumstances that had led them to this point in time. She would have been less surprised if he would have started with a demand of vindication, but Theodine Gray did none of these things.

Instead, he took her gloved hands into his and kneeled before her, bowing his head in fealty. Reaching into his cloak, he removed her father's piece of White Stone. It swung on the silver chain that held it, glowing in a translucent way that reflected the magic it held.

Surah kept her eyes from narrowing, and managed to keep most of the accusation out of her voice as well.

"Why do you have my father's White Stone, Hunter Gray?" she asked.

Theo raised his head, his face open and seemingly earnest. He remained on bended knee before her.

"I removed it from your father's body, for safe keeping." He bowed his head once more. "I'm giving it to you now as your Head Hunter, my queen. I pledge to you my sword, my magic, and my loyalty. I would be honored to serve you, if you will have me."

Surah stood in shocked silence, waiting for Sam to chime in, but the cat said nothing, only looked on with an amused glimmer in his amber eyes. Surah found she had to swallow before she could speak.

In truth, other than her tiger, she had no idea who she could trust. She knew only that she was traveling in murky waters, and she needed to tread carefully.

It was always easier to catch flies with honey, and keeping ones suspected enemies close wasn't a bad idea, either. Also, if she were being one hundred percent honest, a piece of her wanted to be able to trust Theodine Gray.

Somehow—probably during those awful moments following her father's death—when Theo had held her while she'd cried tears that seemed would never cease, Surah's heart had softened toward the Head Hunter.

That didn't mean she had any intention of marrying him, or even that she trusted or liked him… It just meant that her heart had… softened.

Now her tiger spoke up. *"Battered hearts are usually tender, my love,"* Samson told her, his deep voice a welcome presence in her mind.

Surah nodded, releasing a slow breath. "I'm honored to have you by my side, Lord Gray," she said, and found only as she said it that it was not a lie. He'd taken her father's White Stone, yes, but he'd given it to her now. That certainly counted for something.

This made the Head Hunter's face light up in a smile, and Surah caught a glimpse of the attractiveness that made Theodine Gray so popular among most ladies. He took her hands again as he found his feet, looking down at her from his taller height.

"To the city?" he asked.

Surah nodded, resting her hand atop Samson's back for comfort.

"To the city," she agreed.

* * *

Surah, Theo and Sam landed in a back alley near Zadira Square, where the kingdom-wide meeting had been held just the other day.

The jump was not jarring, as all three travelers were seasoned at moving by portal, but the abrupt change in atmosphere was enough to make all three take pause.

The sounds of the chaos were not muffled out here as they were within the castle walls, and the blaring of alarms and yelling voices, the crashes of breaking glass, and the somewhat thick smell of panic and adrenaline filled the air.

People ran by the mouth of the alley in which Surah and her companions stood. Some of them were swinging their cloaks over their heads, while others had wrapped fabric around the bottom halves of their faces to conceal their identities as they did unspeakable things.

Surah took a deep breath, her stomach twisting a bit as she took in the slightly apprehensive look on Theo's face. There had not been riots in Zadira since just after the war, and the Hunters were not completely sure of how to deal with things, especially since some of them were no doubt questioning their loyalties as well, after the whole spectacle in the town square yesterday.

"They're acting like humans," Theo said, a small twist to his lips as he said that last word.

Surah pulled the hood of her cloak over her head and walked to the end of the alley, peering out at the madness taking place.

Across the way a barbershop was on fire, and the bakery neighboring it had its front window smashed in. Looters were streaming in and out through the wreckage.

She turned back to face Theo and Samson. The latter held utterly still, his tail and head tucked low, no doubt on edge with all the commotion.

Surah removed her hood and reached into her cloak, taking out her father's piece of White Stone—the piece meant to be held by the ruler of Sorcerer Territory, the largest and most powerful piece of White Stone wielded by anyone in all the land —and placed the chain that held it around her neck, tucking it beneath her cloak, where it glowed warmly against her chest.

A surge of energy ran through her, a serving of hope that had been lost to her only moments ago. The same way that the Black Stone could affect the one holding it in a negative, dark way, the White Stone had the equal but opposite effect.

There was much to be done, and the road that led the way was littered with shattered glass, rusty nails, empty promises, and more than likely, broken hearts.

But she would see it through to the end, and would do her

best to maintain her morals while she was at it. She was pretty sure that was all anyone could ever do.

Perhaps the White Stone had had an effect on Theo as well, because Surah sensed something changed in him that she just couldn't put her finger on.

Coming to a decision at last, she removed her late sister's piece of White Stone. Meeting his eyes and searching them, Surah handed it over to Theodine Gray.

"You start at the east end of the city," she said, "and I'll start at the west."

Theo nodded, turning to go, but Surah stopped him by placing her hand on his arm.

"Yes, my queen?"

"I don't want anyone to get hurt, Hunter Gray," she said.

He was silent a moment before answering. "Nor do I," he said, in a way that made her want to believe him.

But they both knew Charlie Redmine was an exception to that statement, and at some point, this divide between them would force its way closed.

5

SURAH

"*A*re you sure it was wise to give him that piece of *White Stone?*" Samson asked, as soon as Theo had teleported out of sight. *"Doesn't the Head Hunter already have a piece?"*

"Yes," Surah replied silently. *"The Head Hunter does have a piece, but the one I gave him is more powerful, and sending him into this fray without it could be dangerous."*

Sam was silent a moment, considering. *"What I wonder is whether or not giving it to him is dangerous for everyone else."*

Surah didn't disagree, but she was grasping at straws here. *"I need allies, Sam. The kingdom is turning on itself. I don't know what you want me to say."*

"Sorry, love. I've got more on my mind than any one cat would like."

For not the first time in the past couple days—ever since he'd returned from the jungles of his homeland while rescuing her from Black Heart, in fact—Surah felt that there was something Sam might not be telling her.

And if he was worried about it, that meant it was something big. She'd been so busy fretting about her own mess that she hadn't paused to ask him about how he'd found her in that cave, or about what he'd had *to do* to find her in that cave.

"*Sam, is there something bothering you that I don't know about?*"

The tiger licked her hand, then nudged her back toward the open end of the alley.

"*You've got enough troubles on your mind. Let's settle this mess. Then we'll have time to discuss things.*"

Surah wasn't sure she liked the sound of that, but Sam was right; now was not the time or the place. She wrapped her fingers around the stone at her neck, nodded to her tiger, took a deep breath, and stepped out of the alleyway and onto the street.

The view here was even worse. People were running around like maniacs, smashing and breaking things for what seemed like just the hell of it. Theo had not been wrong when he'd said they were behaving like humans, and Surah's first instinct was to grab them all up by their collars and knock them upside their heads.

At first, everyone was so caught up in what they were doing that no one even noticed their queen standing on the street, watching their shameful ways. The first one to take notice of her was a woman with flaming red hair. When she saw Surah, she fell to her knees before her.

"Oh, please, your majesty," the woman with the red hair cried, tears streaming down her cheeks and cutting paths in the black soot there. She gestured back at the bakery, which was just beginning to catch fire along with the barbershop beside it. "Help me save my shop. It's all I have," the woman pleaded.

Surah was more than happy to oblige. With a flick of her fingers, she extinguished the fire, striding over to the building as she did so.

Inside the broken storefront windows, rough-looking Sorcerers were grabbing at anything of value, and smashing everything else. An ugly grin lit up the face of one of the larger men as he took sight of Surah.

"Look what we got here, gentlemen," the man sneered. "It's the traitorous princess."

Surah's face was free of emotion. She had to tilt her head back to do it, but she met the big man's eyes and shook her head once. Her voice registered soft and even when she spoke.

"I'm afraid you're mistaken," she said. "I am your queen."

The man spat at the floor of the bakery, making the other two men that were with him smirk.

"You ain't no queen of mine," he said, but the last word came out a touch choked, and he took a few stumbling steps back.

Surah did not have to turn around to know that Samson had stepped up behind her.

After that, the men nearly tripped over themselves trying to get out of the building. Samson lunged at the big one who had spoken out of turn to Surah, making the coward nearly fall flat on his face and squeal like a pig as he scurried away.

Surah could not help a smile at Samson's antics, though she raised an amused eyebrow at him.

"What?" he asked. *"I was just inviting him to pick on someone his own size."*

"Sam, no one is your own size," she replied with a laugh.

She took a deep breath to steady herself. She was going to use a lot of magic today, and it would take its toll on her. Her hands flew through the air, spells pouring rapidly from her lips as she used her magic to set the bakery to rights.

It only took a few minutes to repair and reset everything, but by the time Surah was done, a sweat had broken out over her brow.

"There," she said, nodding at her work.

The ginger-haired woman came in through the now-fixed front door of her shop, her eyes wide and still filled with tears. Once again, she fell to her knees before Surah. It was something

Surah would never get used to, nor enjoy, but she accepted the gesture graciously.

The woman grabbed Surah's gloved hand and kissed it what seemed like a million times. "Oh, thank you so much, my queen," the woman said. "Thank you so much!"

Surah took the hold of the woman's hands and pulled her to her feet. She rolled her wrist and summoned a handkerchief that was the same shade of red as the woman's hair. It appeared in her hand like the magic it was. Surah gently swiped away the woman's tears with it.

"What's your name, my lady?" Surah asked.

The woman looked so startled at the question that she had to swallow twice before she could get the words out.

"Gertrude Baker, my queen," she said, holding out the sides of her skirt in a curtsy.

Surah nodded, her face soft and lovely despite the turmoil turning within her.

"It's a pleasure to meet you, Gertrude," Surah said. "It was an honor to help you, and I want you to know that the accusations against me are false, and as your queen, I will protect you from whatever comes next."

The hope and faith that passed behind Gertrude Baker's eyes then was enough to make Surah's breath catch in her throat.

"Does that mean King Syrian has passed on, then?" she asked.

Surah swallowed hard, wondering how many times she was going to be asked that question on this day that was shaping up to be endless.

Each time it was asked, the scene of her father's death came back to the forefront of her mind, the pain tightened its rough grip around her heart.

She nodded, because she did not trust herself to speak. At this, her tiger's deep voice spoke up in her head.

"Sometimes it's beneficial to show a little vulnerability among

those whose loyalty you seek, my love. If they think you incapable of suffering, they surely believe you cannot relate to their lives."

"My entire existence is made of suffering, Sam."

"I know... but so is that of everyone else. It is the one thing all two-legs seem to have in common."

"How'd you get so smart?"

"I'm a cat. I was born that way."

A single tear escaped Surah's eye, and Gertrude took her gloved hands once more and squeezed them tight. The pain Surah felt was reflected in the gaze of the other woman, whom Surah had never met, and whom likely had never met her father, either.

Gertrude Baker hesitated only a moment before pulling Surah into a tight hug, the motherly, warm smell of the older woman somehow comforting. Surah had not felt the likes of it in years.

"I'm very sorry to hear that, your majesty," Gertrude told her.

Surah let the woman hold her for a moment before pulling back and giving a genuine smile.

"Thank you," she said. "I'm going to set things to rights, but until then, close up your shop and lay low, and tell your neighbors to do the same, please."

Gertrude Baker nodded, and Surah turned to go, opening the bakery door manually in an effort to conserve magic. Samson slipped out first, but before Surah could do the same, Gertrude called out to her.

"Your majesty?"

Surah turned back to face her, eyebrows raised.

"I believe you," said Gertrude. "You're going to make a wonderful queen, and the Sorcerer people are lucky to have you."

With a small smile, Surah nodded, thanking the kind woman before slipping back out onto the chaotic street with her tiger.

Samson stood with his tail tucked low, his ears swiveling and amber eyes sweeping.

"And that is how you win back a kingdom," he told her.

"It's not really the winning it over I'm worried about, Sam. It's the keeping it."

Sam fell into stride beside his mistress as she strolled down the street, her hands freezing wrongdoers in their tracks with magic and fixing broken things one by one.

The Great Tiger was more than enough incentive for the people to take notice of their queen, and to fall to their knees as she passed by, some of them looking ashamed, others shocked, and others still, angry.

"One step at a time, dear one," Sam said.

6

SURAH

It took several draining hours, shared tears, and a whole lot of magic, but by the time the sun began to sink behind the buildings in Zadira, order had been restored.

Surah had hugged and cried and reassured more people than she could ever remember doing in one day in all her long life.

The loss of King Syrian really did have an impact on the people. As word of his death spread, sadness seemed to grow thicker in the air, and by nightfall, a sort of eerie silence had fallen over the place.

The mourning was evident on the faces of everyone she met, the sympathy and commemoration enough to choke Surah up to a point that was nearly overwhelming. It was both heart wrenching and incredible to see how much her father had meant to so many.

Stranger after stranger told her stories of encounters with him, of how he had impacted their lives or helped them in some way, and Surah could only hope that at the end of her life, people would say things half as wonderful.

She was biting back yawns, exhaustion weighing heavy on her, listening to yet another tale involving her father. The banker who was telling her was on the portly side, with side-burns that were as wide and hairy as the rest of him.

"I wouldn't be what I am today if not for King Syrian's mercy," the banker said, plucking a stray thread from his fine cloak and pushing up the spectacles atop his nose.

He launched into a story that Surah had heard a similar version of all day. The banker had found himself is some sort of trouble, and while her father had no other agenda, no obligation to help, help he did.

In a matter of hours, her respect for him as a king grew beyond a measure she had anticipated. And her love for him as a father kept hold on her heart.

She was just about to thank the banker for his kind words and condolences when a commotion near the road that led into the city grabbed her attention. A woman was screaming for help in a tone of voice that Surah recognized instantly. It was the kind of cry one makes when they've just lost someone they love.

Her fractured heart sank down in her chest, skipping beats as it did so. She quickly thanked the banker, jumping atop Samson's back as the Great Tiger crouched so that she could do so.

Portaling to the commotion would have been quicker, but Surah had used enough magic today to knock out the strongest of users, and her tiger knew this.

She rode atop his back, gripping the black and blue fur around his neck for balance and hopping down with a nearly feline-like grace when they reached the crying woman.

The small crowd of people gathered parted to let her pass, and Surah had to lock her knees so that they didn't give out beneath her when she got a look at what all the fuss was about.

A young woman was sitting on the ground in the middle of the dirt road leading into Zadira. Her mousy brown hair was disheveled and stuck to her dirty forehead with sweat.

Her eyes, the same brown as her hair, were red and filled

with tears, and exhaustion and grief colored her features the way the dark paints the night.

And on the young woman's lap, lying atop her tan gingham dress was the body of a lifeless child—a little boy who could be no older than six. The boy's eyes were closed, his chest still, his face void of the light that only life can carry.

Surah crouched before the woman, her own violet eyes filling with tears over the loss of a life so young, so innocent to the horrors of their world.

When the young woman looked up and met her eyes, Surah couldn't help but cringe under the fiery hate emanating from them. She found she could not breathe, either, could only wait until the young woman spoke.

She half expected a lashing, but after several seconds of silence, the woman's shoulders slumped in a way that suggested being crushed under the weight of the universe, and her voice came out low and choked. It was a voice Surah could relate to more than she wished she could, the voice of someone who has been consumed with loss.

"They killed my baby," the young woman told her. "They killed my little Kai." She stroked the lost child's hair, wrenching Surah's heart with every beat. "They burned the whole town… the houses, the fields… all of it… gone." She screamed her next words, jolting the crowd collectively that had formed around them. *"They killed my baby!"* she screamed, the high-pitched, broken sound of her words scraping across Surah's soul.

She took the woman by the shoulders, wary of being slapped or blamed for this, which Surah was sure she would ponder later, but the woman only looked at her as if she were lost, as if she'd stumbled into someone else's nightmare, and only wanted to return home.

"*Who* killed him?" Surah asked, her voice low and soft, as gentle as she could manage.

She supposed she knew the answer, but a part of her needed

to hear it. Once she heard it, she felt as though whatever she did next, no matter how brutal it may be to her enemies, it was justified.

"Those fucking *fairies!*" shouted the young woman. Her voice fell to a whisper again, her brown eyes turning back to the lost child in her arms. "They killed my little Kai."

It took effort on Surah's part to ignore the murmur that ran through the gathered crowd, which seemed to be thickening by the moment. She concentrated on the woman before her, pulling her into an embrace that she half expected to be rejected, the child between them. But the young woman fell into her arms like a child herself, sobbing into the expensive fabric of Surah's cloak.

Samson stood silently close by, huge head and tail held low, keeping a careful eye over the unfolding situation.

Something settled deep in Surah's chest, like a heavy stone shifting place in her soul, and she knew that after today, there could be no avoiding it.

War was coming, and it was going to do what wars did—tear apart families and break hearts.

She stroked the young woman's hair, whispering gentle words. Eventually, she got the young mother to release her dear child, and had the gravediggers come and take the body away, preparing it on the royal dime.

The tears in her violet eyes now could not have been stopped even with all the composure training in the world, and when Surah spoke, it was the voice of a queen that came out of her.

"Your Kai will be set to sea with my father, my lady, if you will allow it," Surah said.

The young woman could only nod, and Surah lifted her chin with her fingers so that she could look in her eyes as she said her next words.

"And I'm going to kill the Fae Queen and everyone who

follows her. I'm going to make them pay for Kai's death. You have my word."

The grieving young mother gripped Surah's hands hard enough to hurt. "That won't bring him back," she said, before allowing herself to be led off by some of the other Sorceresses who'd gathered.

Surah had used her magic to send a message to all of the innkeepers whose hotels she had just repaired, telling them to let anyone who needed a place to stay to do so on the royal tab. She felt it was the least she could do.

She watched the woman go, her words playing and replaying on a loop in her head.

That won't bring him back.

No, it would not bring the little boy back, and it would not bring her father back for that matter, either.

But it would make Surah feel a lot better to spill some Fae blood, and that was just what she intended to do.

7

———

SURAH

*M*ore people began streaming back into the city, having returned to their homes in the various towns and cities dotting the Sorcerer Territory to find that their houses had been burned, and those they'd left behind had been killed.

Others still had been injured and killed during the attack at Zadira Square, where Surah's uncle had accused her of treason in front of a good portion of the kingdom's citizens.

Surah's damage control had worked to a certain extent. Theo had done a good job restoring the places in the city he'd visited, and was as visibly exhausted as Surah. Both of them had used an incredible amount of Magic for one day, and it had taken its toll.

Now they sat on the balcony outside of what used to be her father's office, the glittering stars hanging over their heads in the clear night sky.

Samson was perched on the stone ledge of the balcony, over-looking Zadira below, with its neon lights and fine architecture. He had not spoken a word since their return to the castle, and the look in his amber eyes was far-off.

Surah was anxious to get this discussion with Theo over with, so that she could see what was so upsetting her tiger.

Theo swirled a drink in his hand, his eyes also distant. "The Fae burned every border town in the Territory before leaving," he said. "People are still streaming into the city now with no where else to go, and terrified that we can't protect them."

"That's why we have to send the Hunters to the towns and cities, as well as patrolling the roads. We need them to be anywhere there are our people. Their presence alone will offer comfort," she said.

Theo was silent a moment. He turned in his chair, facing Surah until she looked up and met his gray eyes. "That's just not wise, my queen," he told her. "We need the Hunters here. Protecting the castle. Protecting *you*."

Surah waved a hand at this. "I don't need their protection. The people do. Besides, I'm not going to be here, anyway. There are matters to attend to."

Theo blinked at her. "Forgive me," he said, "but you're queen now, the last of the Stormsong line. You have to rule. You can't just go charging into the battle like you used to."

"The best rulers are the ones who stand beside their men on the battlefield," she said. "I would not send them to die over something I'm not willing to die for myself. That's a coward's way of doing things."

Theo seemed to accept this, if reluctantly, though it was obvious they were in disagreement.

"We'll need to name a new Head of Council since your uncle is gone, and a new Keeper also… unless you intend to hold that position as well."

Surah did not miss the slight snap to his tone, and after the day she'd had, it pissed her off more than it probably should have.

"If you've got something on your mind, Hunter Gray, just say it. We've both been drained physically and emotionally today, and if we're going to work together to save this kingdom, we need to clear the air, anyway. So say what you've got to say already, and let's be done with it."

There was no façade to her demeanor, no royal composure to speak of. Theo sat up a bit straighter, his face becoming as serious as the grave.

"Fine," he said. "Do you love him?"

Though she probably should not have been, Surah was taken off-guard by this question. There was no need to ask to whom he was referring, because they both knew very well.

"I don't know," she lied.

She waited for him to say something, but Theo was silent for so long that Surah had to steal a glance at him to try and read his reaction.

The Head Hunter stared out at the city below, the profile of his handsome face all fine lines and edges, a picture of intro-spection. It was a side of him she had never seen before, though she'd known him for most of forever.

Just when Surah was getting ready to say something else, the silence somehow too much for her to bear, Theo released a heavy sigh and surprised her by turning toward her on the bench the two were sharing and taking her hands into his.

She had removed her gloves after they'd returned to the castle, her fingers nearly on fire after all the magic that had flowed out of them, and she was surprised to find Theo's hands were pleasantly cool, if a touch rough.

He met her eyes with a sincerity that nearly took her aback. "Your father offered me your hand in marriage before he passed," he said.

And like that, Surah was pissed off again. She opened her mouth to protest, but Theo smiled, speaking again before she could.

"I don't want you to marry me because your father agreed to it," he said, his voice lower and more apprehensive than she'd ever heard it. "I've loved you since we were children, Surah. I used to try so hard to get your attention." He laughed, his eyes going distant again.

"I was always climbing trees or doing flips or attempting dangerous spells, in hopes that you would just look my way. I forced myself to date other women, thinking maybe you would get jealous and realize my affections." He shook his head. "I was a fool."

For the life of her, Surah did not know what to say to this. Her mouth fell open, but once more, Theo beat her to the punch.

"I know now that I need to earn your love and trust. I want to stand by you in this dark time, and prove to you that I can be worthy of you." His hand came up and rested on her cheek, and Surah did not push it away.

"I don't know what to say, Theo," she said, her heart jackhammering in her chest. It was as if the entire world were spinning out of focus, the picture blurring and the sound jumbling.

A half smile pulled up his lips. "That's the first time in nearly a thousand years that you've called me by my given name," he said.

Surah found that it was becoming harder to breathe. She swallowed and looked down at her hands, his stare somehow too much to hold.

"I don't think I can give you what you want," she whispered.

Theo's hand came up and he gently lifted her chin with his fingers, forcing her to meet his eyes.

"I'm just asking for a chance," he said. "I want you to choose me over Charlie Redmine. Not for any other reason than that you want to. Just give me a chance at making you fall in love with me."

Samson lifted his head, his eyes flicking between the two of them and narrowing, his ears swiveled toward the intimate exchange.

For Surah, the entire world seemed to have paused, as if the heavens and earth were holding their breath.

Her answer came before she could think about it, the word falling from her lips the way one falls off a ledge.

"Okay," she said.

"Okay?" he asked, his eyes lighting up with a hope that was enough to make her insides twist.

She nodded. "Okay."

8

SURAH

Theo left her shortly thereafter, kissing her hand and bidding her good night.

Despite being wiped out both mentally and physically, Surah found that her mind would not stop turning over, her thoughts refusing to shut off even though her body desperately needed a good sleep.

Samson remained out on the balcony while she showered and donned fresh clothing. After brushing her hair and teeth, she climbed into her bed and snapped her fingers, the light in the room extinguishing with a last bit of magic that took way more effort than usual.

When Sam slipped into bed beside her, the enormous weight of him making the mattress dip deeply, she wrapped her arm around his neck and rubbed the soft, thick fur there.

She spoke aloud to him in the darkness, the way she had done for as long as they'd been together. "What's bothering you, my love?" she whispered, her violet eyes staring into the amber of his, his lovely feline face close enough to kiss.

Sam's large chest rose and fell in a deep sigh, and his

soothing voice sounded in her head. *"I may have to leave you soon,"* he said, *"but I will return."*

For several heartbeats, Surah couldn't respond. Her fingers tightened in his fur and she pulled herself closer to his warm, soft body, burying her head in his strong chest. His mitt-sized paw went around her, holding her in return.

When she spoke, her voice was much smaller than she would've allowed it to be with anyone else.

"Where will you be going?" she asked.

"Back to the jungles of my homeland."

The way he said this made Surah's heart ache, though she could not say why. The cat's tone was somehow anguished, nostalgic, and resigned all at once.

"When will you return?"

"I'm not sure, love... Will you be all right in my absence?"

"If I say no, will you still leave?"

"Have I ever been able to deny you something you've asked of me?"

This brought a smile to her lips, but it was shadowed by the darkness surrounding them. "But you don't want me to ask that of you," she said. It was not a question. "You have to go do whatever it is you're going to do."

Samson's warm, rough tongue licked Surah's cheek. *"I'm afraid I do."*

"Is it something you promised to do to be able to find me when Black Heart had me captive in that cave? Is it because of me?"

Sam said nothing to this, only breathed deeply the scent of his mistress. Surah cried herself to sleep that night, something she could not remember doing since she was a child, after she'd lost her mother and sister.

The thick fur of her tiger absorbed the tears, and though the road ahead was looking bleaker by the moment, she felt safe while the Great Cat held her, his heart beating just under her ear.

The thought of losing Samson, her best friend and most trusted ally, haunted her thoughts as they grew slower and thicker with approaching sleep. But the final thought to cross her mind before sleep took her fully was of Charlie Redmine.

It was a prayer, in fact, a hope that all was well wherever he was.

And that maybe, before all this mess was over, she'd get to see his face one more time.

* * *

MORNING CAME the way mornings always do, as if by magic.

Surah opened her eyes to the golden glow of a new day, the sun shining down on her as she lie in her bed.

"Good morning, beautiful," Sam said, nuzzling her face with his cool nose.

Surah sat up and stretched, yawning. "Good morning, Sam."

When a knock sounded on the door, Surah let out a growl that made Sam's mouth twitch in amusement.

"The duties of a queen never end."

Some of her strength had returned during the night, the sleep doing its job and recharging her body. She had slept like a rock, and though her heart was as heavy as a boulder, Surah felt she could face the day, which would undoubtedly be a challenging one.

Today, she would lay her father to rest and take his place as ruler of the Sorcerer Kingdom, with all the people of Zadira bearing witness.

She told the caller to hold on for just a moment, and got dressed the old fashioned way, deciding a conservation of magic would be wise in the foreseeable future.

Better to be able to throw a powerful fireball in a dire situation than to be lazy and use up strength on the mundane tasks.

Not having the magic had certainly increased her appreciation of it, as the absence of things is prone to do.

Sam retreated to the balcony, taking up perch on its stone ledge, as he was apt to do whenever their room received visitors. Surah felt her heart break anew when she remembered what her cat had told her last night; that he would be leaving her soon. He'd promised he would return, so why did the thought of it make her feel like crying?

She sighed and opened the door to her room... and was nearly tackled to the ground immediately after.

Her personal guard, Noelani, was not muted in her show of affection. She swept Surah up into a hug that was almost crushing under the female Hunter's muscular arms. Surah hugged her in return, realizing how much it comforted her, and how much she'd needed it.

"You had us so damn worried," Noelani whispered, and the sincerity in her tone brought a small smile to Surah's face.

"I'm sorry," she said.

"Let her go before you turn her fragile bones to dust," Lyonell said, standing behind his wife and rolling his eyes, making Surah's smile grow wider.

"Who're you calling 'fragile bones'?" she teased.

Another voice spoke up, deep and chocolaty, and Surah peered around Lyonell to see Bassil.

"I believe he was referring to you, my dear," said the Warlock, kissing her cheek as he also entered the room.

Surah shut the door behind him, feeling instantly better with just their presence. It was easy, in times of hardship and grief, to forget how many wonderful people she really did have in her life.

"I'm glad you're all here," she said.

Bassil took her hands into his large ones. "And we're all very sorry about the loss of your father," he said, his head bowing in respect. "King Syrian was a good and honorable man."

Both Noelani and Lyonell nodded their agreement, heads bowing in respect.

"When would you like to hold the ceremonies?" Bassil asked.

"Today," she said.

Bassil nodded, but Noelani and Lyonell exchanged a look.

"It doesn't have to be so soon," Noelani said gently. "You can have some time to mourn privately. You're the queen now."

Surah shook her head, exhibiting a strength she wasn't sure she owned. "It needs to be today. I'm not the only one grieving, and there's the important business of protecting the throne. The Fae's attack can't go unanswered."

She swallowed hard, thinking of Charlie. Always thinking of Charlie. Sighing, she added, "None of what's happened can go unanswered."

Silence fell between them for a few moments. They knew Surah was right, and they knew they would mourn and commemorate over great deaths today, only to go out tomorrow and cause more of the same. Death after all, could only be paid for with death.

"Not true, dear one," Sam spoke up in her mind, having slipped back into the room silently. *"Only life can balance death."*

Surah sighed deeply. *"You may be right, Sam, and yet..."*

The Great Tiger brushed against her side as he went to stand beside her.

"And yet," he agreed.

"Bassil, please schedule and prepare the ceremonies for this afternoon," she said, and drew some strength from Samson, because she was fresh out. "Invite the entire kingdom. I want to send off anyone who's lost someone during the Fae attacks along with my father. And after that's done, we'll hold my coronation, and I'll address the people as their new queen."

Another silence followed this, and this time it was Lyonell who spoke up. "We don't know how smoothly any of that will go, my queen," he said. "The people are frightened and angry. They want blood."

The sound of these words, so plainly and truthfully spoken, made Surah want to cringe, but she bit back her grimace, and her voice was equally plain and truthful when she answered.

"And blood is exactly what I'm going to give them."

9

CHARLIE

When the Fae Queen came to see him, Charlie was sitting in much the same position he'd been sitting in for hours, his head resting in his hands and his handsome face impassive.

A silence preceded her arrival, the forest growing quiet and still in a way that made the hair on the back of Charlie's neck stand on end. Her tinkling, almost childlike laughter reached him first, and then the strong floral scent of her as she drifted across the forest floor toward him, the light pink fog hovering near the ground parting in wisps as she approached.

Tristell the Fae Queen halted just out of reach before Charlie's cage, looking down at him with a devious smile and slanted eyes. Her long, feathery dress shifted color as she did so, as if it were somehow alive. Her wings were larger than any Fae female he'd ever met, the feathers that composed them two feet long. Every once in a while, one would dislodge itself and float merrily down to the forest floor.

The devil in disguise, she was.

"Michael's brother is a pretty one," she said, her voice deceptively juvenile. "Prettier than Michael, even."

Charlie said nothing to this, his lip curling slightly. This did not seem to faze the Fae Queen a bit. Her slanted eyes studied him for an uncomfortable moment, then they darted around the trees, as if she could see things there that he could not, and really, she probably could. The true power of the Fae rested in Mother Nature and all of its offerings.

"The Fae children like you, Michael's brother," Tristell said, revealing sharp teeth with a smile that was somehow both terrifying and beautiful. "The females have been hanging around, haven't they?"

It was a question they both knew she already knew the answer to, so again, Charlie said nothing.

"You are pretty," she repeated, eyes narrowing, "but what is so special about Michael's brother that he can capture the heart of a Sorcerer princess as well as that of the Forest Children? I don't see all the special they see, but yes, yes, Michael's brother is pretty, indeed."

"What do you want?" Charlie asked, growing tired of listening to the Fae Queen's annoying ability to hold entire conversations with herself.

"It's obviously not a great mind," she said, "asking stupid questions all the time."

"You've started a war," growled Charlie. "The Hunters will come, and they'll burn this whole forest to the ground."

With those words, a switch seemed to flip within the Fae Queen. She threw her head back so far Charlie thought it might detach, and let out a screeching caw that sounded both birdlike and insect-like.

From her crouched position, her wings spread out to their full eight-foot span, and she shot up into the trees like a fairy rocket.

Tufts of pastel-colored, cottony leaves fell from above, and a host of exotic birds squawked angrily and took flight as well. Charlie watched in both shock and utter amazement as the Fae

Queen bounced from tree to tree like the mad creature she was.

Only certain words were even intelligible, most of it spoken in the chirping language of the Fae people, but one did not need to speak Faevian to know that whatever was coming out of her mouth was surely curse words and angry proclamations.

After an indeterminable amount of time, she came crashing back down to the floor of the forest, the pink fog whooshing up in plumes around her clawed feet. She landed very close to Charlie's cage now, her enraged face near enough to kiss.

"That was a terrible thing to say, Michael's brother!" she exclaimed. "You will have to pay for that!"

She snapped her long-nailed fingers, and the thick, thorn-riddled vines enclosing him began to tighten in a way that made the plant appear almost intelligent.

Charlie's heart picked up pace as the inch-long thorns drew nearer and nearer his skin, slowly, as if it knew the anticipation was terrifying.

As the vines made contact with his skin, the thorns tearing through the flesh as easily as would the teeth of a Wolf, Charlie had to bite down on his tongue hard enough to draw blood so as not to cry out in pain.

"There is no greater travesty than burning a forest, Michael's brother!" the Fae Queen screeched. "To even speak of doing so is blasphemy! Why, you Sorcerers are no better than humans!"

With this, she snapped her fingers, and the vines yanked him to the ground, the thorns digging in so deep on the side on which he fell that this time he could do nothing to keep back the scream that tore up his throat.

He was bleeding from minor lacerations from neck-to-toe now, and the combination of all of them was somehow worse than the larger injuries he'd had in the past. Charlie spat a mouthful of blood onto the ground, and it dribbled down his chin, his cheek pressed against the forest floor.

The earth absorbed the blood as though it were drinking it, and the very clear misfortune of his situation was brought home to him.

This land he was being held captive in was as foreign as they came, and if Surah were to bring an army here, he wasn't entirely sure they wouldn't be at a terrible disadvantage. Every leaf, tree and vine seemed to be under the intimate control of the mad queen.

One more swift kick to his midsection that knocked the last bit of remaining air out of him, and the Fae Queen turned on her heel and stomped haughtily off into the trees, the natural sounds of the forest returning gradually with her departure.

Charlie could not draw in a full breath of air, the thorny, green vines remaining as tight as she'd commanded them, the pain dizzying, making his mind and vision blurry.

He needed to get out of here, and fast, but he lie where he was, the lively green vines encasing him like an angry blanket, paralyzing and leaving him helpless.

Charlie had seen the type of crazy that reflected out of the Fae Queen's slanted eyes, and he knew better than most that it would bring hell and havoc to everyone she crossed.

And, of course, before the pain of his circumstances pulled him under the dark veil of unconsciousness, his last thought was of Surah.

1 O

———

SURAH

She was numb, and glad for it.

Standing before the long mirror in her bedroom, staring at her reflection, Surah found that she felt nothing at all.

It was as if she were merely a body, floating from place to place, but void in a way that lacked something essential.

Dressed in black from head to toe, her violet eyes and hair the only color to speak of, she did not recognize herself. Who was that girl staring back at her, with the empty eyes and face free of feeling? A queen? A ruler?

Of this, she was not sure. And since she was no longer a daughter, a sister, a lover—or anything else, for that matter, she wasn't truly sure she was anyone at all.

Samson brushed against her leg, unusually silent as she sorted through her thoughts. This incited the little bit of emotion Surah was able to feel just then, worrying her. Sam had said he would stay for the ceremony, but would need to take his leave shortly after, and he seemed to be so deep in his own thoughts that it made her stomach twist as though she might be sick.

Noelani and Lyonell came to retrieve her, knocking gently

on her chamber door. They were also dressed in the customary all black, their faces long and their lack of words evident. After all, what does one say to someone who has outlived every member of their family? The answer is, nothing. Because in such situations, there is nothing to be said.

She trailed her two personal guards through the cold stone hallways of the castle, unable to look at the paintings of her lost loved ones adorning the walls for fear that she would lose the composure she needed to maintain.

Surah was no fool. She was aware that there were people who opposed her rule, and to show weakness—even in this appropriate setting—was not wise. As much as people would "understand" were she to break down, at the same time, they were afraid for their safety, and no one wants a blubbering leader in dark times.

They wanted a warrior. Which was fine with Surah, because she wanted blood.

Samson followed close at her side as Lyonell opened the door that led out to the castle's courtyard. Noelani went through first, her harshly pretty face on the lookout for threats, as always. Samson chuffed a little at this, and Surah knew it was because the tiger thought Noelani's actions were silly. No one would harm Surah with him near.

Surah rubbed at Sam's ears for comfort, pausing before stepping out into the courtyard, where the royal families were no doubt gathered in the best of their black clothing. She found it more difficult than it should have been to step into the rectangle of golden sunlight that was cast upon the floor in the open doorway.

"You don't have to go out," Lyonell whispered to her.

Surah shook her head. "Thank you," she said, "but, yes, I do."

One last deep breath, and she stepped out. She held her chin high as she walked through the courtyard, and the people bowed to her as she passed. They offered their condolences, and

Surah accepted them with nods and gracious thanks, but she was on edge, and could not pinpoint why.

Perhaps it was because every time there was a gathering of a lot of her people lately, the crap seemed to hit the fan. Or maybe it was because there were those present who wanted to see her off the throne. Maybe it was both.

"I almost want one of them to take a go at you," Samson told her in his silent way. *"They all reek of fear, and it's had me on edge for days. Trust those instincts of yours. They're almost catlike."*

"But I can't hide. Not right now," was her silent response. *"I need them to see my strength."*

Sam's watchful, amber eyes flicked up to hers. *"I'm happy to show them mine."*

"Sam, what will I do without you?"

"You will do just fine, dear one. That's what you will do."

Surah crossed the courtyard in a daze, hanging on to Sam's words. This place was the same as always; filled with fountains and exotic flowers that crawled up the stone walls, giving the place a pleasant perfume. But, somehow, it all felt different now, as if the glow it had once carried had died along with her father.

She thought she would find comfort in stepping out of the walls of the courtyard, and in a sense, she did. As she stood overlooking Zadira, on the edge of the hill her castle sat on, she saw that thousands of people had turned up for the ceremonies today, and it made her chest ache to see this.

More Hunters fell into stride around her small party. When she reached the bottom of the hill, she found Theo waiting for her, his gray eyes filled with a sympathy she'd thought he was incapable of, and was still not sure she trusted.

When Theo held his arm out to her, it snapped her out of these thoughts, and she slipped her arm through his without hesitation. She may not be entirely sure she could trust the Head Hunter, but a show of solidarity might not be unwise.

Overhead, the sun shined with a cheery indifference to the

darkness that hung over the people below. The day was warm, bright, only a few wispy clouds lazing their way across the sky.

There had to be nearly ten thousand people lining the streets of Zadira, but for all those in attendance, a silence hung over the place like a blanket.

Arm in arm, Theo began to lead her through the city. The people, all donning dark clothing and heavy hearts, bowed as the two of them passed.

She would never be able to do this with Charlie, not after all that had passed, and the random, unwelcome thought made a dull ache in her numb chest. After all that had transpired, they could never do something as simple as walk through the capital city of her kingdom arm in arm. The prospect made her sadder than she wished it would.

Passing through the city this way, with her tiger and the Head Hunter at her side, along with the rest of the Royal Hunter Guard, felt surreal.

It took nearly twenty minutes to reach their destination, but it felt both longer and shorter to Surah. She seemed to be dragging lead in her feet.

Then, it was as if she blinked, and Bassil was standing before her and the dark waters of the Lake of the Lost Ones stretched out beyond his back.

Unlike humans—and a select few of the other supernatural creatures, like the Fae—Sorcerers did not bury their dead. They built a pyre and set them to sail on a body of water.

The Lake of the Lost Ones was the equivalent of the largest cemetery in their Territory. Over the centuries, hundreds of thousands of Sorcerers and Sorceresses had been set to rest here.

Today, it would be her father.

Someday after, it would be her.

But not before she killed the people responsible for this.

Of that, she was damn sure.

11

SURAH

*B*assil's face was filled with sympathy.

She could tell the Warlock wanted to hug her, but was thankful when he didn't. With all these people looking on, she wanted to be a comfort to them, not for them to think she was the one in need of comfort.

Standing by the edge of the Lake of the Lost Ones, the memories of the times she'd stood in this very spot before came flooding back to her.

For a small moment, she could see herself as a child, dressed in black from head-to-toe, her small cloak a rich velvet that she wore like a brick wall between her and the world. Her violet hair had been set into curls by Noelani earlier on that long ago morning.

The Hunter had held her as she cried, the only female left in the world whom she felt close to since her sister and mother were dead. Noelani had only hugged her, her harsh face softer than Surah had ever seen it, the same way it had been just this morning when she and Lyonell came to retrieve her.

Surah's brother and father had stood beside her that day, their backs straight and their heads held nobly high. Even back then, despite thinking this was the greatest amount of pain she would ever go through, despite the hollowness in her chest and the fracture in her heart, she'd stood silent and strong like the princess she was.

These memories floated away on the breeze, which smelled faintly of lilies, as the white flower grew in long stalks all around the lake's shoreline, like tombstones for all those these waters had sent away.

Next came the memory of her not so long ago, one of only a few months back, though it seemed like an eternity between then and now. Her father, King Syrian, had stood beside her, his last child, as they set her brother Syris sailing. Again, she had thought that day that she was feeling the most pain she would ever know.

Surah was given a slight nudge by Samson, and this brought her back to the now. She realized that Bassil must have already spoken, and saw that it was time for her to approach the pyre atop which her father's body lie, and say her final goodbye.

It was as if she were walking through a dream, or perhaps, a nightmare. Her movements felt slow and heavy.

It took every ounce of strength she possessed to look down at her father for the last time. Her eyes began to burn, and she stared out over the water, taking a deep breath and gaining control over herself.

Finally, she looked down at the lost king, at her fallen father, and into her soul. It was there that she saw that she did not want a war, and why her father had always tried so hard to avoid it.

Where Surah had always wanted to take swift justice, to strike back when struck, King Syrian had insisted on trying every method of diplomacy first. It was a quality of his she'd never quite understood until just now.

Looking to her left, she saw the mother she'd attempted to console in the city yesterday, the one who'd been holding her fallen darling in her arms, the one to whom she'd promised revenge.

The mourning mother stood beside her son's pyre, which was half the size of that of Surah's father. She stared back at Surah, her eyes filled with grief and a burning need for vengeance. Surah knew the look well. She'd seen it in the mirror more often than she'd like to admit.

Surah wished she could tell the mother that killing all the Fae in all the realms would not bring her baby back, and all of the death and destruction in the underworld could never fill the hole she'd forever carry inside her.

But Surah knew she could say no such thing to the poor mother. She could say no such thing to her people, either. There was a time for diplomacy, but there was also a line, and that line had been crossed.

Beyond the grieving mother, others stood atop the long wooden docks that led into the lake, their lost loved ones silent and still before them. Turning her head to the left revealed more of the same.

She had yet to receive the official count of how many had been lost, but she could see that there were dozens, if not hundreds. The Fae Warriors had torn through the unsuspecting crowd and towns like the mongrels they were.

There were thousands of eyes on her. She could feel them from all around the way one can feel the weather. She could also feel the divide among her people. Some of them truly did love the Stormsong family enough to know that Surah wanted what was best for the kingdom, and others among them were just here for the show.

But the ones whose gazes she could feel on her cloak as though they were a second skin had a fiery distrust, obviously thinking she wasn't suitable to sit on the throne. Or worse, they blamed her for all the misfortune that had befallen Sorcerer kind as of late. Or both.

Surah was as lost as all those who ever burned atop the dark waters of the lake. A single tear fell down her face, and she did not wipe it away.

To love was not weakness, but strength. For love, she would face whatever and whoever dare threaten the peace of her people. For love, she would fight, she would kill, and if need be, she would die.

Bassil handed her a torch ablaze with a violet flame, the fire as brilliant as a star in the dark night. All along the edge of the shoreline, more violet flames sprang to life, dotting the perimeter of the lake like a ring of purple diamonds.

Only the insects spoke into the shadows, the rest of the souls present holding silent in respect. It was as if they were collectively holding their breath, pausing the beating of their hearts.

With a final exhale, Surah placed the torch atop her father's chest, where the substance that covered the pyre and body made the flame spread and cover its entirety in a matter of seconds.

Placing her black boot on the edge of the pyre, she shoved it out into the lake, where the ever-shifting violet blaze grew brighter and brighter.

All around the lake, pyres large and small, depending on the size of their occupant, were set aflame and afloat, and soon, the night was glowing bright with the fire of all the Lost Ones, the lake's dark surface reflecting the glow like a mirror.

It was in this brilliant purple light that the shadow of the first Demon appeared, and then the screeches of dozens of the denizens of darkness were filling the dark sky.

Someone in the crowd screamed, and a palpable terror filled the air.

Fire filled her, and Surah reached behind her and removed her two silver sais, letting her cloak fall into a puddle at her feet.

A grin that held no humor pulled up one side of her mouth, and she spun the weapons around in her hands, her heart picking up pace in anticipation of battle, the tiny hairs on her neck standing on end.

Screams and screeches filled the scene, hell descending from above as the chains of vengeance slowly wound tighter around the new queen's battered and hardened heart.

54

SURAH

They'd picked the wrong person, the wrong day.

A sort of slow motion overcame Surah, a tunnel-like focus. She thought if Alexa Montgomery—the brave young Sun Warrior who was fiercer than any creature in all the Territories—could see her now, she would give Surah a crooked smile and a nod of approval.

Surah was going to kill them all, and she was going to do it by herself, for all to see. Or she was going to die trying.

Sais gripped loosely and comfortably in her hands, in all the panic that was on the edge of erupting, Surah turned to the Warlock and held his dark eyes for a stolen moment.

"Cast a barrier spell to protect the people," she told him, slipping her queen's piece of White Stone from around her neck and handing it to him. "And then freeze the people in place below the barrier. I don't want them running. I want them to watch what happens next. I want their full attention."

Bassil hesitated only a moment, a look of both concern and newfound respect for her passing behind his eyes. What she was telling him to do was crazy, and would take an enormous amount of magic from both the Warlock and the stone.

Also, it would leave her to fight the Demons solo—without the help of magic. She had not brought the Black Stone with her for the ceremony, as the presence of her grief was dark enough.

The Warlock took the stone into his large hand, meeting her gaze steadily. "Kill them all, my queen," he told her, and then braced himself, closed his eyes, and cast the spell.

The barrier spell took effect just in time, the move both risky and clever on her part. Surah watched as it blanketed the people like an invisible ceiling, the dozens of Demons rebounding off it in a way that was almost comical.

Almost, because nothing about this would be funny. No matter what happened in the rapid moments that would follow, nothing would be funny at all.

The Demons were intimidating physically, with their scaly, black, and winged bodies, long horns atop their ugly heads, and sharp claws on their hands and feet. They would scare the daylights out of most people. But Surah was not most people, and as far as intelligence went, these dark creatures left much to be desired.

Slowly, the Demons began to recognize that they could not reach the people below, who were now under the binding spell Bassil was casting, and could not move but for their eyes, which were as wide as disks.

A Demon noticed Surah still standing atop the dock with that crazed smile on her face, and came soaring at her, flashing sharp teeth and long-clawed feet outstretched for the kill.

Surah spun her sais, waiting, but before the creature could reach her, Samson tackled it out of the air, his enormous blue and black body moving faster than one would think possible.

Surah charged, her black leather boots moving atop the invisible barrier Bassil was impressively maintaining as if she were running on air. She reached the first Demon a heartbeat later, and skewered it the way one might meat on a stick.

The creature let out a screech of pain that could be heard in the heavens.

Spinning gracefully, she skewered another Demon on her opposite side, the sharp, silver points of her sais going through the creature's neck, spraying black and sticky blood into the air and across Surah's face.

Below her, the frozen people of her kingdom looked on, Hunters, royals and common folks alike, watching her deliver death above them as if a war had erupted among the stars. The barrier blocked the spilling and spurting black blood of the Demons from the people, but it splashed against it the way mud would on glass.

Samson also leapt atop the barrier, fighting alongside his mistress with a grace and penchant for killing that only true beasts could ever obtain. The hisses and feline sounds that issued from his belly as he tore through Demon bodies with teeth and claw were the only things louder than the screeches of the Demons, which was pain-filled music to Surah's ears.

She killed two more, ducking out of the way of the swipe of a Demon's sharp claws just in time and skewering him from below, right into its gut, spraying herself with more of the icky blood.

Time was moving both fast and slow. She killed one Demon after another, receiving scrapes and a few deep gashes on her arms and legs that went unnoticed for all the adrenaline that was running through her.

"I wish these creatures tasted better," Samson's voice spoke in her head at the same time as he tackled another Demon swooping at Surah from above.

Sam gripped the thing by its scaly throat. Its claws were digging into him, trying to free itself, so he whipped his huge head to the side, ripping out its throat and flinging the piece of tough, gamey meat to the side.

It hit the magical barrier below them the way an insect

smashes into glass, and the people beneath did not have to have control of their movements for Surah to know they'd just cringed internally.

Surah shook her head, her face streaked with the black blood, making the smile she gave her cat eerie, to say the least.

"What?" Sam asked. *"You wanted to put on a show, did you not?"*

In answer, Surah stuck her sais deep into the stomach of another Demon, which lashed out and scratched her deep enough to scar above her eyebrow, mixing her red blood with that of the black gore that covered her.

Climbing up the Demon's tall, lanky body as if it were a ladder, she set her boots on its shoulders, tucking her sais into their leather holders on her back, and snapped the Demon's neck with her bare hands.

The rotten bones there cracked as loud as thunder, and the Demon, blood spilling from its gut, and neck creased at an unusual angle, fell dead beneath her.

Rolling to her feet, Surah slipped the long knife from its holster on her thigh and ran up the back of another Demon, which she realized was the last one still alive. There was a mess atop the barrier that Bassil was still holding between Surah and the people like a glass ceiling.

Demon bodies and bits lay strewn all around in the way that only battle can achieve; careless and haphazard. Blood obscured the invisible glass of the barrier, but the people below had not been spared the sounds.

Samson sat on his haunches atop the barrier, licking the black blood around his mouth and sticking out his tongue in distaste.

Surah gripped the horn of the last Demon, yanking its head back and exposing its throat, her long knife gripped tight in her right hand. She slashed at the bony part that held its wings to its back, disabling the creature's flight.

They both fell to the barrier, Surah maintaining her advantageous position. Its claws scraped at the air above its head, and it screeched like a bat out of hell, but Surah knew that Demons were like crustaceans; if you gripped them in the right place, you had nothing to worry about.

She held her blade to its throat now, looking down at all the people standing below her, meeting the eyes of as many as she could. She wanted them to see her face. She wanted them to see what was behind the mask she'd worn for as long as she could remember, and for the first time in her life, she didn't care whether it scared them.

Hell, they *needed* to be scared. When she spoke, her voice came out that of a queen, the question of her strength more than answered in the deeds her people had just witnessed.

"I promised you my protection," she told all those present, speaking loudly enough to be heard by all, and giving the Demon's horn a sharp yank when it tried to screech in frustration.

She placed her blade to its throat, and in one swift motion, drew it deep into the creature's scaly skin, a fountain of steaming black blood spraying out into the air. She released the horn she was gripping and the Demon's head hit the barrier with a cringe-worthy *thwack!*

Wiping her blade off on her thigh and replacing it in its holster, Surah strode calmly over to Bassil and placed a hand on the Warlock's large shoulder, letting him know he could release the spells. Sweat rolled down his ebony brow, and his dark eyes were bloodshot when he opened them.

With a *splat!* that made even some of the stronger stomachs in the crowd twist, the gore of the deceased Demons fell free of the diminishing barrier and covered some of those below, who stumbled and coughed and took long, wide-eyed breaths as they regained control over their bodies.

As they did so, Surah climbed to the top of the royal dock from which she'd just barely said goodbye to her father. It was elevated higher than the others, and though it was nighttime, the blazes of the lost ones atop the lake were still burning strong.

The moon was full and round. The crowd was massive and silent, and their eyes were only for her. She stood before them now, covered in the blood and body parts of those who would dare threaten them, and she did not bother to wipe it away, not even from her lips.

"I promised you my protection," she repeated, her voice loud and larger than one would think possible from such a petite woman. "Is there anyone among you who thinks I'm incapable of this? If so, step forward now."

She paused, her heart racing faster than it had even during the killing. "If not, bow before me now as your queen, and follow me as I defend our Territory against those who have wronged us."

Time slowed in the handful of seconds that followed, the world freezing before her as if this were all some dream.

Then, slowly, like a wave rolling out to sea, the Sorcerer people began to take to their knees, bowing before their new queen, chins tucked and eyes cast down in respect.

Bassil smiled despite his obvious exhaustion. He came forward and replaced the queen's piece of White Stone around her neck, where it glowed brightly enough for all to see.

1 3

CHARLIE

When his eyes peeled open sometime later, night had fallen in the Fae Forest.

For the split second before swimming back to full consciousness, Charlie awoke to find he didn't know where he was.

He'd dreamed he was back home at his cabin in the countryside, a warm fire blazing in the fireplace, and his guitar resting in the corner.

Surah had been there. She'd been curled up on the couch beside him, her long, soft legs stretched across his lap, reading a book about some imagined world full of imagined people with imagined problems all their own.

And then he'd been pulled back to consciousness, blinking and heart sinking as the slow realization of reality came over him. The scents filling his nose, the sounds in his ears, and even the air of the place confirmed its identity.

He was on the floor of the Fae Forest, amidst the odd pink fog, his body wrapped in thick, thorny green vines from shoulder to feet. He could not feel the right side of his body at all, and thus came to the conclusion that the plant life restraining him must be of the poisonous sort. His head was pounding and his vision blurry, and his heart felt like it weighed a hundred pounds in his chest.

He could not remember ever feeling so lost and hopeless.

Charlie rolled over onto his back with a grunt, the thorns there making fresh digs into his skin, which he hardly felt for all the paralysis the plant's poison was holding over his body.

Above, the fluffy, pastel-colored canopies of the trees danced lightly in the sweet-scented wind, and beyond that, three moons and millions of stars lit the night sky.

If not for the absolute awfulness of the whole situation, Charlie would have to admit this small, strange Territory owned by the Fae was quite lovely in its otherness.

Rustling in the trees around him, the Fae children had returned, their high-pitched voices a mixture between the chirps of morning birds and the songs of nighttime bugs. Their eyes, wide and slanted, glowed in the darkness, a stunning color of earthy-green that was a wonder to look at, despite the effort it took Charlie to even turn his head and do so.

Their glowing gazes stared back at him in the dozens, and the foliage of the forest floor rustled and shook as they darted around the way children of all species are apt to do. Charlie began to fade in and out of consciousness, listening to the strange children and catching glimpses of the moons between the trees.

He was not sure how much time had passed, how deep it was into the night when the girl approached him. At this point, he had no concept of time. In fact, it took a couple slaps to his face before he actually awoke and took notice of her. Her face was so lovely that he thought he must have been dreaming of an angel.

"Wake up," the girl whispered, slightly slanted green eyes as bright as emeralds staring down at him. Soft fingers touched his chin, holding his head in place, the girl sighed. Her breath smelled of flowers and sunshine. "Wake up, Sorcerer," she repeated.

It took enormous effort on his part for Charlie to clear his mind enough to keep his eyes open. The girl with the angelic face and stunning eyes was running her fingers lightly over the vines around him, whispering in a way that seemed oddly motherly, and after a few moments, Charlie realized that the pain of all the thorns stabbing into the various parts of his body was subsiding. The vine itself was pulling out the hooks, and instead of the poison they'd been administering, a cool, burning sensation filled the wounds, the way a disinfectant might.

After ten minutes of whatever the girl was doing, Charlie felt almost completely better, though he was still restrained by the plant. He found he could breathe again, and his eyes looked up at the strange girl in wonder.

"Thank you," he said, with the genuine gratitude of someone who has just been liberated from considerable suffering.

The girl sat back on her haunches, her long and wavy reddish-brown hair falling over her shoulders. Her emerald eyes—a deeper, somehow shinier shade of green than Charlie's, with a slight slant that gave away her Fae descent—narrowed as she looked down at him.

"You're welcome," she said, her voice strong but somehow musical.

A moment of silence passed between them, and then, with one last look all around, the girl sat cross-legged beside him, her eyes never leaving his face.

"Who are you?" he asked.

The girl smirked, and Charlie wondered if she knew that each of her expressions was more beautiful than the last.

"Don't you mean, *what* am I?" she replied.

Charlie raised an eyebrow. "That, too."

She smiled now, and sure enough, this made her even lovelier.

"My name is Aria," she said. "I'm a Halfling." When Charlie only blinked at her, she added, "I'm half Fae and half human. I act as a liaison between the worlds."

He let this sink in. "Well, my name's Charlie, Aria, and I'm the guy trapped in your forest."

Another smile, only half of one, but somehow twice as lovely. She pushed a lock of thick, red-brown hair behind her ear, which was not pointed like a Fae's, but rounded like a human's.

Actually, the closer Charlie looked at the girl, the more he saw that she could pass for completely human. As a liaison in the human world, she no doubt did.

"The forest isn't mine, Charlie," Aria answered. "The forest doesn't belong to anyone." She was keeping her sweet voice low, her eyes glancing all around before settling back on him.

Charlie craned his neck and saw that she was dressed in human clothes, with black leggings and black combat boots, a gray t-shirt and black leather jacket. Tucked behind her back, Charlie caught a glimpse of a wooden staff. He nodded at it as best as he could with his limited mobility.

"What's that for?" he asked, though he knew the answer.

Aria's hand reached behind her jacket, stroking the weapon before falling away. Half-smile still pulling up her lips, she reached up and brushed a piece of Charlie's dark hair off of his forehead.

"All the realms are dangerous places, not the least of which the human world," she said. "A girl's gotta be careful."

Charlie gave a small nod, looking down at his restraints. "Seems a guy's got to, too."

Her face grew serious, eyes darting around the dark forest once more before settling back on him.

"You're the brother of the dark Sorcerer, right?" she asked, her words taking on a haste that had not been present a moment ago.

Charlie sighed. "Yes," he said. "But it seems he's chosen your queen over his blood."

Her head tilted back, her face taking on a knowing look. "The same way you chose the Sorceress queen over him?"

Charlie's brows furrowed. "How do you know that?"

"It's my job to know things," she said, dismissing this question with a wave of her hand.

By the red nail polish on her fingernails, Charlie gleamed that this girl spent most of her life in the human world, and though she was not nearly as out of place in the Fae Forest as he was, she was not right at home, either.

A cool, sweet-scented breeze went through the trees, ruffling the fluffy leaves and lifting Aria's red-brown hair from her shoulders. Once again, urgency filled her eyes as she looked down at Charlie.

The Fae children were growing antsy, disappearing to wherever they went when not staring or laughing at Charlie, slipping away, the voids they left filling with a silence that made Charlie's heart pick up in pace.

He knew what it meant. The Fae Queen was approaching.

Aria spoke quickly. "War is coming, Charlie," she told him, green eyes locked on his. "Not just between the Fae and the Sorcerers—a big war."

Something in the way the girl said this made goose bumps break out over his skin, the hair on the back of his neck standing at stiff attention.

Aria leaned in closer, her young face filling with a wisdom beyond her years, her expression as grave as the dead. Her voice was lower now, somehow older than it had been just before.

"I've known my share of loss, Sorcerer," she told him, and swallowed before continuing, her eyes darting to the south, where the forest itself was beckoning the Fae Queen's arrival.

Aria placed her small, cool hand on his cheek, the floral scent of her surrounding him. "Answer me a question, Charlie," she said. "In the battles that lie ahead, which side will you be fighting on? That of the darkness, or that of the light?"

Charlie did not consider lying. He didn't see the point. Also, he felt that somehow his next words to the strange Halfling girl were going to determine something important, that they may mean the difference between life and death.

"I'm gonna be fighting on whatever side Surah Stormsong's fighting on," he said.

Aria gave a crooked smile, and something mischievous flashed behind her earth-green eyes.

Then a hole opened up in the forest floor beneath him, and Charlie was sucked into it like liquid in a straw, falling through the abyss with a neck-jerking quickness, his beaten heart lodging itself somewhere in his throat.

14

SURAH

Surah watched as the blood of the Demons she'd slain circled the drain near her feet.

She'd been in the shower for five minutes, and still the water falling over her had not run clear.

The icky substance was in her hair, under her nails. It had streaked her face and soaked her clothes. She could smell its rank, sewage-like aroma when she breathed in deeply, could taste the rottenness of it in her mouth.

She shut off the shower and stepped out onto the cold floor, wrapping a towel around her body and another around her head. Samson was out on the balcony, letting the cool rain that had begun to drizzle clean his fur of the gore that covered him.

Surah stood watching him through the glass doors of her balcony for a moment, her heart breaking anew at the thought of him leaving her.

His enormous, black-and-blue striped body stood overlooking the city below, his ears flattened against his head and his amber eyes squinted against the rain. He stood as still and stoic as a statue, while Surah stood inside the warmth of her bedroom and fought hard against the urge to crumble.

As if he could sense her there, the large cat hopped gracefully down from the balcony's ledge and pushed his way inside the room, kicking the glass door shut with his rear paw in a way that was oddly human.

"If I were human," the cat told her in that silent way of his, his deep voice a welcome presence in her mind, *"then things between us would be interesting."*

He brushed the side of his body against her bare leg, making her shiver. Surah wanted so badly to tell him he had to stay, that he just could not leave her. She wanted to cry, and have Sam lick the tears from her face with his rough tongue, the way he'd done since they were both but cubs. But she would do no such thing.

She rubbed at his ears and spoke aloud, happy when her voice came out steady. "If you were human, Sam, we'd run away together, we'd leave all this behind and go where no one could find us."

She sat back on her bed, and he came forward and rested his huge head in her lap, sitting back on his haunches. She found it was harder to hold his amber stare than it should've been. Her eyes were beginning to burn, but she blinked it away.

"You will return, won't you, Sam?" she asked.

"Nothing could keep me from it," he answered. *"And I don't need to be human for us to run away together. You say the word, say the word and I'll take you away from this place. We'll go live among the beasts. You will be mine, and I will be yours."*

Surah knew he meant this, knew that every word was spoken from the heart. She responded silently now, preferring the intimacy of their shared minds.

"I'm already yours, Sam, and you are forever mine."

"But your heart calls for him, doesn't it?" he asked, and she did not miss the jealousy and heartache that rode the cat's words. It was rare for Samson's tone to take on any inflection at all, and it

twisted at her soul to hear it, because they both knew he was right.

"We both know you love him, that you belong together."

It was hard for Sam to say this, and it was even harder for Surah to hear it, but the love between the Sorceress and the feline was too great to allow for pretense.

The cat would stand by her forever, and would sooner die than speak false words to her, even if the words were too true for her to even admit to herself.

To have this pointed out by her most trusted friend, her soul mate in cat form, brought on a sense of clarity that was nearly paralyzing in its enormity. Surah realized with this epiphany that she had to get to Charlie, had to save him from whatever trouble he was in.

Let's be serious, a little voice in her head—one that did not belong to her cat, but her conscience—pointed out. *You've got to save him from whatever situation* you *left him in.*

This thought came like a slap to the face, and urgency surged through her. Her lovely face fell, and Samson only stared up at it, knowing that she was at last coming to terms with what he already knew.

"I've got to get to him, Sam," she said, the words an unintended whisper. "I've got to make sure Charlie's okay."

Samson said nothing to this, only licked her hands with his warm, rough tongue.

"I've got to save my kingdom, kill the Fae Queen, and get to Charlie," she said. "I don't know if I can, Sam. I don't know if I've got what it takes."

The cat lifted his large head and took to his feet. With her sitting on the bed before him, they were eye level, and Sam moved in close so that their noses were nearly touching, his amber eyes closing to slits as he breathed her scent in deeply. She dug her fingers into the fur around his neck and pulled him even closer.

"You will do all these things, Surah," he told her. *"You will protect your people, and when the time comes, you will watch as the life leaves the eyes of that crazed fairy... and you will find your Charlie."*

Sam was silent a moment, turning his head so that he could meet her eyes. *"I'm beginning to think there are no forces upon this earth that could keep the two of you apart... There's not much else you need to be sure of beyond that."*

"Oh, Sam," she said holding him close. "What have I done? What if it's too late? What if Black Heart decided to just kill him?"

Sam blinked at her, his beautiful, feline face as expressionless as always, though she knew he was as reluctant to leave her as she was to leave him.

"There's only one way to answer those questions, dear one. You need to go find your fate."

"Is that where you're going, Sam?" she whispered. "To find your fate?"

The cat was silent a moment, the time to part drawing near. They both could feel it, so there was no need to speak the words.

"I guess we all are, aren't we?" he said, and licked her face. Stepping back from her, he lifted his large head, his eyes taking on the gleam of a predator's. *"Will you open a portal for me?"* he asked.

Surah stood from the bed and went to the closet, disappearing inside for a moment. When she returned, she was fully dressed, royal cloak over her squared shoulders, royal stone around her neck, and the determination of a queen upon her lovely face.

She would never know how proud Sam was of her in that moment, how his heart thudded in his chest just at the sight of her. There were beasts in all the jungles that did not have the strength of the two-leg before him, beasts that did not have the might of his dearest one, of his Surah.

Two-leg or no, there wasn't a creature in all the Territories in all the realms that would ever compare, and he thought if he wanted to tell her so, he ought to do it now, because if he was being honest, he wasn't sure if he would ever see her again, and this broke the heart inside his chest that had been unbreakable before he and the Sorceress had met.

Surah stepped up to him. She would do what needed to be done, and that was that. "Where would you like to go, Sam?" she asked, the White Stone glowing around her neck.

"To the jungles of my homeland," he told her.

She did not look surprised. She had somehow known this was where he would go. *To find his fate,* she thought.

And with a wave of her hand, a swirling portal large enough to step through opened before them. The slight suction of it lifted her lavender hair from her shoulders, and it danced around her face in a rhythm Sam would never tire of.

The Great Cat hesitated just before jumping through the wormhole, rubbing his head against his dearest friend one last time.

"I love you, Surah Stormsong," he told her. *"More than any cat has loved before."*

"I love you, too, Sam," she whispered, and waited until her Great Cat had stepped through the portal and it had closed behind him before falling to her bedroom floor in a puddle of heartache that did not feel queenly in the least.

15

CHARLIE

The hole that had opened up in the floor of the Fae Forest sucked him in spat him back out on an old couch in a small apartment that smelled faintly of floral and old wood.

When Charlie landed, his head struck the armrest of the couch. He rubbed at the back of it, letting the nausea pass over him before sitting up.

Aria landed on the floor in the middle of the small living room, but she rolled right into an agile stand with the expertise of someone who was no stranger to whatever Halfling transportation method she'd just used to bring him here. She smirked when he gave her a slightly annoyed look.

Aria placed a hand on her hip. "What?" she asked. "I think the words you're searching for are 'thank you', seeing as how I dropped you on the couch. It's not easy to land and roll the way I just did. I could've busted my head open on the coffee table. I've seen it happen before."

Charlie said, "Why did you bring me here?"

Aria made a face like this was a stupid question. "Because

Tristell would've killed you if I hadn't," she said. "And I can't imagine that would've pleased your queen."

"My queen?"

Again with the stupid-question face. Charlie had forgotten how annoying teenage girls could be.

"Surah Stormsong?" she said. "Your Sorceress Queen? Your beloved? The lady who's half the reason you're in this mess? Ring any bells?"

Charlie took a minute to absorb this information, though he supposed he should have already known, as he knew King Syrian had passed when the magic flooded back into their world. But somehow, in all the thinking about her he'd done, Charlie hadn't put two and two together.

"You'll have to forgive me," he said. "I've been a little kidnapped and held against my will."

Aria smiled, its radiance lighting up her face. "Well, now you're free. And, again, you're welcome."

She wandered into the small kitchen connected to the living room in which he sat, opened the refrigerator (which Charlie could see ran on electricity, not magic, meaning they were indeed in the human world, as he'd suspected) and took out a red apple. "Want one?" she asked.

Charlie nodded so fervently that Aria chuckled as she tossed it to him. He caught it out of the air. He couldn't remember the last time he'd eaten, and just the sight of the fruit made his mouth water.

"Again," she began, "You're wel—"

"Thank you, Aria," Charlie interrupted, swallowing a large bite of the sweet apple. "Thank you for freeing me from the Fae Forest and dropping me on the couch instead of the floor." He held up the already half-eaten apple. "And thank you for the apple."

Aria sat in the armchair across from him and gave a satisfied nod. "You're welcome, Charlie Redmine."

"Now, will you tell me what's going on here?"

He looked around. The apartment was small, but had tall ceilings, with modern furniture and neutral colors. There were paintings on the walls of various scenes, mostly of shadows in alleys and sunsets over a city, all done by the same unknown artist. Two tall windows hung on the eastern wall, which revealed closely spaced multi-colored houses, and the light of a new morning just beginning to brighten the sky.

"And where is 'here'?" Charlie added.

Aria bit into her apple, her black-booted feet flat on the floor, as if she were ready to hop out of her seat at any instant, though her posture suggested ease.

"We're in the human world," she said, as if transporting out of the supernatural realm was no big deal. "In a place called Blue Hook, New Jersey. You ever heard of it?"

Charlie had been to the human world a handful of times, for no other reason than curiosity, but he'd always found it to be a disappointing, somewhat sad place. Humans polluted their oceans, dug up the earth and trees, and seemed to have little to no regard for the quality of air or the sacredness of all life.

Then again, Charlie thought, he knew plenty of Sorcerers with the same qualities.

"I visited New York City some years back," he said. "Dirty, crowded place full of crooked humans and smelly sewers and more Accursed than any one place I've ever been outside of Vamp Territory."

Aria grinned. "You've got a particular distaste for humans, don't you, Sorcerer?"

Charlie had forgotten that the girl was half human, and suddenly felt a little foolish.

"I'm sorry," he said, rubbing at his chin, which needed a good shave. "I guess I'm a little on edge, and in truth, I really don't know enough about humans to judge them like that. In my experience, there's good and there's bad people in all the races."

Her smile softened a bit. "I knew you were a good one," she said, and leaned forward, her arms resting on her knees. She pointed a red-painted fingernail at him. "But if I turn out to be wrong about you, I'll kill you quick as a Christmas goose." Her grin returned. "Got it?"

Charlie held his hands up, trying to keep a small smile from his face. If he was sure he could trust her, he would probably like the girl, but he wasn't sure of this in the least. He also had no idea what the heck a "Christmas goose" was.

"Okay," he said. "Why'd you bring me here, then?"

"This is my apartment," Aria said, obviously proud of the fact. "And you'll be safe here until she comes to get you."

"Where are your parents?" he asked, knowing the girl could not be older than seventeen. "And safe until who comes to get me?"

At the mention of her parents, Aria's face darkened. It was a look he knew well, a distance to the eyes that spoke of loss and heartache, anger, and a need for revenge, and he did not need for her to speak on the matter of her family. It was clear that the girl did not have any family left. Charlie knew this because he'd seen the look on his own face so many years ago, when he'd been not too much younger than her.

Aria's chin lifted, and her eyes remained dry and focused as she spoke, causing Charlie's respect for the girl to grow.

"It's just me," Aria said. "And until Queen Surah comes to get you." She paused, her dark brow lifting and some of the humor she wore as a safeguard against the world came back to her face. "You're not the sharpest tool in the shed, are you?" she asked.

"Why do you think Queen Surah is coming to get me?"

Stupid-question face. "Because you two are 'getting it on,' aren't you?"

Charlie almost choked on the last bite of his apple. "Excuse me?" he said.

Aria smirked. "You're lovers, right?" she sighed, taking on the dreamy look. "Star-crossed lovers," she added.

"How do you know that?" he asked, but before she could give him the stupid-question look again, he held up his hand. "Wait, I know. It's your job to know stuff, right?"

Another radiant smile. "Bingo! We have a winner!"

Charlie rubbed at his chin, his large shoulders falling a fraction. "Well, I hate to break it to you," he said, "but I don't think she's coming after me."

"But you love her, don't you?" Aria asked.

What was the point in lying? How could it make the situation worse? It couldn't.

"Yes," he said. "I love her."

Aria's bright green eyes narrowed, her full lips pursing in thought. A moment of silence passed before she leaned back again, kicking her feet up over the armrest of the chair in which she was sitting, boots dangling in the air. She closed her eyes and laid back against the chair in a position that only really young people and cats would be comfortable in.

Without opening her eyes, she grabbed a small beanbag from the end table beside her and threw it at the western wall behind her chair. The beanbag struck the light switch there with a thud, and the lights in the room went out, casting early morning shadows into all the corners.

"She's coming for you, Charlie," Aria said, shifting a little in her seat. "Get some rest. You're gonna need it."

Charlie sat quietly for a moment before lying back on the couch and closing his own eyes. When he finally spoke, he was not expecting a response from her, because he thought she'd fallen asleep.

His deep voice was just above a whisper when he asked, "How can you be so sure, Aria?"

She didn't answer for so long that he decided she actually was asleep, and just before he decided to take her advice and try for some rest himself, Aria lifted her head and looked at him, her bright green eyes glittering like emeralds in the soft, dim light of the morning.

"Have you looked in the mirror lately, Charlie?" the half-Fae, half-human girl asked, a mischievous smirk pulling up her pink mouth. "I'm not sure there are too many women who *wouldn't* come after you. Now sleep, Sorcerer, and don't you worry, if someone attacks us, I'll totally protect you." Her straight, white teeth gleamed in the darkness. "With a face like that, you gotta be careful," she added with a wink that was way too charming for her own good.

Charlie would not have thought it possible, but he let out a laugh—the first real laugh he could recall in what seemed like a lifetime, and found that sleep came easy after all.

16

SURAH

*S*he rose well before the sun, standing before the glass doors of her balcony, which overlooked the city of Zadira below.

At this early hour, the city was awash in a sweet blue and violet light, the night not quite completely receded from the corners, where deep shadows clung tightly before slowly giving way to morning.

Last night she had allowed herself a breakdown. She had locked the doors to her chambers, added an extra barrier spell around the room for good measure, and just sat on her bed and cried into her pillows for what seemed like hours.

The absence of her father in the castle was as noticeable as would be a twenty-degree drop in temperature. The place, with its high stone walls and endless labyrinth of rooms, felt empty and cold and a touch forsaken now that she was the last of the Stormsong line that would likely ever dwell between its walls.

Or any walls, for that matter.

The absence of her tiger in her bedside was just as felt, just as palpable. After an indeterminable amount of time, the tears finally ceased, and she'd drifted off to a mercifully deep and dreamless sleep. When she awoke this morning, she felt as ready as she supposed she would ever be to take on the world.

A knock sounded at her door, and without turning, she flicked her wrist, knowing well who would be on the other side.

Sure enough, Theo entered with a hesitation uncommon of him, as if he could sense her need to be approached with caution, despite the expressionlessness on her face.

"Good morning, my queen," the Head Hunter said with a bow.

"Good morning, Theo," she said, not completely comfortable with this informal way of addressing him, but remembering her promise to give him a real chance at being more than just a piece in her royal court.

The address clearly pleased him, and a half smile pulled up his mouth, making his handsome face even more so. However, there was a seriousness to his gray eyes that Surah knew predated bad news.

She took a deep breath and asked, "What's the word?"

The smile was gone from his face now. "Demons have been popping up in the small villages at the edges of Sorcerer Territory. As you ordered, I sent a good majority of the Hunters to protect them, and they've been very effective in doing so, but this has spread our manpower dangerously thin."

"How many Hunters are here protecting the city?" she asked.

"One hundred, counting your personal guard, and myself."

She nodded. "Focus them on protecting the city, not the castle," she said.

Theo was silent a tick. "My queen… Is it wise to do so? That would leave us very vulnerable to attack."

Surah turned to face him now, her violet gaze inscrutable. "By 'us' you mean the royals, Hunter Gray."

It was not a question, but he answered anyway. "Well… yes… of course."

"Instruct them to take to their hideouts if they fear for their wellbeing."

This made him smirk, and she could see by the look in his gray eyes that her decisive way of handling things only deepened his affections for her. A voice that sounded eerily like that of her tiger's spoke up in her head, telling her to tread lightly with the Head Hunter, to remember that when a woman played with a man's emotions, she tended to end up absorbing the blunt end of his darker side.

"I expect the lords and ladies will not be pleased with that," he told her matter of factly.

"No, I suppose they won't." She thought for a moment. "If any of them complain too much, send Noelani and Lyonell to double protection."

Now Theo looked displeased. "My queen, that would leave you without protection."

In answer, Surah went to her floor length mirror, the rounded corner of which was draped with her long cloak. Hidden in the folds of that cloak, all of her weapons were stored.

She slung it over her shoulders, her eyes never leaving his. "I'll need you to stay here and hold down the fort, Theo." She came forward and took his hands into hers when he looked apprehensive, and again that small warning voice spoke up in her head. "Will you stand beside me as you've promised?" she asked, her head tilting back in order to meet his eyes.

He only hesitated a moment, then the Head Hunter gave a slight nod. "Do I get to know where you'll be running off to?" he asked, his voice a little huskier with her so near.

The lie came easily. Really, it was only half a lie, and she would never know if Theodine Gray totally bought it that day, or if he just truly was done fighting her, prepared to let her make her own decisions and see just where they led.

"Only Dark Lords can command Demons and open portals

into our world," she said, "and there's only one Dark Lord I can think of that dislikes my family enough to help the Fae Queen and Black Heart with whatever they're planning."

She tied her cloak around her shoulders and back, running her fingers over her silver sais tucked neatly into their folds, taking comfort in the feel of them there. "So I suppose I'll be paying a visit to that Dark Lord," she said. "Have a word or two with him."

"The Underworld isn't a place to be wandering alone," he said.

"You mean, it isn't a place for *me* to be wandering alone."

He shook his head, and she didn't miss the earnestness in his gaze. "No, I mean it isn't a place for *anyone* to be wandering alone."

"But you'll stay while I go?" she asked.

Theo sighed, and with a touch of wariness, tucked a lock of her lavender hair behind her ear. "I'll do what you've asked of me, my queen," he said. Then, "Is that the only place you'll be going?"

Here was the lie. The half of her story that she suspected they both knew was untrue.

"Yes," she said. "To the Underworld, and then back here to take action accordingly."

Whether or not the Head Hunter believed this, she would never know, because all he did was nod and bow deeply, kissing her hand before taking his leave. She watched him go, the tall, arched double doors of her chambers clanging shut behind him, wondering if he had read the silent words in the air as clearly as she had.

To the Underworld, yes.

But, first, to Charlie.

17

CHARLIE

When he awoke he found he was alone in Aria's apartment.

He sat up, feeling more rested than he would've expected, staring out the two tall windows to see that he had slept a good portion of the day away.

He stood, stretched, and found his way to the bathroom, which was just a tiny square of space with an old sink, shower, and toilet. There was a note stuck to the time-stained mirror hanging above the sink.

It read: *Go ahead and take care of your business, and shower while you're at it. I'll be back when I'm back. ~Aria*

Charlie plucked the note from the mirror, shaking his head. Deciding the idea of a hot shower was too tempting to pass up, he stripped out of his clothes and hopped in, turning the temperature to as scalding as he could stand.

The small wounds all over his body burned as the water hit them, making him cringe as he watched the scarlet of his own blood circle the drain at his feet.

Once he was finished, he stepped out and dried off with a

towel Aria had set out for him. He pulled his jeans on, slung his shirt over his bare shoulder, and stepped out of the bathroom, drying his now too-long hair with the towel.

While he was making himself at home, he decided to see if the girl had any tea or even coffee. He was in the middle of making a cup when a breeze brushed by him. Charlie's heartbeat kicked up in pace before he turned to see Aria climbing in through the window, a small gasp escaping her as she took in the sight of him.

He suppressed a sigh, regretting the decision not to put his shirt back on, despite it being filthy and in tatters. The Halfling girl came forward slowly, dropping the bag she'd been holding in her hand without a thought, and approaching Charlie with a look of sympathy that he'd learned to hate over the years.

She stared at his bare chest, his shoulders, and shamelessly moved in a circle to study his back. "So many scars," she said, almost as if to herself.

He ignored this. "I don't suppose you have any clothes that would fit me?"

Aria's eyebrows arched, and she couldn't seem to keep her gaze from all the scarring on his golden skin, but she wandered over to the bag she'd dropped earlier, pulled out a plain black t-shirt, and tossed it over to him.

She continued to watch him as he pulled the shirt over his head, the fabric sliding easily over the lean, strong muscles in his chest and waist. Leaning against the counter that separated the kitchen from the living room, she shook her head slowly, a slight smile pulling up her lips.

"She's coming for you, all right," she mumbled.

Charlie suppressed a half-annoyed, half-amused shake of his head. The girl had an odd way of making light of things.

"You're making this whole thing a bit uncomfortable, you know that?"

Aria picked up the cup of hot tea he'd made for himself and took a sip, as if people just left random cups of tea around for her to drink all the time, and waved her free hand at this.

"People tell me that a lot," she said, and shrugged. "I'm never quite sure what they mean."

"How many of your kind are there?" he asked.

Another shrug. "Not many," Aria said. "The Fae don't mix with humans the way your kind and some of the others do. When Halflings are born, we are taken and trained for a specific purpose."

As she said this last part, her shoulders sank just the tiniest of fractions, as if this were a statement that brought her heartache to speak. A less perceptive person than Charlie would've missed it. The girl was young, but she was good at hiding emotions.

He steered away from the subject in consideration of her not-so-obvious feelings. "So what's your stake in this?"

Aria tossed her leather jacket aside and picked up some fingerless gloves from the coffee table, sliding them over her small hands.

Then she went to a metal workout bar that was mounted on the wall and jumped up, grabbing it with both hands. She began to knock out pull-ups the way old Sorcerers tend to knock back beers. She carried on the conversation with Charlie as she did so, not in the least out of breath.

"My stake in this is the same as my stake in all things," she answered, as if this explained everything. She finished more pull-ups—making fifty in all—and jumped down, turning back to face him. "To keep the peace between the races."

"But you still haven't told me anything about anything, Aria. For all I know, that's not even your name, and this could be some magic spell-reality, rather than a town on a coastal part of the human world."

Aria hopped up on the countertop on which she'd been leaning and crossed her legs beneath her. The girl never seemed able to stay in one place for too long, but instead just bounced from here to there.

"How do you know you're in a coastal town? Did you leave the apartment?"

Charlie smirked. "You've been around humans too long. I can smell the salt in the air, same as you."

She crossed her arms over her chest. "Aria *is* my real name, and this *is* a coastal town in the human world. Beyond that, all you need to know is that I'm going to help you reunite with your beloved queen, and hopefully stop Tristell from causing a war."

He blinked at her, half impressed, half in disbelief. "Okay… but *why?*"

Sighing, Aria leaned forward and held his gaze. "Because war isn't good for anyone, Charlie Redmine," she snapped. "I told you, I'm trying to keep the peace. It's my duty and honor."

He was silent a moment, mulling this over. He supposed it really didn't matter what her reasons were. What options did he really have? The human world, as undesirable as it was for most of his kind, was probably the safest place for him right now.

"You're smarter than you look," he told her. "You know that?"

Aria rolled her eyes, the joking half-smile on her face again. "People tell me that a lot, too."

"So, Halflings are drafted to be peace-keeping liaisons between the worlds… Does that sum it up?"

She shrugged, and he thought that it must be a default gesture of hers, as it was for many teens of all races. "It sounds more exciting than it is. Most of the time I'm just here sitting at my post, living like a human among humans… Only I'm not human."

"There are worse lives to live," Charlie observed.

"And better ones, too," she countered.

Charlie swallowed before responding. "So the plan is to wait here until someone comes for me?"

"Your excitement mirrors my own," she said, getting down from the counter. "If you're hungry, you can help yourself to whatever you want in the fridge, but you gotta be quiet. I have an essay due tomorrow."

"You attend the human schools?" he asked, fascinated and slightly bewildered.

It seemed such an odd way to live. To be *taken and trained.* He suddenly felt sad for the girl. Aria was forever a stranger in a world full of strangers.

But if it was as sad and lonely of a life as Charlie expected it to be, the young lady had become a master at hiding it. She sighed.

"Yes, genius. I attend the human schools. I eat the human food, and wear the human clothes, and rescue stupid Sorcerers who ask stupid questions from sticky situations."

She grabbed a backpack that looked as if it weighed a ton from a hook by the door and tossed it down on the coffee table. "I also enjoy video games, reading, and ninja training. Anything else?"

Charlie didn't know whether or not to laugh at this, because he had no idea what a 'ninja' was, so he just held his hands up in surrender.

"Okay, I get it. You want me to shut up and sit tight."

She winked at him.

"You're very strange, Aria," he said.

"Another thing I hear often," she replied with a roll of her eyes.

Aria flopped down onto the couch and pulled several large books out of her overstuffed backpack. She spread them out all around her, and opened a silver computer atop her lap.

Charlie decided there really wasn't much else to be done on his part at the moment. He would listen to the young Halfling girl and wait for a little while, but not because he was waiting for Surah to rescue him, but because he needed some time to formulate a plan.

After all that had happened, after all these years of hoping Michael could change, of having his trust and his love for his older brother betrayed again and again, a slow realization had finally settled over him.

Michael could not be saved, because Michael no longer existed. Though it had taken Charlie longer than it probably should have to really see it, to really come to terms with it, there was no way of avoiding the truth of it now.

Michael Redmine, the older brother who had chased away Charlie's nightmares as a child, who had knocked out bigger boys in the schoolyards in Charlie's defense, who had gone hungry on many a night in their youth after the war so that Charlie could put in his belly whatever little bit of food they'd managed to get a hold of… That Michael, he was dead.

And a vengeful, cold-hearted Dark Sorcerer had taken his place. Black Heart, they called him, and Charlie knew for certain it was a name that fit.

He also knew for certain that Black Heart and the Fae Queen Tristell had to be stopped. It was no longer just for Surah. It was for the young Charlie's and Michael's of their world, for the strange children who dwelled deep in the Fae Forest, for the girls like Aria, who was so young and so green, but obviously wiser and deeper than she most likely received credit for.

Because the girl was right: War was good for no one, and one needn't have lived through the horrors of a war to know that. One needn't, but Charlie Redmine had.

And as he sat looking at the Halfling girl, her feet tucked under her as she read her human books and wrote her human essays and lived forever as an outsider in the human world,

Charlie knew for the first time in his life that if it came down to it, if the only way to stop the coming of another war was to kill his older brother, the former Michael Redmine, the current Dark Sorcerer plaguing their world, then so be it.

This thought settled on his shoulders and in his gut with the weight of the universe.

18

SURAH

She stared into its depths, at the darkness in its endless, unflawed prisms.

The Black Stone reflected in the vibrant violet of her eyes, as if casting her under a trance. But Surah Stormsong was under no spell. She was fully aware of what she was doing, and equally aware that there would be consequences for the use of this stone of dark magic.

When the door to the secret chamber opened behind her, she nearly dropped the stone, startled as though she'd just been snapped out of a trance she would've sworn she was not under.

Bassil stood in the entryway of the chamber, his dark eyes narrowed as he shut the door behind him. "Surah..." he cautioned.

Though she knew he was only concerned for her wellbeing, her back went up a touch at the look the Warlock gave her.

"If you've got any other suggestions, Bassil," she snapped. "I would love to hear them. If not," she paused, and her hand tightened around the large stone, which was so big that it shined through the cracks of her fingers, "then save the lecture."

The Warlock said nothing for a long while, only folded his

hands into the long sleeves of his patchwork cloak and stared at her with onyx eyes. The small, secret space was dim and musty, and Surah was just going to teleport out of there when he sighed.

"You are the queen, Surah," he said slowly, "By divine right and law, the Black Stone is yours to do with whatever you see fit."

Surah's purple gaze narrowed, and she waited, knowing the old Warlock well enough to anticipate the *but* that would surely follow this.

But Bassil said nothing, only stood staring at her, offering every opportunity for her to leave, Black Stone in hand.

And she almost did. There was a big part of her that wanted nothing more than to snap her fingers and teleport out from under the arbitrating gaze of the Warlock. But there was another part of her that wanted to be talked out of this madness, brought back from this ledge she'd been pushed out on.

Still, the Warlock said nothing, because the truth was, they both knew there weren't any other options. Surah had to go to the Underworld and seek out a Dark Lord. Not just any Dark Lord, but a Dark Lord who had hated the Stormsong family for as long as any of the descendants could remember.

Any of the descendants, Surah thought, the words in her head as small and dark as the space she was standing in. *I'm the only one left. Utterly alone in the world.*

She slapped this thought away, because it was counterproductive. Lifting her chin, she asked, "You'd rather I visit the Underworld without the protection of the Black Stone?"

Bassil placed his large hands on her shoulders, his smooth, ebony face full of love and sympathy.

"Dear child," the Warlock said, "what I would rather makes none the difference… I would *rather* you not have to go into the Underworld at all. I would *rather* we not be at war with the Fae. I would rather…"

Surah waited, and when he didn't finish, she took a deep breath. "You'd rather what? Just say it."

The half-smile that pulled up one side of Bassil's full mouth was colored with sadness.

"I would rather that you didn't love Charlie Redmine," he said at last. "Not because he's not worthy, not because he's not a good man, and not because I don't think he loves you as much as you obviously love him."

He shook his head, his gaze going distant, as if remembering a time from long ago. When he spoke next, his deep voice was barely above a whisper. "But simply because it would make things a hell of a lot easier, wouldn't it?"

Surah's lips pulled up at this, but her heart remained as sunken as a sea-swallowed ship. "You ever known me to do things the easy way?" she asked.

He chuckled and pulled her into a hug that was as close to a fatherly embrace as she would ever get again. As small as it was, she decided it was something to be grateful for.

When he pulled back, Bassil kept hold of her shoulders, meeting her gaze. Surah placed her hands over his and squeezed.

"I don't want to do any of this either," she admitted. "But you agree that it must be done?"

Bassil smirked. "You're asking for my permission before doing something dangerous and crazy?" he laughed. "Who are you, and what have you done with Surah?"

"So you're not here to stop me, then?"

"Would I even be able to stop you if I were?"

She shook her head. "I don't suppose you could."

His dark face grew serious, and he took the Black Stone from her hands, tucking it gently into a pocket on the inside of her cloak.

"And that is the point, dear child," the wise Warlock told her. "Whenever there has been something you've really wanted, all the powers and magic and crossed stars in the universe have never been able to stop you from getting it. You'll be keeping that stone of dark magic so close to your heart… I just don't want you to lose sight of things. Don't let it change who you are. Don't let it corrupt you. There is the greatest of lights within you, Surah Stormsong, but even bright lights can be doused with shadows."

Surah said nothing to this, because there was nothing to say. How could she tell him that it was too late, that she had long been corrupted, that she had spent years fighting off the shadows, only to have them creeping in like creatures of the night right now?

How could she tell her old friend, her lifelong mentor, that sometimes one could not fight the darkness with light, that sometimes one had to take a torch in hand and battle fire with fire, darkness with darkness, hate and revenge with hate and revenge?

She could not say these things to Bassil, because he would not understand. Only those who were as lost as she could possibly comprehend.

So what she said was, "Okay, Bassil. I'll do my best."

The smile he gave her then was enough to break her heart, had there been any part of it left unbroken.

"That's all any of us can do, dear child," he said, and kissed her forehead.

Before he could see the moisture that was beginning to fill her eyes, the start of salty tears she hadn't the time nor the patience for, Surah gripped the piece of White Stone around her neck and teleported out of the secret space in which they'd been standing.

Using the power of both the stones combined, she commanded them to take her to Charlie Redmine, and Gods help whoever stood in her way.

* * *

Surah landed in a small apartment, her mind a bit fuzzy from the use of so much magic in one burst.

She had crossed realms. Of that, she was sure, and she could smell a slight saltiness to the air that suggested close proximity to an ocean, but other than that, she had no idea where she was.

"Holy jumping jacks!" said a sweet voice.

Surah spun on her heel, her hands gripping her sais, the silver weapons slipping free of her cloak as she braced herself for an attack.

Her eyebrows rose as the owner of the voice hopped up from the couch she'd been sitting on, a large book spilling to the floor in the process.

"I've never seen a portal open like that," the girl said, her pretty face lit up in a smile.

Surah only looked at her, wondering if the stones had somehow taken her to the wrong place. She glanced around the small space, determining that she was in the human world, but that couldn't be right. Why would Black Heart have taken Charlie here?

Before she could ask these things, the over-excited girl held out her hand, her bright green eyes locked on the sais in Surah's.

"You must be Queen Surah," she said with a bow. "I'm Aria Fae. It's nice to finally meet you."

Surah's voice was poised, careful. She returned the bow mostly out of habit. "The pleasure is mine, Aria," she said. She studied the girl closely. "You're a Halfling," she observed. It was not a question.

Aria grinned, tossing some of her thick, red-brown hair over her shoulder. "So you're the smart one in the couple, huh?" she said, as if in jest.

Surah was growing more confused by the moment, but before she could ask the girl what that was supposed to mean,

Charlie stepped out of the back bedroom. He opened his mouth to speak, but the words seemed to jam up in his throat as he saw Surah.

For a moment, as she took in the sight of him, it was if the world stopped. The small apartment, with its slightly sea-scented air, dropped away around her, and all she could see was Charlie.

Her gaze traveled the length of him, checking for injuries, nearly convinced she was seeing a ghost. Until just this moment, she had not realized that a part of her had suspected she might never see him again.

Not alive, anyway. And the sight of him now, so obviously alive and as transfixed by the sight of her as she was by that of him, took on a somehow surreal quality.

And then she was in his arms, not even aware of having moved. Their bodies pulled together like magnets, or the way gravity holds things to the earth. With his strong arms around her, the clean, masculine smell of him filled her senses.

"I thought I'd never see you again," he whispered in her ear, making her suppress a shiver that ran all the way from her toes to the top of her head.

They may well have stayed in that manner for eternity, wrapped in each other's embrace and hearts beating side by side, had Aria not cleared her throat behind them. Surah had totally forgotten the girl was there, and that she didn't know where *there* even was.

The Halfling girl quirked an eyebrow at Charlie. "Told you she'd come for you," she said.

Charlie sighed in a way that suggested he'd grown used to the girl and her somewhat crass way of speaking. "That, you did, Aria," he agreed, his eyes never leaving Surah's face. He traced her soft cheek with his thumb, the look in the emerald of his gaze full of words unspoken.

Surah didn't want to speak about all the things that needed

addressing between them. Not yet, anyway. Not until they were alone. She pulled herself out of his arms more than reluctantly and turned to face the girl.

"Aria," she began, "how did you come to be in possession of a wanted Sorcerer?"

Aria plopped back down on the couch, settling herself in the middle of her books. "I stole him from the Fae Forest when the Fae Queen wasn't looking," she said.

Surah raised a half-amused, half-disbelieving eyebrow at Charlie, who spread his hands and nodded.

"She's telling the truth," he said. "She talks a lot, but she sure saved me from a pinch."

Aria rolled her eyes. "Says the guy who asks the world's dumbest questions," she retorted.

Surah couldn't help a smile at this. She looked sideways at Charlie. "I think I like her," she said.

Charlie nodded again. "Somehow, she manages that, too."

"Uh, hello," Aria said. "I'm right here. And if you two don't mind, I've got homework due tomorrow." She looked at Charlie. "And, again, you're totally welcome. No big deal at all, you know, for stealing you from Tristell and all that."

Slowly, Surah realized whom, or rather *what*, this girl was.

"You're a Faevian Peace Broker," Surah said.

Again, it was not a question.

Aria grinned. "Like I said, you're the smart one."

"Why haven't your people reached out before now?" Surah asked. "Where have you been while all this mess between the Fae and the Sorcerers has been brewing?"

"I've been right here," Aria replied, a slight snap to her tone. "Following orders. Don't shoot the soldier. Besides, it's not an easy decision to decide to counter one of the most powerful rulers in the supernatural world. The Peace Brokers had to try diplomacy first."

She rolled her eyes as if this would not have been the way

she'd have done things. She shrugged. "I guess Tristell has finally gone too far." Aria met Surah's gaze square, with more backbone than most people whom Surah met. "We don't want a war."

Surah gestured to the chair across from the Halfling girl. "May I sit?" she asked.

Aria waved a hand. "By all means, your majesty."

"Thank you," Surah said, taking a seat across from the girl. She crossed her legs and smoothed out her cloak. "I don't want war with your people either, but I'm afraid it may be too late. Your queen hasn't left me much of a choice."

She thought of her father, lying on the pyre, of the Demons that hadn't even allowed her the chance to say goodbye.

"Your queen enlisted the help of a Dark Lord. Demons have been attacking the Sorcerer Territory. Hundreds are dead." Surah shook her head, removed her hood, and held the girl's eyes. "There's no way back now. Tristell will die. I'm going to kill her myself."

Unexpectedly, the Halfling girl grinned, as if this was exactly what she'd wanted to hear. She gave one nod, her long, red-brown hair falling over her shoulders.

"With all due respect, your majesty," Aria said, "Tristell isn't *my* queen, and I know you're going to kill her, because I'm going to help you do it."

19

SAMSON

For a cat that was not used to traveling by portal, the trip to the jungles of his homeland would have been a dizzying feat, to say the least.

But Samson was no ordinary cat, so he emerged in the jungle with a clear head, but an aching heart.

He had not wanted to leave her, and she had not wanted him to, either. Sam knew Surah understood that their last goodbye could be their last *ever* goodbye; he had seen it in her beautiful violet eyes.

He may never return from this trip, this insane agreement he'd made with the King of the Beasts.

Sam had made the deal to save Surah when she'd been captured by Black Heart and kept in a cave in these jungles. In exchange for information, he'd fought and defeated the pride's greatest fighter, but that had been only half of the deal.

The other half was a promise he'd made to the king. A promise he was here to fulfill, or to die trying. Not particularly out of moral regard or even honor, but because Sam knew that if he'd made the King of Beasts come and find him, everyone around Sam could get hurt in the process. Surah was the only two-leg he cared about, but she was more than enough to hold the cat to his word.

There could be no avoiding it. He walked slowly through the trees, his large, padded paws moving lithely over the undergrowth. His large head and long tail were held low and still, the powerful muscles in his back rippling on his shoulders.

When in the Jungles of the Beasts, one had better always be on the lookout. He headed in the direction of the pride's field, where the Great Cats spent most of their time when not on the hunt.

The closer he drew, the faster his aching heart seemed to beat in his chest. His senses were filled with the clean, pleasant smells of the jungle; green vegetation and clean water that hung in the humid air.

The sun had not yet fully risen, but the soft blue light of morning was began to scatter the shadows that ruled the jungles at night.

If not for the nearly palpable feeling of loss that had settled somewhere in his gut after saying goodbye to his Surah, Samson would have to admit that the jungle was a much better place for a cat.

Here, the air was not polluted with the stenches of two-legs, who reeked of such fear at the sight of Sam that refraining from hunting them had become a constant battle, had taught him self-control he wasn't sure any cat was meant to have.

The only sounds were the soft chirping and clicking of insects, the occasional rustle of the trees. In the jungle, when the weather was such, one could listen to the music of rainfall for hours, could fall asleep to it and awake again to find it still gently playing. When a cat was tired, he simply found a place among the brush to rest his head. When he was hungry, he went on the hunt, and if successful, was rewarded with the inimitable taste of fresh and hot blood as he tore through the neck of a fresh kill.

He loved Surah for all the effort she put into obtaining different types of meat to sustain him, but there simply was no replacement for a good hunt in the jungle, nothing better than taking down a Great Dear—

"And sharing the spoils with your pride," a familiar voice spoke up in his mind.

Samson's head jerked up, looking to the thick green canopies above him.

Among the greenery, he spotted her, with her jet-black coat and bright green eyes, Mila was unmistakable.

"I didn't think you'd return," she said, speaking only in his mind, communicating in the way of the Great Cats.

"I gave my word," Sam said.

Her beautiful feline head tilted to the side. *"Right... that and you knew my father would come after you if you didn't. Couldn't risk putting your beloved Sorceress in harm's way."*

Sam did not miss the touch of jealousy in Mila's tone, and he couldn't really say he blamed her for it. He was her betrothed, after all, and had been long before he'd ever met Surah.

Mila hopped down from the tree limb on which she was perched, the powerful muscles in her legs catching her with ease, the pads on her paws landing silently on the jungle floor. Sam came forward, but paused when he saw the wariness in the green of her eyes.

"I never meant to cause you pain, Mila," he told her. It was a very two-leg thing to say, to admit to such regret, but Samson thought she deserved to hear it, and it was the truth.

When he'd been a cub, he'd had every intention of honoring the marriage arranged between his father and hers... but life just hadn't turned out that way.

"Who says you caused me pain?" she replied, ever the cat, willing to go to the death rather than admit to emotion.

Sam moved forward again, but did not stop this time. He came so close to her that their noses nearly touched. When she did not move away, but instead held rigidly still, he rubbed against her soft side, his larger body pushing against her.

He could hear her heartbeat pick up in her chest, and knew she was lying. It was odd, but he felt both glad and sad for this. He had indeed hurt her, and that meant that she really cared.

Mila pulled away at last, spinning around to face him. *"How can you be so calm, so confident?"* she asked, her tone taking on a snap that he suspected was there to cover the sudden harshness of her breathing. *"Have you forgotten what our betrothal entails?"*

Now it was Sam's turn to grow slightly nervous, but he hid the emotion as well as any cat.

"I have not forgotten," he replied, and that was all. There really wasn't anything else to say.

Silence hung between the two felines, the only sounds that of the bugs and the breeze in the jungle. The sun was beginning to break over the horizon, the golden glow of early morning replacing the light blue paint of pre-dawn.

Mila broke the silence first. She sat back so that she could look him in the eyes. *"Are you ready?"* she asked. *"I mean, do you think you can actually win?"*

"Honestly, Mila, I don't know."

For another long moment, neither said anything. Then Sam swallowed, his tongue feeling a touch thick in his mouth, and asked the question he wasn't sure he wanted to know the answer to.

"Do you want *me to win, Mila?"* he asked.

With a silent sigh and a small shake of her head, she met his gaze. *"Honestly, Sam,"* she said, *"I don't know."*

He considered her a moment before heading off again toward his destination. Mila fell in line silently behind him. Neither cat said another word. Sam could not stop replaying her response in his mind, though he supposed it was not the worst she could have given. After all, what had he expected her to say?

Samson had been promised to her at birth, and then he'd disappeared from the jungles with Surah, who'd saved his life and given him a new one. Mila had thought him dead for all these years.

Then, out of the blue, he returns, asking for help in locating a woman he loves, the woman he'd essentially left her for. Now, he was all but being forced to return and fight Mila's father to the death for the title of King of the Beasts, for Mila's hand, for the position fate seemed hell-bent on seeing him in.

So, really, what exactly had he been hoping she would say?

When they reached the edge of the clearing where the pride waited, Samson paused before stepping out of the cover of the trees.

Mila stepped up beside him, staring out at the gathered Great Cats beyond with the same dread and anticipation that Sam felt in his own heart.

"No running away this time?" she asked, the slight break in her voice enough to make Sam's stomach tighten.

He found he had to take a deep breath before answering, despite the fact that doing so required no air.

"No running away this time," he agreed. *"How many suitors has your father defeated over the years?"* He pulled his amber eyes away from the scene before him and looked at her now. *"How many have fallen in my place?"*

She hesitated, as if she was not sure she wanted to tell him. She could not meet his eyes when she said, *"One hundred and thirteen."*

Though this number didn't surprise him—there was a reason her father was named *King of the Beasts*—there was nothing Sam could do to stop the shiver that ran up his spine, from the hair on the back of his thick neck from standing on end.

He took one more deep breath, nudging Mila with his nose, forcing her to look up at him. Cats did not cry the way two-legs did, but one would have to be blind to miss the heartache in the green of her eyes. Either way, she would lose someone she loved on this day.

Sam licked her face, catching her off-guard with the intimacy of the act, and taking a small rejoice in the fact that though he'd surprised her, she hadn't pulled away from his affection.

He made sure to hold her gaze when he told her, *"No matter what happens next, Mila, either way, I'm sorry. I hope you can forgive me. I hope you can forgive me for all of it."*

Now the pain on her face was almost too much to look at, but her voice was strong like the Great Cat she was when she said, *"If you could... even now... you'd still return to her... wouldn't you? You'd still choose her over all of this."*

Samson stood looking at her, but found he could not bear it much longer. With one last lick to her cheek, which Mila sighed and leaned into, he turned on his heels and exited the trees, head held high as he went to face his fate, Mila's question to him answered in his silence.

Before the sun set on this day, Samson would either take his place as the King of Beasts, or die trying.

2 0

———

SURAH

*S*urah came to the nearly immediate conclusion that she could trust the girl. It was so sudden that she questioned the feeling for its oddity.

It was true that the new Sorceress Queen had a knack for being able to detect lies from most people, and her gut instincts most often did not prove her wrong, but the very fact that the Halfling girl was so intensely disarming intrigued her.

She'd never met a Fae/Human Halfling before. She'd met Halfling Wolves and Vamps, Halfling Witches and plenty of Halfling Sorcerers, but never anyone like Aria. The girl had a way about her that just made one want to like her.

Surah told her as much, not seeing the need to mince words.

The girl waved a hand with short, red-painted fingernails, a gesture Surah suspected she didn't realize was humble.

"That's part of being half Fae," she said. "Apparently I've got some sort of draw." She rolled her vibrant eyes. "Believe me when I tell you it can be as much a curse as it is a blessing."

"I do believe you," Surah said, and paused, watching the girl closely. "At a time when I should be believing hardly anyone, I believe you… That's part of this 'draw' you have?"

Aria shrugged, her signature grin pulling up her lips. "I guess I just have one of those faces. And on top of that, you really can trust me. My only agenda here is the objective I've been given by my superiors. Keep you both alive and ensure that you kill the Fae Queen," she paused, her eyes switching to Charlie. "And her accomplices."

By the look on his face, Surah could tell this was the first Charlie had heard of this.

"You mean my brother," he said. It was not a question.

Again, the girl shrugged. To her credit, she met Charlie's stare dead-on when she said her next words.

"If it comes to that, yes," Aria said. "But the dark Sorcerer is hardly our biggest concern at the moment. The Dark Lord he's consulting with? *That's* our biggest problem."

Her gaze went to Surah now, who had not taken her violet eyes from Aria. "We can't have Demons running free in the Territories. The balance of things is already tipping. People of all races are concerned. That includes the Peace Brokers."

Surah thought the girl said this almost as though it were recited, something she'd heard so many times that she truly believed in it. She'd had a few dealings with Peace Brokers over the years, but not much. They were an elite organization whose only purpose was to maintain the peace among the races.

The Peace Brokers were created nearly one thousand years ago, as a part of The Great Compromise. Halflings of every race made up their ranks, and their movements and activities were clandestine, to say the least. It was rare that they got noticeably involved in things, but only a fool would think they weren't present in one form or another for most of the happenings in the supernatural world.

That was about the extent of Surah's knowledge concerning the Peace Brokers. Sorcerers were notorious for keeping to their own kind, and staying out of the dealings of other supernaturals, so dealings with them had never been necessary.

Surah tilted her head back. "I'm aware that Demons aren't good for business," she said. "You can assure your people that I'm going to take care of it."

Aria sat back on the couch, her legs folded beneath her. She nodded at Surah, her eyes going to her rich cloak, which felt horribly out of place in this world.

"Is that why you're carrying the Black Stone?" the girl asked.

This surprised Surah, and her eyebrows shot up at the same time as her eyes narrowed. Charlie was deadly still beside her.

"How do you know I'm carrying the Black Stone?"

Aria closed her eyes and took a deep breath. "I can feel it," she said, exhaling slowly. Her eyes opened, and there was such understanding there that Surah once again felt disarmed. "It's part of being what I am. I'm always aware of the emotions of all the life around me."

Her green eyes began to fill with moisture, and she closed them tight and took another deep breath. "Miles away from here a forest is on fire, and if I listen hard enough, I can hear the trees screaming as they burn." Her eyes popped open, and she smiled a smile that was just bound to break hearts. "But that's neither here nor there. I think it's wise that you're taking the stone with you."

Surah's eyebrow quirked, and though there were dark feelings stirring in her, she could not be critical of this child. She felt a sudden rush of sympathy for Aria, at how lonely the girl must be, living with one foot in this world, and one foot in the others, not quite fitting here, and not quite fitting there. Living alone in this small apartment, brokering peace while writing essays to be graded by a human teacher. Following orders. Playing her part in a game she'd been born to play, though had probably never agreed to.

"I'm glad you approve," Surah told her, and for a moment, the darkness in her seemed to subside, the light of this young

Halfling girl chasing it away. Surah took Charlie's hand in hers. "Thank you for your help, Aria."

The girl smiled and the room lit up as if with sunlight. "You're welcome, your majesty," she said, with a bow of her head. "And for what it's worth, I really hope everything turns out right for you two."

Her cheeks grew slightly pink, and she added, "I've been following your story in notes and updates passed down from my superiors, and I think what you two have is amazing… I want your love to win, to rearrange the stars, if that's what it takes."

Surah and Charlie did not know what to say to this. Aria's cheeks bloomed even more roses with their silence.

She cleared her throat and added, "I'm sorry. Like I told your boyfriend, most of my job is just sitting around and going through the motions of human life while I await orders. Rescuing Charlie was the most exciting thing they've had me do so far, and that was only because the person above me—"

She cut off abruptly, letting out another deep breath and forcing away unwanted thoughts Surah could only guess at. Surah let the subject drop. She had places to go, people to see, and a couple more questions she'd like answered.

"So what did your people tell you to do next?" she asked. "How do they intend to help stop Tristell?"

Aria bit her lip, as if she were trying to decide something. "Wish I could tell you, but to be completely honest, they don't intend to help you any further. My orders were only to save the fugitive Sorcerer and keep him safe until the Sorceress Queen retrieved him."

"But I thought you said you were going to help kill the Fae Queen."

Aria nodded. "And I am. But not because the Peace Brokers have ordered it."

A darkness swirled behind the girl's eyes that Surah recognized well. It was the look of someone who has a personal stake in matters. She'd seen it most recently in her own reflection in the mirror.

"I see," Surah said, considering the girl. She may not know much about the Peace Brokers, but what she did know suggested that what Aria was saying could get her in trouble. She said as much to Aria.

Again, Aria waved her hand, but just under that tough façade Surah also recognized so well, she could see that this was a concern Aria was well aware of.

"Some things are worth getting in trouble for," was all she said.

Silence fell in the small living room, and Surah couldn't help but feel for this girl in a way that was something like motherly. Aria reminded her so much of herself, and she remembered that not long ago she had jumped into a fight that was not her own because of a personal stake.

That fight had been a civil war within the Territories of the Vampires and the Wolves, and the person she'd come after had been Alexa Montgomery. The King of the Vampires and Wolves had convinced Surah that Alexa was responsible for her brother's death, and Surah had gone in headfirst and challenged the young Sun Warrior to a fight.

Had Alexa's Accursed sister not stepped in, Surah would likely have been dead, because while Surah was a hell of a warrior, a Sun Warrior was *the* warrior of *all* warriors. Everyone knew this. But grief and vengeance had a way of blinding one to things like this, the same way Aria was clearly blinded by whatever debt she had to settle with Tristell the Fae Queen.

Once Surah had figured out it was actually King William who was responsible for Syris' death, she'd told Alexa that she would kill the King of Vampires and Wolves, and the young Sun Warrior had smirked and told her that she could get in line.

And then there was the night in the Silver City, where she'd witnessed a civil war between two of the most physically brutal races in all the realms, and also her vengeance exacted by the Sun Warrior.

She chose her next words carefully, scooting forward on the couch and taking Aria's hands into her own with a motherly gentleness. Aria's gaze was guarded, but she did not pull away.

"Aria," Surah said slowly, "Tell your people that the Dark Lord will be dealt with, that I intend to deal with him personally… And you can rest assured that Tristell will suffer for everything she's done."

Aria swallowed hard before she could speak, and even then her soft voice came out a whisper. "You don't understand," she said.

Surah squeezed the girl's hands gently, completely sure of being able to trust the Halfling now that they'd made contact. It was a funny sensation, touching Aria, because Surah had a gift of being able to tell when people were lying, and Aria had a gift for sensing true emotions.

In truth, these two abilities were not far from each other, despite being gifts of their separate races. It was something akin to Soul Searching, and while holding hands, it was as if the two were staring into the soul of the other.

All things come from one, Surah remembered her mother telling her so long ago that it seemed only a dream now.

"I do," Surah said. "I do understand. I can see the good in you, same as you can feel the darkness in me. I would rather you keep the light in you untainted for as long as possible, as inevitable as the darkness may be."

Aria said nothing, only stared at Surah with wide, conflicted eyes. Her voice was hardly above a whisper now, and there was such pain in it when she spoke that the fractured pieces of Surah's hardening heart gave a squeeze.

"But… she has to pay," Aria said. "For what she's done, she *has* to pay."

Surah nodded. "And she will, Aria. You can look at me now and know that she will… Tell me, what do the Peace Brokers do with those who don't follow orders?"

The girl's face darkened, her eyes going distant. Instead of answering, she only shook her head, her long red-brown hair rippling over her shoulders.

Surah nodded. "Trust me when I tell you it doesn't matter who does the killing, as long as the killing gets done." She held Aria's gaze with a strength that was impossible to deny. "So let me be the one to do the killing this time. If you live long enough, there will come a time when you'll have to be the one to do it… but that time is not now."

Same as killing King William had not been mine, Surah thought, and could tell by the resignation that fell over the girl's face that she understood, though it did not help ease the pain that was in her.

"I knew I'd like you," Aria said, her eyes flipping between Charlie and Surah. "Who doesn't route for the star-crossed lovers?"

Her lips pulled up in a half smile, but the sadness reigned in the green of her eyes. She took one last deep breath, giving Surah's hand a squeeze. "Go, then, Queen Surah Stormsong, last of her name. See the Dark Lord and gain back control of your kingdom. I'll sit here and await word of your tale… I've gotten pretty good at waiting."

Surah nodded, but when she tried to pull back from Aria, the girl kept tight hold of her hands. That swirling darkness was back behind her eyes.

"You have to cut off her wings," Aria said. "They hold the power, the privilege of the power she's abusing."

Now it was Surah's turn to smirk, and any doubt the girl may have had about Surah's ability to carry out the tasks ahead of her was washed away when she saw the look that came into the Sorceress Queen's eyes.

"Sweet child," Surah told her. "I'll take her wings, and once I've done that, I'll take her head… as well as that of anyone who should stand in my way."

21

SURAH

_S_urah and Charlie thanked Aria before taking their leave.

Night was beginning to fall, the light of the day fading from the sky as the shadows crept in to take its place.

"You're welcome to stay here to work out your plans," Aria said. "There's only the one bed, but the couch isn't so bad."

Surah smiled, then surprised them both by pulling Aria into a hug. After a brief hesitation, Aria returned the embrace.

"As long as we're here, you're in danger," Surah told her. "I'd rather not take the chance."

Aria nodded, though she seemed disappointed by this. It was the slight drop of her shoulders that spoke of how lonely the poor girl must be. But hanging out with Charlie and Surah was about the most reckless thing one could do right now.

The Fae Queen might not know where they were, but a Dark Lord was a different story. It might take a little while, but sooner or later, he would find them. Which was why Surah intended to save him the trouble and visit him first.

"You should take a walk along the boardwalk before you go," Aria suggested, folding herself up on the couch and opening her laptop with a drudgery all school kids of every race exhibit time to time. "Even the human world can be really beautiful, and the ocean always helps me think."

Surah smiled at this, a real smile, despite the fact that the longer she had direct possession of the Black Stone, the darker her mood became, like the shadow of the moon slipping in front of the Earth, blackening the entire world below.

"Maybe we will," she said, casting a spell that made her cloak appear to be just a gray t-shirt and jeans, which would undoubtedly fit better in the human world.

She and Charlie left after that, walking out of the small apartment complex near the slightly smelly back bay of this small coastal town, rather than portaling to another destination.

Surah had never bothered to visit any of the oceans in the human world, and it seemed as good a place as any to have the words with Charlie that they both knew needed to be had.

Per Aria's instructions, they followed the sidewalk toward the direction of the ocean, the waves of which Surah could hear in the close distance, the squawk of strange seabirds flying overhead a gentle soundtrack to the scene.

The little seaside town the Halfling girl lived in was much like many of those along the eastern seaboard of what was called the United States of America. The homes here were both large and small, the yards clearly maintained by professionals, the medians decorated with fountains and trees that were just beginning to bloom with the new season.

Cars drove slowly and lazily down the streets, their exhausts pumping out pollutants, the effects of which were beginning to show even on Surah's separate side of the world.

Overhead, the sky was painted a soft pink that truly was magical, despite the apparent lack of magic in this realm. The setting sun was a fiery orange ball, and it sank into the endless, blue ocean as if being swallowed bit by bit.

"Such a strange world this is," Charlie said, almost as if to himself. They reached the ramp that led up to the boardwalk, which flanked the ocean with its white, ever-rolling waves. The saltiness of the air was somehow pleasant, somehow soothing to the mind.

As Surah took in the sights from the top of the boards, she saw that Aria had been right; staring out into that vast ocean, walking alongside it as it danced its endless dance, was as close to magic as anything could truly come.

She realized with a small jolt of surprise that this world was not so different from her own, and neither were the humans who called it home, as much as she would deny this if asked. There was magic all around them, the only difference was, here, they called it *nature*, they called it *science*.

Glancing over at Charlie, she got the feeling he was thinking the exact same thing. And both of them were avoiding the real issues at hand. They walked on a little longer in silence, passing by an older couple on a double bike who offered smiles as sweet as the colors of the setting sun painting the sky.

"It's funny," Surah said, "All the races fought so hard over the Territories… We're still apparently fighting over them, but we left one of the greatest realms, the greatest Territories, all to the humans… and what do they do with it? They drive machines that stink up the air, fill their fearsome oceans with plastic and trash, dig up their ground to fill it with more."

There was a sense of something foreboding to what Surah was saying, an air of prophecy that was too terrifying to consider in its implications.

Charlie took her hand, pulling her to a stop, forcing her to look at him. His brilliant eyes stared at her, his strong form silhouetting the rolling waters behind him.

"Surah," he began, "I—"

"Just tell me I'm not a fool for loving you, despite it being the absolute craziest thing a woman in my position could do," she said, cutting him off.

Charlie pulled her to him, his arms going around her waist and settling there as if that was the very purpose for which they'd been created.

She leaned into his embrace, wishing she had the power to stop time, to freeze this moment, this moment just before the Scales of Balance tipped in whatever direction they were destined to tip.

But that was the thing about time; all the magic in all the worlds could not stop it.

Charlie held her close, looking deeply into her eyes. When he spoke, his deep, slightly accented voice was as sincere as a man's could be.

"I can't tell you that loving me isn't foolish," he said, "but I can tell you that hearing you say that has made me the happiest man in all the realms, no matter what happens next. I don't have any regrets as far as that goes. None at all."

Surah was not aware of it, but her arms had tightened around him, her hands clutching tightly at the fabric of his shirt as if at any moment he could be ripped away. And, in truth, she supposed that was so.

"But it's like Aria said, Charlie… To be together, we'd have to rearrange the stars." Her voice lowered, her words nearly lost in the gentle sea wind. "Aren't you afraid?" she asked. "Because I am. I think I'm more afraid than I've ever been in my entire life."

Charlie held her tight, his breathing steady and deep, the strong pace of his heart beating under her fingers. "Of course I am," he said. "I've never had something so worth living for."

Surah did not miss that for the first time she could recall, Charlie had referred to his brother as Black Heart, rather than Michael, but it seemed poor taste to mention it. It would've spoiled the moment, and Surah knew enough to know that these types of moments did not come along often.

She found she had to swallow twice before she could speak,

and that the words were harder to say than perhaps any she had ever spoken.

"So then tell me you love me, Charlie Redmine," she whispered. "Tell me you love me and you'll do whatever it takes to help me untangle the stars that have crossed themselves against us." She held his green gaze with her violet eyes. "Whatever it takes."

They both knew what she was really asking; the exact question need not be spoken. She hated to ask it of him, but before she let this thing get on any further, she had to know.

She had to know that if it came down to it, Charlie would choose her over his brother, because Black Heart was beyond saving now, and they both knew it.

Surah found she could not breathe in the small space between her question and his answer, and despite it being exactly what she'd hoped it'd be, it still made her slowly freezing heart ache in her chest.

"I love you, Surah Stormsong," Charlie told her. "Like the moon loves the night and the sun loves the day, and I'll take on the stars with you… Whatever it takes."

2 2

SURAH

Rather than risk returning to their world, Surah and Charlie agreed that finding a hotel here in the human world to prepare themselves for their next steps was the safest option.

They passed by several quaint and charming bed and breakfast places dotting the seaside, and Surah chose one where the units looked like tiny log cabins built beside the sea.

Charlie commented that they reminded him of home, and Surah smiled at this. It reminded her of his home as well, which was why she'd chosen it.

Using some magic, she'd conjured some of what passed for money in this world and went into the office—which was an even smaller cottage unit in the center of the others.

After securing a room, she left the office, the small bell on the door chiming above her head, and her stomach tightened as she caught sight of Charlie, still standing on the boardwalk that flanked the charming, if out of place, cabins.

This would be the first time she'd been alone in a bedroom with him since, well, the last time she'd been alone in a bedroom with him.

Suddenly, her heartbeat picked up in pace. She wondered if this man would ever stop making her feel this way, and simultaneously hoped the answer was no while fearing the possibility that it was yes.

She climbed the wooden ramp that led back up to the boards, and said nothing as she stepped up beside Charlie. For a moment, the two of them only stared out at the vast ocean in this strange world.

Gulls cried overhead and the churning waters danced their endless dance. It was easy to feel small standing here, no matter how big the problems resting on one's shoulders. Surah could see why the Halfling girl loved it so.

After some time had passed, Surah took her lover's hand in hers and led him toward the cabin she'd secured for them. He followed her with a certainty she'd only ever seen in the eyes of her tiger, and the pace of her pulse kicked up to a near hum.

Neither of them said a word as she stuck the key she'd been given in their cabin door, turning it in the lock and pushing it open, sunlight spilling into the dark interior of the cabin in a bright rectangle. Surah wondered if Charlie's heart was beating as fiercely as hers. She was not aware of it, but the answer was yes.

The interior of the cabin was cozy and clean, the smell of the salty sea air lingering between the dark walls. It was one room with a bed, a small kitchen separated by a half wall with an open top, and a sliding glass door that led out to a little porch with views of the ocean where two rocking chairs rocked gently in the wind. There was an outdoor shower, and a door that led to a tiny bathroom with a sink and a toilet.

In other words, it was about as intimate a setting Surah had ever seen. Or maybe she was just that nervous.

Charlie was watching her, his handsome face expressionless as he shut the door to the cabin behind him and wandered through the room. His green eyes seemed to pin her where she stood, and she had the feeling he was well aware of this.

"You look like you're afraid I'm going to attack you," he said.

Actually, she thought, *you should be more afraid that I'm going to attack you.*

She swallowed away the thought and said, "Don't be ridiculous," in as queenly a manner as she could manage.

Charlie studied her for a moment before going to the sliding door in the east side of the cabin and pushing it open.

"Come out and sit with me," he said. "Let's talk."

Surah felt both relieved and disappointed. Following his instruction, she stepped out into the cool and pleasant evening air, seating herself in the rocking chair beside his. They listened to the soundtrack of the world for a moment.

Then, Charlie said, "What's next, Surah?"

Surah released a deep breath, staring out at the sea. "Next, I visit the Underworlds. There's a certain Dark Lord who needs to be paid a visit."

Charlie nodded. "I'll go with you."

"You don't have to do that. You should be safe here. I doubt anyone suspects us to be in the human world."

"That's neither here nor there. If you're going to the Underworlds, I'm coming with you."

Surah nodded at this, grateful that he didn't want to leave her to do this alone.

"Okay," she said. "But I'll have to use the Black Stone to protect us. It's the only thing that's powerful enough. It'll take me a few hours to prepare the Spell." She cleared her throat. "Which is why we needed the cabin."

A small smile was tugging at the corner of Charlie's lips. Surah wondered if he realized how attractive he was when he did this. "Is that the only reason we needed the cabin, my queen?" he asked.

Surah kept her gaze on the waters before her, but a tiny grin was pulling at her lips as well. "Among other reasons, Mr. Redmine," she said.

He chuckled, and already the mood between them was lighter, despite the heaviness that always seemed to be hanging over their heads.

"What are we trying to accomplish, going down to the Underworlds?" he asked. "What's the best case scenario here? I don't have much experience with Dark Lords."

This was a question that was hard to answer, because Surah wasn't sure there *was* anything to be accomplished. In fact, if she was being honest, odds were that visiting this particular Dark Lord would only make matters worse.

Dagon was not known for being reasonable, and his history with her family was surely the reason he'd thrown his hand in with the Fae Queen and Black Heart.

But Surah's late father had always insisted that a good leader tried every manner of diplomacy before subjecting his or her people to a war, where surely the losses would be even greater than those already had.

And if that failed, there was always the backup plan: Kill anyone who posed a threat, be it Fae, Sorcerer, Demon, or Dark Lord. Kill them all.

"Honestly," she said, turning to face Charlie, "I don't know what I hope to accomplish. Dagon is not one who usually sees reason… but if there's any chance, any chance at all, that all-out war can be avoided, I have to give it a shot."

"Spoken like a true queen," Charlie said.

Rather abruptly, Surah stood, the chair rocking gently with her motion. She slid open the glass doors and paused in the doorway, looking over her shoulder at the man she loved, the man she'd risked everything for.

"Come inside, Charlie," she said. "We've got other business to attend to."

Charlie stood and followed without a word, closing the

sliding door behind him and drawing the curtain that accompanied it.

SURAH

*D*espite the boldness with which she'd just spoken, Surah found that her hands were shaking slightly, her breathing growing a touch uneven.

She knew what was coming next, and somehow the prospect of being alone with Charlie Redmine was even more intimidating than going to the Underworlds to visit a Dark Lord.

She let the magic spell that was disguising her real clothing drop, her long cloak and otherworldly attire becoming visible once more. Charlie stood as still as a statue, his brilliant green eyes watching her the way a lion observes a gazelle. Surah wouldn't have thought it possible, but her heart kicked up in pace further still.

Violet eyes locked on him, she unclasped the front of her cloak, and with a flick of her fingers it lifted from her shoulders and folded itself into a neat square, settling down on the dresser pushed into the corner of the small room.

Slowly, she unzipped her black boots and set them aside. Charlie continued to watch her, his chest rising and falling as his gaze traveled up and down her and back again. Her full lips lifted in a smile, her palms a bit moist at the prospect of sliding over his skin.

She was well aware that the world of their kind hung in the balance, that some terrible people were after them, that death was waiting around the bend, and only time would tell exactly whom it was waiting for.

This only drove home the fact that she needed this. *They* needed this. Charlie and her needed to steal this time that was ever working against them and just *be together.*

Because he knew as well as she that this could be the last, the light of their love as brilliant and as short-lived as that of a shooting star, gracing the skies with its beauty for only a few stolen breaths.

Charlie came forward slowly. His hands were clenched into fists at his sides, his muscular shoulders tight with tension, only stopping when he was within inches of her, when she could smell his clean, masculine scent mingling with the salty air.

Silence hung between them, the only sound that of Surah's heart beating in her ears, of the ticking clock in her mind. His hand came up and rested on her cheek, and she leaned into his touch, her violet eyes squeezing tight, trying to commit to memory the sensation of his skin against hers.

His voice was a deep whisper in the dim light of the room, the soft murmuring of a lover. "No regrets, Surah," he told her. "No matter what happens, know that I've got no regrets."

His rough thumb stroked her cheek, brushing away a single tear that had fallen there. "No matter what, no matter how short our time is together, for me, it was worth it." He sighed, staring at her like he might never see her again. His next words were barely audible, as if spoken only to himself. "So much more than worth it."

Surah gripped the bottom of his t-shirt, lifting it over his head. The hard muscles in his wide chest captivated her, the tan skin there scarred in various places, reminders of wounds received long ago.

He stood silent and still under her appraisal. Slowly, she let her fingers wander over the smooth scars that marked his shoulders, chest, and abdomen, wondering if fate would allow them enough time together for her to learn the story behind each of those marks, or if most of him would forever remain a mystery to her.

She swallowed hard, her chest rising and falling more rapidly as each intake of breath brought with it Charlie's scent. He had not moved an inch since she'd removed his shirt, as if he was afraid his touch might break her. Surah could not help a small, sad smile at this, because in a way, she supposed it had.

One last deep breath, and she pulled her shirt over her head, tossing it aside, standing bare before him. Still, Charlie did not move, only stared into her eyes as if an eternal fire burned there. Her fingers barely made it to the button on her pants when his paralysis broke, and he lifted her into his solid arms as though she weighed nothing.

The feel of her bare chest against his made a fire swirl in her stomach that she was sure would scorch her soul were it not extinguished with a hurry.

Then his lips were on hers, her eyes squeezing shut and her mouth exploring his with a hunger that rivaled that of a Great Beast. Tears broke free despite her closed eyes, but for the first time in what felt like forever, they were not tears of sadness, but those of joy.

She knew then that he was right. All of it, everything that had happened, and everything that was still to come, was worth it.

His strong hands gripped her thighs as he held her aloft, her legs wrapping around him and squeezing tight. Her fingers trailed over the hard muscles in his back, her head falling back and a sigh escaping her lips as his warm tongue drew small circles on the tender skin of her neck.

Charlie carried her over to the bed, laying her down gently, his large body poised over hers, his emerald eyes drinking her in.

She pulled him down to her, their bodies flush against one another, their hearts beating perfectly in time. Her fingers dug into the tan skin of his back, her legs encircling his waist.

Charlie braced his strong arms on either side of her, pushing himself up so that he could stare at her bare body. Her chest rose and fell, as she lifted her bottom and removed her pants, wearing nothing now but her sheer thong underwear.

When he dipped his head and kissed the spot between her breasts, his lips warm and soft, a shiver ran through her body. He chuckled lowly against her skin, his mouth trailing kisses up to her sensitive nipple, which he flicked twice with his tongue before taking it into his wicked mouth and making her arch up off the bed in pleasure.

"Charlie," she gasped.

"Mmm," he mumbled, his fingers stroking circles on the hard planes of her stomach as his mouth continued its exploration.

She reached between them and unbuttoned his pants, needing to feel every inch of his bare skin against hers. Charlie lifted and kicked them away, and Surah held his emerald gaze as he bit his lip and looked down at her.

"You're beautiful," he said.

Surah was surprised she could speak. "So are you."

A low growl rumbled in his throat, and he kissed her before moving his mouth to her neck, his tongue teasing the sensitive skin there.

Surah reached between them and gripped him in her hand, the proud length of him smooth and warm. She stroked him once before opening up and guiding him into her.

As he filled her, his head lifted and his eyes slipped closed as he groaned in pleasure.

She bit her lip as he pushed slowly deeper, and gasped in ecstasy.

She flipped him onto his back and climbed atop him, guiding him back into her. Her head fell back as she stared up at the ceiling and began to move atop him.

One of his hands went to her waist while the other gripped her breast, the former guiding her movements while the latter stroked gently.

They finished together, their bodies uniting and melting into one another. When they were done, Surah collapsed into Charlie's strong arms, and Charlie held her as if he would never let go.

Surah could not remember ever being as happy and content as she was in this moment, and more than anything, it made her realize that she would fight to the death to keep this man at her side.

Her mouth opened and the words fell out before she could stop them. "I'll kill anyone who tries to take you from me, Charlie," she said, and her cheeks immediately reddened as she heard how crazy that sounded spoken out loud.

Charlie only chuckled. "I love you, too," he said.

2 4

BLACK HEART

Tristell the Fae Queen fell to the side, sliding off her lover, the air still tearing in and out of her lungs.

Her lover lie at her side, staring up at the sky through the canopies of the strange trees that made up the Fae Forest.

"Michael was distracted," she said, her sweet, high voice close in his ear.

He turned his head to the side and raised a dark brow at her. "By the sounds you were making, I wouldn't think so," he said.

The Fae Queen waved a sharp-nailed hand, her slanted eyes narrowing. "Just because Michael's still a good lover when he's distracted does not change the fact that he was distracted." Her red lips pushed out in a pout.

He sighed, crossed his hands behind his head, shifting on the soft makeshift bed of leaves below him.

"You'll have to forgive me," he snapped. "I've got a lot on my mind."

Her sharp grin widened, and he wondered at the way his anger only ever seemed to excite her. Say what you want about Tristell the Fae Queen, but she was one unique creature, any way you cut it. He just wasn't much in the mood for her games

126

at the moment. Too much was still hanging in the balance, too much still to be done.

"You're still worried about involving Dagon," she said. It was not a question.

"Dark Lords are even more untrustworthy than Leprechauns. Of course I'm concerned."

She hopped up with that animal-like agility that was so common among her kind, and began rubbing her back up against the bark of the nearest tree, the large, feathered wings attached there shifting this way and that.

"Michael needs to stop being afraid of the Dark Lord. It's not attractive."

He climbed to his feet, grabbing his pants from a bush near the base of a tall tree and pulling them on, his movements harsh and aggravated.

"Only fools don't fear the Lords, Dark or Light. Is that what I am to you, Tristell, a fool?"

She stopped her back scratching and approached him, a wide-eyed look on her beautiful face that Michael was beginning to question.

"You agreed that taking the magic away was a good idea. We killed a king because of it!"

His eyes narrowed, his hands clenching into fists at his side. "And yet I'm no closer to the Sorcerer throne. The kingdom has rallied behind the Sorceress despite her indiscretions." He fixed her with a look that made her fold her arms over her chest. "And your people are concerned as well. I'd be surprised if the Peace Brokers aren't all over this."

Tristell's face darkened like a sky during a thunderstorm. "Peace Brokers? You're concerning yourself over those insects, those *cowards*? They do nothing but sit in shadows and whisper in corners! Besides, you knew what you were getting in to. You can't collect honey without rattling a few beehives. Michael wanted to overthrow a kingdom, but now Michael is *scared*."

His hand shot out and gripped her throat, but for all the darkness in his black eyes, the Fae Queen only stared back at him with the darkness in her own, her sharp teeth bared in both excitement and anger.

"I'm not scared," Michael told her.

One of her fine eyebrows arched. "No, of course not. *Of course* Michael isn't scared."

Releasing a heavy breath, he freed his grip and rested his hands instead on her shoulders.

"Forgive me, my love," he said.

Her sharp grin pulled up at one corner of her mouth, her slanted eyes glittering. "Don't apologize, Michael. *Kings* do not apologize."

She jerked out of his hold and spun on her heel, her long, multi-colored dress fluttering around her ankles. "Besides, I know what's really plaguing Michael." Her voice lowered to a near mocking tone. "I know what his real weakness is."

"Watch your tongue, Tris," he threatened.

"Or what?" she spat. "You'll cut it out? I know you Sorcerers are fond of doing that. And we both know it's your precious Charlie-Boy who's got your stomach all in knots. *He's* the thing Michael is really worried about."

"He's my brother."

"He betrayed you!"

"I betrayed him first!" He shouted back.

In the pastel colored canopies above, a bird or two took flight, and following the small sound of beating wings and fluttering leaves, the eerie silence of the Fae Forest hung over the place, making the thought that he'd never meant to speak aloud seem to hang in the air before him.

I betrayed him first.

Tristell scaled a large tree and perched on one of the lower branches, crouched the way a cat might, looking down at

Michael with those ever-taunting slanted eyes, though there was no joke in them now.

Her magnificent wings were tucked behind her, the dark cobalt feathers ruffled in both the literal and the figurative sense. She stared down at him for so long that if Michael had a weaker poker face, he would have squirmed on his feet.

Instead, he only stared defiantly back at his crazy Faevian lover, the darkness in his own eyes reflected in hers. There was a devil sitting on both of their shoulders, constantly whispering of ill things, muttering bad omens on a loop that was so consistent it had become background music in their minds.

Though Michael was only dimly aware of it, for lack of want to see the true nature of things, this was what truly united the two—a common desire to wreak havoc wherever they went.

As far as Tristell the Fae Queen knew, this was what one called love.

But Michael had not always been black at heart. There had been a time, be it long ago, that he'd known true love, had received it, as well as given it.

And this thought, this brief, if completely earnest utterance of guilt, shook him down someplace deep and long unvisited within him. He could not deny its truth, not with it being in such plain sight.

He had betrayed Charlie first. Gods knew he hadn't meant to, but he had.

Tristell dropped in front of him like an angel cast out of heaven, her feet landing squarely on the ground before him and her strong, muscled legs bending with ease to absorb the shock. She stood from her slight crouch, as tall as Michael, eye to eye with him. She grabbed his chin with her long fingers, her sharp nails digging into the soft skin on his face.

Her lips came close enough to kiss as she leaned forward, dark eyes boring into his. Her deceptively sweet voice came out in an intimate whisper, a rarity from her that never failed to set his blood afire.

"You are going to be a king, Michael," she said. Her tongue flicked out across her full lips, drawing his eyes and stirring up heat deep in his stomach. "And when Michael is king, he will see that justice is finally served to all those who deserve it. He will finally avenge the lives of his parents, and he will be a champion of the common people. They will sing his name in the streets, write songs about him, build statues that will be bowed before for generations."

He was becoming lost in her words, in the sweet way she spoke them, in *her*. His hands came up and gripped her hips hard, his fingers digging deeply into the soft flesh there, earning a small gasp from her. Her head tilted back, eyes rolling, and Michael tasted the smooth, sweet skin on her neck.

Her slanted eyes stared up through the trees and at the sky, a grin pulling up her mouth as she urged him onward, clutching at his back with one hand while burying her fingers deep into his hair with the other.

"And when Michael is king, we will merge our Territories and get back what was taken from us."

Michael pulled back, his dark eyes wide with what he thought she was suggesting. "Tris," he said, "you mean…?"

She nodded, devil on her shoulder and glint in her gaze. "That's right," she said. "Once we take the Sorcerer throne, we can settle things down and start our family." She rubbed at her stomach, which was just beginning to bulge. "I am with Michael's child."

With those words, Michael Redmine felt a new surge of resolve, his black heart thudding loudly in his chest.

"You're pregnant?" he asked, because part of him just couldn't swallow the news down. He had to hear her say it again.

"Yes!" she said, and jumped up and down, her hands clapping in her characteristic way.

Michael wrapped her in his arms and spun her around in a circle. When he set her back down, she fixed him with a serious look.

"You see?" she said. "We must finish what we started. We must make our worlds better for our little one. Does Michael see that now?"

He nodded, devil on his shoulder and glint in his eyes. "I see," he said. "Clear as crystal."

CHARLIE

As a simple common man, Charlie had never had much use for magic, but if he could, he would use all the magic of the Sorcerer kind and freeze time. He would live in this moment for an eternity, her in his arms, her body tucked closely against his, forever.

But they needed to get a move on, that clock hanging over their heads had begun to tick again now that they'd had each other and had satisfied the hunger they ignited in one another. For the time being, at least.

Her head was resting on his chest, her lavender hair spilling over him like silk. He'd taken her three times already, and thought if she shifted at all he would toss her onto her back and do it again.

Hell, if she even looked up at him again with those vibrant violet eyes, the two of them may never leave this cabin. The entirety of all the realms could be burning down outside these walls, and Charlie Redmine would not give one damn.

He ran his hands slowly up the soft skin of her arms, his fingers trailing lazy patterns.

She shivered under his touch, making that warmth spread

through his stomach again, stirring a part of him that should be more than exhausted.

"I don't want to leave this room," she mumbled, lifting her head and trailing kisses up his chest.

Would he never get enough of this woman?

"You read my mind," Charlie said, his voice low and rough. "And if you keep doing that, we won't."

She laughed, a sweet and throaty sound that only made him want her more.

Looking up at him through dark lashes, she said, "Tell me again why we have to?"

This made him smile, and he kissed her forehead before sighing and staring up at the ceiling. "Because a Dark Lord, a crazy Fae Queen and a dark Sorcerer—"

"Walked into a bar?" she interrupted.

Charlie laughed and shook his head. "I wish. That might do them some good. Instead, they want to take your throne and start a war."

He paused, looking down at her beautiful face. Her chin was resting atop her hands, which were resting atop his chest. "But if you want to just say fuck it and stay here for the rest of forever, you won't get an argument out of me."

"Fuck it, then," she said, a twinkle coming into her eyes.

"If only we could live with that."

Surah let out a slow breath and pulled reluctantly out of his arms. He watched her naked form as she gathered her clothing, wondering at how every inch of her could be such perfection.

Surah was all muscle and curves, the smoothest of skin and the fairest of features. She moved like liquid, with a fluidity that made her seem as though she was always dancing. Such queenly demeanor—a certain confident set to her shoulders, a straightness to her back—mixed with the ability of the best of warriors, a skill she'd no doubt honed over the years.

The sheer amount of admiration he had for her was enough

to stun him into silence as he lay in the bed they'd just shared and watched her move about the cabin.

Pulling her shirt over her head, she turned and saw him staring at her. A crooked smile pulled up one corner of her lips and her head tilted ever so slightly to the side.

"If you weren't so attractive, Charlie Redmine," she said, "the way you're staring at me right now would be creepy."

He chuckled, sitting up and grabbing his t-shirt from a nearby chair. "I guess it's a good thing I'm so attractive, then."

Surah folded herself into one of the chairs accompanying a small round table in the corner. Taking a deep breath, she set out the two stones, one black, and one white. They gleamed against the wood of the table in stark contrast.

Charlie came over and sat in the chair across from her, the mood in the small space abruptly serious.

"Is it dangerous?" he asked, unable to pull his eyes away from the Black Stone for a moment longer than he was comfortable with.

Surah lifted her own gaze away from the Black Stone, but its reflection gleamed in the violet of her eyes, making them look nearly onyx.

"You're asking me if casting a dark spell and visiting the Underworld is dangerous?"

Charlie sat back in his seat, a sheepish grin on his face. "I guess it sounds pretty stupid when you put it like that. I'll just… uh… keep quiet."

Surah winked at him, making his heart skip a beat in his chest. "That's just how I like my men."

He chuckled and watched her as she took one last breath and sat up straight, resting her hands atop the table.

She closed her eyes, her pretty features smoothing out in concentration. Her hands lifted from the table, fingers hovering over the Black Stone, which began to glow against the wood where it rested.

The shift of atmosphere in the small cabin was immediate. It seemed to Charlie that the heavy feeling was all around, but somehow within as well, as if it were radiating out of his stomach. The small crease between Surah's eyebrows was the only indication that she felt it just the same.

Time passed. How much, Charlie could not be sure. It felt like both seconds and hours, a certain thrilling agony that came with being so near to such dark magic.

It was harder to breathe, and the harsh rise and fall of Surah's chest, the thin sheen of sweat that broke out across her brow, matched his own. The temperature in the cabin seemed to have gone up about twenty degrees.

Charlie sat at the edge of his chair, his face slightly strained and his eyes locked on his queen. He wasn't sure how much more of this he could stand, and realized with something of a jolt just how powerful the woman he loved truly was.

Her eyes popped open, startling him. Instead of the deep shade of violet he'd come to love, they were all black, no whites to speak of, only ebony orbs. Surah's lips moved quickly, speaking in the language ancient dark magic, her voice but a mumble and two tones deeper than normal.

Black magic filled the cabin. One could not see it, but as a Sorcerer, Charlie could practically hear it dripping down the walls, could smell it permeating the carpet, the air.

Just when Charlie thought he was going to lose what little food there was in his stomach, that he could take being so close to such magic no longer, Surah's eyes cleared back to normal, the onyx leaking out of them like oily tears.

He felt the spell she'd cast to keep them safe settle over him like a warm, black blanket.

Surah took three short breaths before slipping the Black Stone around her neck and placing the smaller piece of her royal White Stone around Charlie's. Then she reached across the table and clutched his hands in hers. Though the magic had clearly taxed her, the amount of determination on her face alone was enough to take his breath away.

Squeezing his hands in hers, she said, "Are you ready, Charlie?"

He nodded and told her yes, though he was sure that wasn't entirely true. How can one ever be *ready* to visit the Underworld?

A look passed over Surah's face that suggested she could see this thought written on his forehead, and her mouth pulled up at one corner in a sympathetic smile.

And then she portaled them both out of the small cabin near the seaside in the human world, and to the Underworld that lie below.

Ready or not, there was no turning back now.

Not for Charlie Redmine, and not for Surah Stormsong.

Perhaps there never had been.

2 6

SURAH

Surah's battered heart beat like a drum in her chest.

The Black Stone rested there, hanging flush against her skin. It thrummed slightly, sending out vibrations that radiated all the way to the core of her. She had not told Charlie of the consequences of using such black magic. There would've been no point to that, because she had no choice in this.

Consequences or no, this had to be done.

As soon as they landed in the Underworld, a drop of sweat rolled down her spine, a jarring contrast to the chill that had just run up it. The temperature in this cursed world was much as one might expect it to be; hellishly hot.

They were in the Underworld, had landed right in the heart of it, and though Surah had heard tales of this place since childhood, nothing could have prepared her for what she was seeing now.

Charlie stood beside her in a silence as shocked as her own. All around them, fires blazed, offering the only light to speak of. The sky above was an endless, unadorned black, as if stars and moons refused to shine here.

Tall, dilapidated structures made up the landscape, fires burning in them as well, their surfaces black and crumbling, as if they'd been ablaze for eternity.

Gut-twisting screams of agony filled the dark sky, coming from every direction, from every burning building and flickering dark alley.

The screams and the crackling of the endless flames were the soundtrack, the only noise to be heard other than the rapid beating of Surah's heart.

Surah felt someone take hold of her hand and remembered that Charlie was with her. Looking all around at the hell she'd brought them to, she wished that she hadn't let him come. There was a good chance they would not leave this place alive.

As if this thought had summoned them, Demons began to slink out of the darkness, their glowing red eyes glittering with an insatiable hunger for death and chaos.

The winged ones took to the dark sky, screeching like diseased birds, the beat of their wings only serving to fuel the endless blazes surrounding them, sending the flames soaring higher, showering sparks into the air.

Surah reached into her cloak, removing a sword, its deadly blade tucked into its hilt with magic. Quickly, she cast the spell that released the blade, and handed the weapon to Charlie.

"Don't let them bite or scratch you," she said, her voice eerily calm, even to her own ears. "Demon venom is not fun."

Charlie took the sword and nodded. She had to hand it to him, most people would be cowering in such a situation, and though she could see the fear in his eyes, he stood strong and steady at her side.

Reaching into her cloak once again, she slid her sais out of the straps on her back, a hunger for death and chaos filling her own eyes as she stared defiantly back at the approaching Demons.

She gripped her sais tightly, her knuckles going white, and

called out, adding a little magic to her voice so that it echoed into the endless world around them.

"Dagon!" she called. "Come out and face me!"

The Demons moved in, and Surah burst forward first, skewering the one nearest her right through the chest, where its heart would be had it had one. The creature let out a screech that stung her ears, and its black blood sprayed out into the stifling air, the stench as rotten as its soul.

Behind her, Charlie spun around and beheaded another Demon approaching from behind. Its horned head rolled into some flaming trash near the gutters, sharp jaws still snapping at the open air.

More Demons came on their heels, their scaly bodies swarming around Charlie and Surah like enormous wasps, glowing red eyes dead but for that ceaseless hunger. Their agonized screeches filled the sky as Surah and Charlie sliced and skewered one after the other.

To an observer looking on—as several Dark Lords were no doubt doing—the battle could be said to be quite lovely in its passion.

Surah's movements were much like a dancer, fluid and practiced to perfection. Her cloak fluttered and flowed around her as she used her magic to portal through the air; popping up here to slide her sais through the lizard-neck of a Demon, and then disappearing and popping back up somewhere else to stab another Demon through its red eyes.

Charlie's movements were less beautiful, but equally deadly. His strong arms wielded the heavy silver sword with ease, arcing it through the air, trailing steaming black Demon blood in its wake.

It streaked across his handsome face, which was set in a way that spoke of how many battles he'd faced in his lifetime, of having had to fight for his life on many more occasions than this one.

But the truth was, they could not kill every Demon in the Underworld that belonged to Dagon. There were too many. The bodies of the creatures could pile as high as the burning buildings all around them and still more would come, for there was never a shortage of lost souls, never a drought of ill deeds.

Having gotten out some of her blood lust—which was stronger than Surah ever remembered it being, no doubt thanks to the Black Stone hanging around her neck—Surah slay one more Demon, crushing its throat beneath her boot with a sickening crunch.

Sheathing her sais, she gripped the Black Stone and cast a barrier spell around her and Charlie. Demons began to slam into it again and again, scratching and snapping at its invisible surface with their clawed hands and sharp teeth. They fell away dazed and all the more angry, screeching into the air.

"Dagon!" Surah called out again. "Come face me, you coward!"

Charlie stood beside her, panting. He pushed his hair back, which was slick with sweat. The muscles in his arms bulged as he caught his breath, ever ready for battle.

The Demons began to slink away, the winged ones taking flight and hovering in circles above like vultures. As they disappeared into the shadows, which were undoubtedly the true rulers of this forsaken place, she knew that her last words had not gone unheard.

Holding the barrier spell in place was not an easy task, and she could not do it and fight at the same time. The spell took concentration, but it would offer them protection against any magic the Dark Lord might try to use against them.

Once the army of Demons had scattered, Surah spotted him leaning against one of the buildings to her east. She spun on her heel to face him. She had only ever seen pictures in story books from hundreds of years ago, but he had not aged a day. Dark

Lords and Lords of Light were immortal, the most feared of all the supernatural races, Gods in their own rights.

Dagon was not in his Demon form, but rather that of a mere mortal. He wore a tailored black suit, black shiny shoes that gleamed in the flickering firelight. His demeanor was relaxed, his ankles crossed and his hands resting loosely in his pockets. If not for his soulless eyes, he could pass for human.

His handsome façade did not fool Surah, just as she was sure her delicate one did not fool him. Still leaning against the dilapidated building, Dagon looked up and met her eyes.

"Big words for such a little Sorceress," the Dark Lord said, taking neither note nor notice of Charlie. He watched Surah the way a cat watches a mouse.

Surah lifted her chin, refusing to show intimidation. "Dagon, I presume."

His dark eyes flashed and narrowed. "You presume nothing, child. You know who I am."

Surah's fist clenched tighter around the stone, her violet gaze ablaze with anger. "I also know you've been sending your Demons to attack my Territory, and I'm here to tell you to stop."

Dagon laughed hard at this in a way that could not be taken as anything but insulting. It was an ugly, grating sound that revealed the darkness hidden beneath the pleasing mask.

He pushed off from the wall of the building and strode over to her, his eyes flicking uninterestedly to Charlie and back again.

Surah had never found any gaze in a thousand years of life as hard to hold as the Dark Lord she was facing, and she had faced a Sun Warrior in her time.

It took enormous effort not to avert her eyes, and to maintain the barrier spell as she did so, but she managed. To show weakness right now would mean certain death, and the Black Stone around her neck was lending her all its power.

Dagon's face suggested that he knew holding his stare was

more than a feat, and a touch of amusement and perhaps some admiration passed over his fine features, but when he spoke, any jest that had been was gone, as if wiped cleanly away.

"You've come to tell me to stop?" Dagon said. "Or you'll do what? Your family owes me a debt, and I'm only making sure it gets paid."

This was the first of any debt she'd heard of, but Surah's face remained impassive. "I am the last of my blood, and I owe you nothing, Dark Lord."

Dagon wagged a finger at her, his forked tongue—the only part of him that was not disguised—flicking out across his lips.

"Your great grandfather made a deal with me, child, and that deal has not been honored. You come here not even knowing the truth of your lineage," he laughed again. "Did you never wonder how your family came to hold the Sorcerer throne? Did they leave the tale out of your bedtime stories, dearest princess?"

Uncertainty spiraled through Surah as she took in what he was saying. She found she had to swallow before she could speak, and she could feel Charlie's confused eyes on her.

"I'm a queen now, Dagon," she said. "Thanks to you."

The Dark Lord smiled, forked tongue whipping out and disappearing again. "It *is* thanks to me, and you're welcome."

An uncharacteristic anger washed over her so completely that she nearly dropped the barrier spell and charged the Dark Lord. Had Charlie not reached out and placed his hand on her arm, she would have.

"Careful," Charlie whispered. "That's what he wants."

Dagon finally paid Charlie some heed, distain filling his face as his eyes flicked between the two of them.

"Ah, yes, and you must be Charlie," he said. "Your brother and his Fae lover also owed me a debt." He nodded toward Surah. "And they paid it with her father's life."

Charlie met the Dark Lord's glare and said nothing.

Dagon paid this no mind, as if he neither expected nor wanted a response from Charlie. His gaze returned to Surah. The Dark Lord moved closer now, so close that he could kiss the invisible barrier between them. Surah was unaware of it, but she was holding her breath.

"But my debt with you has yet to be settled," he whispered, the sound of his voice sickeningly intimate.

The clenching of Surah's fists was the only physical indicator of the cocktail of emotions swirling through her, and she had her royal upbringing to thank for that. If what Dagon was saying was true, everything she'd believed her entire life had been a lie.

Her curiosity got the best of her, and she asked the obvious question.

"You claim my ancestors made a deal with you to take the Sorcerer throne," she said. "What do you think is owed?"

Dagon grinned. "An heir, of course," he said, his voice once again a whisper. His black eyes ran the length of her, and if she didn't know better, Surah would have sworn there were slimy insects crawling over her skin.

For the life of her, she couldn't think of a thing to say to this. Her face drained of color at the implications. This only made the Dark Lord's smile grow wider still. His hand came up, his porcelain fingers stroking the barrier between them, making Surah shiver despite the heat.

"You want me to stop sending my children topside to your Territory?" Dagon whispered, his voice low and deep, echoing slightly in her ears. "Just drop your magic and we can settle it right here."

His black eyes flashed red as he jerked his head toward Charlie, gaze never straying from her.

"He can watch." Dagon said, his fingers continuing to stroke the invisible barrier separating them. "I'll show him how to really please his woman."

Any intimidation or fear Surah could have been feeling melted away, replaced with a fire as bright and hot as those surrounding them in this cursed place.

Her pretty features were relaxed, composed, but her knuckles were bone-white where they clutched at the Black Stone.

When she spoke, her voice came out eerily calm, her violet eyes holding his stare with the strength of a ruler—of a Goddess in her own right.

"I owe you nothing, Dagon," Surah said. "Send them topside again, and I'll bathe my land in the blood of your Demons, and after I do that, I'll come back here and remove that forked tongue from your mouth, after I separate your shoulders from your head."

Rage filled Dagon's face, and for a flash of a moment, his true form was visible, the handsome façade melting away to reveal scaled and ridged skin, clawed hands and feet, black, loathsome wings that spanned twenty feet when extended.

It was only a glimpse, but it terrified her, and she held tighter still to the Black Stone hanging around her neck.

She portaled herself and Charlie out of there, despite the fact that she'd failed this mission of attempted diplomacy.

Somewhere, between slaughtering the Demons and speaking with the Dark Lord controlling them, she had lost sight of this, reveling in the power she felt with the Black Stone hanging around her neck.

They landed back in the cabin, and Surah gave pause at the look Charlie gave her when his shock over the portaling out of the Underworld wore off.

He looked the way a man might when approaching a tiger… cautious. His green eyes flicked between the Black Stone and her face, and he spoke slowly.

"Maybe you should take that thing off now," he suggested.

Irritation swirled in Surah, and her eyes flashed with something that made Charlie flinch. This diffused her a bit, and she released a heavy breath and lifted the stone off of her neck, tucking it back into her cloak.

Charlie, still moving with caution, removed her piece of White Stone from his neck and slipped it over her head, hesitating only a moment before placing a gentle kiss on her forehead.

Surah closed her eyes, leaning into his touch, letting him pull the darkness out of her with just his proximity. She was afraid to ask, but she had to know.

"Why'd you look at me like that, Charlie?" she said.

He pulled her closer, his arms going about her waist, and his eyes filling with a wonder that she hoped she would never stop evoking in him.

"Because you can be pretty damn scary sometimes, love," Charlie whispered, one corner of his mouth pulling up as he tucked a piece of her lavender hair behind her ear.

Resting her head against his chest, she squeezed her eyes shut, listening to the beating of his heart.

"Charlie," she said, her voice coming out a whisper, "If what Dagon said is true—"

Charlie shook his head, tilting her chin up with his fingers so that she had to look at him.

"It doesn't matter, Surah," he said. "No matter how your family came to the throne, it doesn't matter. You're a better ruler for our kind than Black Heart and Tristell."

A tear fell from one of her eyes, though she had not been aware that she was on the verge of crying.

"But—"

Charlie shook his head again. "But nothing," he said, brushing away the tear with his thumb. "All that matters now is that we finish what we started."

When she had a moment to breathe, Surah was sure that she would have to sort through some of the new things she was learning about herself, but now was not that time, and she knew what Charlie was saying, and that he was right.

This needed to be over. Lives needed to be taken. The scales needed to be tipped, one way or the other. And whether her family had come by the throne by ill means or not, she wasn't going down without a fight.

Gods help us all, she thought, and hugged her lover for what she hoped would not be the last time.

SAMSON

"*I was beginning to think I'd have to come find you,*" said Drake, King of the Beasts.

Samson said nothing, only sat where he was, his demeanor relaxed despite what lie ahead. He knew Drake was referring to the fact that Samson had been absent all these years, and that he had expected Sam to shirk his responsibilities, as he had done in the past.

But it wasn't as simple as that. Samson had not asked to be betrothed to Mila (this was not to say he didn't have a certain affection for her, because he did) and he had not asked to be rescued by Surah all those years ago, and to fall so deeply in love with her that he could not bear to leave her, despite the difficulties of living among two-legs for such a long time.

"*I'm here,*" Sam replied, when the silence between them stretched on too long.

Drake considered him a moment, his amber cat-eyes as piercing as a gaze could be. His long tail flicked lazily behind him, his head tilting as he looked at Sam.

"*Yes,*" he agreed, "*you are here in form... but your mind is elsewhere.*"

The King of the Beasts fell silent again, settling down on the ridge on which the two cats sat, looking out at the jungle below, at the kingdom, which stretched on as far as the eye could see, a rich green crowned with wisps of white cottony clouds.

"It's a curious thing," Drake added. *"Your affection for the two-leg. In truth, I'm not sure how it can even be. In all my years, I've never known any beast to do as you've done."*

There was a certain distain in the king's voice that Sam didn't miss. His throat felt tight, and he settled down beside the king, taking in the sights as well. It would be a lie to say he hadn't missed the fresh air here, the land untouched by man.

"It's a curiosity to me as well," Sam replied. *"I didn't choose to love her. I didn't choose any of it. It just is."*

Drake considered this, the sound of the jungle filling the space between their exchanges.

"I'm conflicted over you, son," the king said at last. *"Half of me is so tired, so ready to be done with this world and move on to the next, to relinquish my title and pass on the crown... but the other half of me doesn't trust the pride to you. Tell me... should you win tonight, where will your loyalties lie, with the pride, or the Sorceress?"*

Samson chose his next words carefully. He refused to lie to the king. He respected Drake too much for that.

"If I should win tonight, I will do my best to rule justly. That's all I can promise you, Drake."

The king's amber gaze flicked over to Sam, looking at him out of the corner of his eye. *"My daughter is in love with you, Samson... You are aware of this, are you not?"*

Sam suppressed a sigh; it was a two-leg quality that the king would not appreciate.

"I am," he said.

"She mourned for you when we thought you'd died. I thought that girl would never stop skulking about."

Sam stared out at the green canopies of the jungle rustling gently in the breeze. Tonight, when the sun set over this land from which he'd hailed, he would face Drake in a battle where only one cat would walk away.

The pride would gather around them in the clearing, and the two would fight to the death, the victor taking the title of *King of the Beasts.*

It was a destiny that had been chosen for Sam long ago by his parents, the path that he'd strayed from, knowing that someday he would be led back to it, for one could only avoid their fate for so long.

After some time, Drake took to his paws, stretching his long body the way only a cat can. He was bigger than Samson, his form all sinew and muscle, built for the kill. His long tail flicked lazily behind him, and he lifted his head and sniffed at the air.

"Come, my son," the king said. *"Let us catch a meal and dine together."* His cat eyes flicked to Sam, and there was sympathy there. *"For one of us, it will be the last."*

Sam took to his paws as well, following behind the King of the Beasts much like a man accepting his sentence, having a last meal and taking his last walk.

It didn't take long for the two to find a Great Stag and take it down, though the buck fought with impressive force.

As Sam ate, he thought of his Sorceress, wondering if he would ever see her again, if he would ever get to feel her fingers running through his fur, or hear her sweet voice in his head one last time.

Sometime between taking his last bites and the sun making its way across the sky, sinking into the trees and giving way to the light blue hue of twilight, Samson decided it didn't matter. If today he should meet his end, it really didn't matter. Had he the chance to go back and do it all over again, he would do everything exactly the same way.

Because it had been worth it. His time with the Sorceress Surah Stormsong, the bond they shared and the feelings he never would've experienced without her, were all so much more than worth it, and if this marked the end of his life, he would say that it was a life well spent.

A life beside his Surah was as good as it got, and a death in her name was all the more beautiful. Because that was really what it came down to, and both alpha cats knew it. The reason he was here, the reason Sam would not run, but instead would face his fate, as unfortunate as it may be.

If Sam hadn't come, Drake would've come after his Surah, and Samson could not allow that. As the day wasted away, passing with no regard as to the consequences, Sam thought only of her, of their time together, and for the first time in his life, he sent up a silent prayer.

He prayed only that Surah was safe, and that no matter what happened, she would come out the other end of all this on top. For that, Samson would die a thousand deaths, would face a million Kings of Beasts.

"Say your goodbyes, Samson," Drake told him, looking up from his meal, rough tongue licking the blood-covered fur of his mouth.

It was not a threat, merely a piece of advice the king had clearly spoken to dozens before him.

Drake stood, his belly full of the deer they'd taken down and his eyes void of emotion, and slipped away into the trees, the jungles growing silent as he passed through them.

Sam watched him go, experiencing an emotion only ever brought on by the idea of losing his mistress.

Samson realized with a start that he was scared. Tonight would decide not only his fate, but also that of all those in the pride.

Tonight, he would either die a disappointment, or triumph a king.

2 8

SURAH

"I don't agree with this at all," Charlie said, for what must've been the millionth time.

Surah sighed, knowing that she would say the same in his position, but being no less irritated with the knowledge.

"You can't very well return to the castle with me, Charlie," she said, for what also was the millionth time. "There's really nothing else you can do right now."

They were back at Aria's apartment, and the young Halfling girl was watching the exchange with apt attention, clearly pleased that they'd returned. Surah would've left Charlie at the cabin, but she knew he would leave if unsupervised, and he had seemed to take a liking to Aria.

Surah decided to try a different tactic. She lowered her voice now. "Also, you need to look after the girl," she added. "Aria could be in danger if anyone finds out she helped you escape."

"No one is going to find out," Aria chimed in, and cringed a bit when Surah's eyes flashed at her. She shrugged. "They won't, though. My people are good at staying under the radar. No one knows of my involvement except my superiors and you two."

"Thank you," Surah snapped, not meaning to sound as harsh as the words came out. She was still very much feeling the effects of the Black Stone, and she clamped down on her uncharacteristic anger so as not to make it so obvious.

Charlie was looking at her with narrowed eyes, not fooled. He placed a hand on her arm, and lifted it away when this only seemed to further her anger.

"Using all that dark magic wasn't good for you, Surah," he said, wary.

Surah took a deep breath, knowing she was directing the dark emotions at the wrong people. "I won't argue with that," she said. "But you and I both know you can't return with me to our land. I can't defend the kingdom if I'm worried about protecting you." Her voice was smaller as she said this last part.

Charlie shook his head, chuckling without humor. "You make me sound like a damsel in distress," he said. "I can take care of myself, love. But how can I sit here while you go off to fight a Dark Lord and a crazy Fae Queen?"

Suddenly, Surah was angry again. She needed to get a hold of herself. She'd underestimated the effects of the dark magic.

"Charlie," she said slowly, between clenched teeth, "I don't want to, but if I must, I'll tie you to a chair and force you to stay here."

"I'll make sure he stays, Queen Surah," Aria said, her green eyes flicking quickly between the two of them. "No need to tie him to a chair." She held up two fingers. "Scout's honor."

Surah had no idea what a "Scout's honor" was, and this must've been evident on her face. Aria sighed and waved a hand.

"Never mind," Aria said. "It's a human thing. It means you have my word."

Surah eyed the girl. "And if he decides to leave, how will you stop him?"

Aria shrugged, a half smile pulling up her lips. "I could

always knock him over the head," she grinned. "But I have other talents…"

She hopped up from where she'd been sitting on the couch, surrounded by her enormous books. Stopping in front of Surah, Aria held her hands out. "Here," she said. "I can show you if you want."

Staring at Aria's hands, Surah raised an eyebrow. "What are you doing, child?"

Aria laughed. "Just take my hands, your majesty, so I can show you."

Surah looked at Charlie, who shrugged. He was apparently as clueless about the abilities of Halflings as she was. Sighing, Surah pulled her gloves from her hands and tucked them under her arms. With narrowed eyes, she placed her hands in Aria's.

As soon as her hands touched the girl's, the strangest sensation washed over her. Surah found that she could do nothing other than stare into Aria's green eyes, a shade that seemed to be constantly shifting, swirling almost, as Surah looked into them.

The girl was lovely. There was no denying that. She had a face that made one instantly trust her, and a voice that seemed to fill Surah's head rather than just her ears.

"I can make sure Charlie doesn't follow you, your majesty," Aria said, her voice sounding both very close and far away. "All I have to do is ask him… You believe me, don't you?"

"Yes," Surah heard herself say. "I believe you, Aria."

Abruptly, Aria dropped Surah's hand, and whatever Faevian magic she'd been using on Surah dropped with it. Surah shook her head, her brow furrowing.

"What was that?" she asked.

Aria shrugged. It seemed to be a default gesture of hers. "It's one of my talents. I have the power of suggestion. People want to do what I say, want to believe they can trust me."

It was curious, because these words alone would've normally

made Surah suspicious, but she found that the girl was right; Surah did still trust her.

She mulled this over for a moment, her gaze switching between Aria and Charlie. She needed to get back to the castle, back to her people, and she had two choices here; either trust the Halfling girl to keep her word, or magic Charlie to a chair until she returned.

"I have the honor of the Scouts that you won't allow him to follow me, Aria?" she asked.

Something about this must've struck the girl as funny, because she grinned and nodded firmly, again holding two fingers up into the air.

"Yes, your majesty," she said. "You have the honor of the Scouts."

"Will you make your suggestion now?" Surah asked. "While I watch?"

Aria shrugged. "Sure," she said, and reached out for Charlie, who backed away.

"Excuse me, ladies," he said, eyeing Aria's outstretched hands. "I'm right here, and I don't want any suggestions."

"Would you rather she magically tie you to a chair?" Aria asked.

Charlie said nothing to this, and Aria moved before either of them had noticed and grabbed Charlie's hands. He instantly became as lost in her gaze as Surah had been moments ago. Surah watched in curiosity as Aria used her gift.

"Charlie," the girl said, "You're not going after Surah. You're going to stay with me, okay?"

Charlie's response was immediate. "Okay, Aria. I won't go after Surah. I'll stay with you."

Aria dropped his hands and flashed a pleased grin at Surah before sitting back down on the couch. "See? All taken care of, your majesty."

"You're a strange girl, Aria," Surah said, more than a bit

mystified at this mysterious gift. She did not mean it as an insult, but merely an observation.

Aria sighed. "That's what they tell me," she said.

"Thank you," Surah said. "I need to go now."

"By all means," Aria replied, waving a hand.

Surah turned to Charlie, who did not look too pleased about any of this, but didn't argue, either. She placed her hands on his face, forcing him to look at her.

"I'm sorry, but this is the only way," she whispered. "I can't go into this with a straight head unless I know you're safe. When this is over, I'm coming back for you. I'll clear your name and we'll be together. I promise."

Charlie sighed, clearly unhappy. "Someone once told me not to make promises I can't keep. This isn't right. I should be with you. I should be helping you clean up the mess my brother has made."

Surah shook her head. There were tears in her heart but not on her face, and she suspected this was a result of the Black Stone. She felt hardened in a way she hadn't experienced before.

"Stop taking responsibility for your brother," she said, and kissed him before he could respond.

Despite his upset at the situation, Charlie couldn't have resisted her had he tried. Surah felt his strong arms go around her, his lips move against hers with a familiarity that she had never known before him.

For the smallest of moments, while she was so close to him, the darkness that had been creeping slowly over her mind receded, and she felt the peace and comfort that she'd come to refer to as the *Charlie Effect*.

Remembering they were not alone, and that things needed to be done, Surah pulled away from Charlie and cast an apologetic glance at Aria, who pretended to be deep in the words of the huge book cracked open on her lap.

"Stay with Aria," Surah whispered, giving Charlie's hands one last squeeze. "I love you, Charlie Redmine."

And then Surah gripped the White Stone around her neck and teleported out of there, leaving Charlie to say *I love you, too, Surah Stormsong* into the empty space in Aria's apartment, leaving a hole in Surah's heart the size of a galaxy.

For they both knew she might never return.

29

SURAH

Her first thought when she landed back inside her castle, back in the Territory of the Sorcerers and out of the human world, was to look for Samson.

In her gut, she knew that her cat had not returned, and a voice inside her head whispered that Sam might *never* return, but she did her best to silence it.

Samson had promised to return to her. He was strong and reliable and could more than take care of himself. She had to remember that.

The same way that you're strong and reliable and can take care of yourself? whispered a voice in her head. *The same way you promised Charlie you would return, knowing that was not a promise you could make?*

"Oh, shut up," Surah mumbled, and jumped when someone spoke behind her.

"Who're you talking to, my queen?" asked the Head Hunter, looking around the room. They were in her father's study, and Theo had just entered through the arched double doors.

"No one," she snapped, and then composed herself. "Now's not the best time to be sneaking up on me, Hunter Gray," she added, more gently, releasing hold of her sais, which she'd gripped in her surprise."

Theo bowed deeply, his fine black cloak swaying with the movement. "Forgive me," he said. "I didn't know you'd returned." Theo studied her in silence a moment. "I take it you spoke with Dagon?"

"Why do you assume that?" she asked.

Theo shrugged and shook his head, because they both could hear the effect of the dark magic in her voice. "Only a guess."

Surah sighed, trying to release some of the heavy anger she'd been carrying since using the Black Stone, and not nearly succeeding.

"My apologies, Hunter Gray," she said, wandering over to her father's high-backed leather chair and taking a seat. "Yes, I visited Dagon."

When she didn't continue, Theo asked, "And how did that go?"

Surah shook her head, thinking of her last words to the Dark Lord. "I told him I would bathe my land in the blood of his Demons should he send them here again, and that I would cut out his tongue and then take his head."

She laughed as she said this. Even though it hadn't been funny at the time, speaking it aloud here was somehow morbidly comical.

Theo's brows shot up. "Was that wise, my queen?"

Surah rested her head back against the chair, staring up at the ceiling.

All of a sudden, she was very tired. Using the amount of magic—be it White or Black—that she'd used would exhaust anyone, and it's not like she and Charlie had gotten much sleep in that cabin.

She pushed thoughts of Charlie away, thinking absurdly that Theo might read them on her forehead or something.

Realizing she hadn't answered his question, she said, "He

wants me to bear his child, Theo. Claimed it's a debt owed to him by the Stormsong family."

Theo's lack of response made Surah sit up straighter in her chair. Her voice came out sharp again. "Did you know about this?"

Theo sat across from her, obviously buying time to choose his next words carefully. "Your father mentioned it to me when I was a boy," he said. "He didn't say exactly what the deal was, but he told me I'd need to look after you someday. Said there was a debt that you shouldn't have to pay. I was so young, I didn't think much of it at the time." Theo smirked without humor. "All I really heard was that you needed me. I guess I just held onto that part."

Surah didn't know what to say to this. She didn't doubt the truth of Theo's words, but that didn't mean they weren't nearly as shocking as hearing that a Dark Lord thought he was entitled to impregnate her.

Her voice sounded far away when she spoke. "My father promised you my hand before he died, isn't that what you said?"

Theo hesitated, then nodded. "Actually, King Syrian promised me your hand when we were children, but he was going to force you to marry me if I saved you from Black Heart when he took you captive."

The Head Hunter looked down at his hands, his voice taking on a quality Surah had never heard before. "But I failed. Samson saved you that day, didn't he?"

He looked up at her with his gray eyes, his handsome face more open than she'd ever known it to be. Her stomach swirled uneasily as the sudden realization came to her that she did not hate Theodine Gray, that maybe she'd been just misunderstanding him all this time.

"Yes," she answered. "Samson saved me."

She didn't add that Charlie had also played a role in her rescue. A huge role, in fact. He'd used his love for her to break the chains of black magic his brother had used to hold her. She suspected Theo knew this anyway, and there was no need to rub salt in the wound.

"But you know that I was looking for you?" Theo asked. "And not just because your father promised me marriage… but because I couldn't stand the thought of something happening to you."

Surah stared at him. "All these years, Theo," she said, "and you tell me these things now? Why? I'll be honest and tell you that I don't know if I can trust you. I don't know anything right about now."

Theo scooted forward on his chair, resting his muscled arms on his legs, his gray eyes as grave as the dead.

"I told you. I finally see that there's only one way into your heart. I can no more force you to love me than I can force the sky to turn green and the grass blue. I've done some things, my queen… some things I'm not proud of. I haven't always been the most honorable of men. I've hunted and I've killed, but I've always loved you, and even though there's a part of me that wants to, I can't seem to stop."

"Theo… I don't know what to say."

Theo stood, looking down at her with a compassion she would've thought was beyond him, and placed a hand gently against her cheek. His fingers were rough and calloused, but warm.

"You don't have to say anything," he whispered.

Just then, there was a knock at the door to the study. Both of them jumped, startled out of the moment. Surah was partly relieved. She wasn't sure she was comfortable with whatever emotions she was starting to feel toward the Head Hunter, and with the effects of the Black Stone still holding her, she couldn't trust *any* of her emotions right now.

She told the caller to enter, and in stepped Noelani and

Lyonell. Noelani's eyebrow quirked as she looked at Surah and Theo, but she only bowed to her queen.

"Glad to see you've returned safely, your majesty," she said.

Surah didn't miss the slight edge to Noelani's voice, and she couldn't say she blamed her. Noelani and Lyonell were Surah's personal guard, and Surah was not an easy Sorceress to keep an eye on.

"I always do," Surah said, giving her usual response.

Lyonell said, "We thought you'd like to know all of the Lords and Ladies have moved to safe spots, and the Hunters are spread out across the land, protecting the people."

Surah nodded, hearing the anxiety in her guard's voice loud and clear. "Good," she said. "It's imperative the people know they're protected…"

"You should've seen the look on some of the royals' faces," Theo said. "If we get through this, your court won't be happy, my queen."

"And if we don't," Surah said, "I won't *have* a court to be unhappy with me." She met the eyes of the three people in the room. "I understand that you may not agree with my decisions, and I know it's because you all care about me and this kingdom, but without the faith of my people, I'm no queen, and whether it puts me in danger or not, I have to do what I feel is right."

Surah paused, her eyes flipping between her two personal guards and the Head Hunter. "However, I won't force you to stay for what's coming next, and I won't blame you if you want to leave. I've sent orders to the remaining Hunters to stay within the castle walls, no matter what comes next."

Noelani's mouth fell open to protest, her spiky hair sticking out on her head and her toned arms crossed over her chest, but Surah cut her short with a single look, and Noelani's mouth snapped shut with an audible click. It wasn't often Surah used this commanding way of hers, but when she did, it was undeniable.

Surah continued, "I'm ordering the three of you to do the same. Stay within the walls of the castle. The protective magic is strongest here, and you should be safe… but if the enemy does get inside, use the tunnels to escape, or portal the hell out of here. Take whoever you can and hide among the humans if you must."

A stunned silence hung over the room for several long moments.

At last, it was Theo who spoke up. "My queen," he began slowly, warily, "with all due respect, you must know we can't do that."

Surah's gaze snapped to the Head Hunter and whatever he saw behind her eyes made him flinch. Subconsciously, Surah recognized this as abnormal, because Theodine Gray was not a man who shook easily.

A tiny voice in her whispered that perhaps she was being more affected by the Black Stone than she realized, but it floated away almost as soon as it landed.

"You *will* do that, Hunter Gray," Surah said, her tone allowing for no argument. Her voice softened as she looked at each of them in turn. "I can't have anyone else I care about dying on me," she said. "I need to know you're all safe."

Lyonell said, "So you're going to take on an army of Fae and Demons by yourself? That's your plan?"

A smile pulled up one side of Surah's face, darkness flashing behind her eyes the way lightning flashes across a black night.

Unconsciously, her hand slipped beneath her fine cloak, and her fingers wrapped tightly around the Black Stone, which pulsed warmly under her touch. She'd never been more angry and filled with battle lust in all her life… and she'd never felt so powerful.

She'd be damned if she would lose anyone else to this mess. So she nodded to her longtime friend and told him that was the plan precisely. She would take on the Fae and Demons, and anyone else who dared challenge her as well.

Surah did not know it, but all three people in the room that day did not know just who exactly they should be worried for—their queen, or the rest of the world.

30

CHARLIE

Charlie stood at the door of Aria's apartment, trying for the millionth time to reach his hand up, turn the damn knob, open the blasted door, and leave.

And for the millionth time, he found he could not.

"What curse have you placed on me, girl?" he asked.

Aria was sitting on her kitchen counter again, her legs folded beneath her and an amused grin on her face. She sipped slowly at a cup of tea before answering. Her nonchalant attitude was beginning to drive him crazy.

"Cool your pants, " Aria said. "I didn't place any curse on you. I just made you keep a promise. You told your queen you'd stay with me, so that's what you gotta do."

Charlie threw his hands up, having the strong urge to kick the damn door down but completely unable to act upon it. It made for a confused and infuriating feeling. He stalked over to Aria, pointing back at the door.

"Open that door," he demanded.

The girl quirked an eyebrow at this, her pretty face clearly amused at the approach. "It's not even locked," she said.

"You know what I mean." Charlie deflated a little, seeing that trying to force the girl to comply was pointless. "My brother is trying to kill the woman I love, Aria. You have to let me go."

The amusement slipped off her face, and she looked like she wanted to say something, but couldn't quite make up her mind. After what felt like forever to Charlie, who reminded himself not to push (he didn't know much about Halfling teenagers, but if they were anything like all the other teenagers he'd met, pushing them to do something often had the opposite effect) Aria sighed and pushed her red-brown hair out of her face.

"Look, I can't break the promise I made to your queen," she said, and when Charlie threw his hands up again, she cut him off with a look. "But if you recall, the only thing I promised was not to let you follow her and to keep you with me."

The implications of this dawned on Charlie, and his heart sank a little at the same time as it lifted.

"So I can leave, but I can't go after her, and you have to come with me?" he asked.

Aria nodded, but didn't say anything else.

Charlie sat down on one of the chairs in the living room, rubbing his hands through his hair. While this was a loophole, it was not a great one. Charlie wasn't exactly sure where he needed to go to accomplish what he needed to accomplish, but he was sure that it was dangerous. How could he ask this girl to come along, and put her in danger?

He couldn't, that was the answer. He didn't know much about her, but from what he did know, she was just a girl, a child, really, having only lived seventeen years of life.

Also, she was a Peace Broker, and she'd fulfilled her mission. If she were to step outside those orders, and get further involved, she could lose her job.

Again, Charlie couldn't be sure of this, but from what he'd seen, the girl didn't have anyone—no family, no support system —outside of her organization. No pictures of parents hung on the walls, no sign of siblings or friends.

Charlie looked over at her and saw that Aria was watching him, as if she could see these assumptions playing out in the air above his head. Her pretty face was free of emotion, and as she looked at him, she breathed in deeply and spoke the kindest words any stranger had ever spoken to him.

"I'll go with you, Charlie," she said, sweet voice soft and low. "Wherever you think you need to go… I'll go with you."

For a heartbeat or two, Charlie was stunned into silence. "I can't ask you to do that," he said at last.

"You didn't," said the girl. "I offered."

"Why? Overlooking the fact that it'll be dangerous, couldn't you get in big trouble with your superiors?"

She shrugged, but in that small gesture Charlie could see that this offer was beyond generous on her part, and would certainly lead to trouble for her, in one form or another.

"I understand wanting to do something you've been ordered not to do," she said, her face blank again, as if slipping into an unreadable mode had become second nature. "Especially when it involves someone you love."

Charlie shook his head. "Isn't there another way? Can't you just take off whatever magic you put on me to make me stay with you?"

Aria only blinked at him. "I told you, I can't break my promise. We both go, or we both stay. It's up to you."

Charlie cursed, rubbing his jaw. He appreciated the offer, but it was a bad position to be put in. In order to help Surah, whom he loved so much it hurt sometimes, he would have to put this girl in harm's way. There was no right choice here, no good way to go.

Hopping off the counter, Aria went over to a closet in the corner of the room and opened the door. She disappeared inside, and then returned dragging a trunk behind her.

It scraped across the wood floor of the apartment. When she was in front of the couch, the trunk in between her and the chair Charlie was occupying, she took a seat and began putting in a combination on the lock securing the trunk.

Charlie watched in silence as the girl opened the top and removed five shiny throwing stars.

"Whoa," Charlie said. "What're you doing?" The stars were beautiful, but dangerous weapons.

"I'm taking the weight off you," she said. She gave the trunk a little kick with the toe of her boot. "Pick a weapon. I'm assuming we'll need them. I don't have any guns, though. I hate guns."

As a matter of fact, most supernaturals hated firearms, and there was magic in the other realms that kept them from working.

"Aria—" he began, but she cut him off.

Tucking a long iron knife into her boot, she said, "Look, I've made the choice. We're going to help Surah, and we're going to put an end to Tristell. She needs to be stopped, and I'm done sitting on the sidelines. To hell with my orders."

"You could die," he replied flatly.

"I'm not as easy to kill as I look," she snapped.

She wasn't looking at him now, but staring fixedly into the trunk as she removed weapon after weapon and tucked them into various parts of her clothing. Her movements were calculated and relaxed, robotic.

Charlie sat back in his seat, in awe of this girl, and curious about what else there was to her story. He'd never met anyone like her, and knew instinctually that her willingness to help had to be personal at least in part.

She'd said she knew what it was like to want to break orders, especially when concerning a loved one, and he could see in the green of her eyes that she was no stranger to loss.

Aria held out a long iron dagger, and he took it with hesitation. Iron was toxic to Fae, a weapon wielded when one meant to kill, and it was clear Aria knew this.

"We're going back to the Fae Forest," he said. It was not a question.

Aria nodded once, her face set and her mind decided.

Charlie took the blade and stared down at it. "I'll also need a silver one," he said.

The girl studied him a moment, forearms resting on her thighs as she leaned forward on the couch, sitting very still and eyeing him.

After some time had passed, how long Charlie was unsure, as he was a bit lost in his own thoughts, Aria said, "Why will you need a silver one too, Charlie?"

Charlie had a feeling the girl knew the answer to this question already, but he replied anyway.

"Because silver works best on Sorcerers, and I'm gonna kill my brother… I'm going to put an end to this mess once and for all."

Aria gave another single nod, then swept her long hair up off her neck and tied it into a knot at the top of her head. "I won't judge you for that, Charlie Redmine," she said. "So long as you don't judge me for whatever happens tonight. Do we have a deal?"

Charlie wasn't sure what to think of this, and he didn't miss the ominous way the Halfling girl said it, but he had a feeling that lost loved one of hers might have something to do with it.

When Charlie hesitated, the girl sighed. "You're not the only one who has business to attend to in the Fae Forest, okay? I'll be straight with you, I need you as much as you need me. Now hold out your hand and tell me we have a deal, and let's get this show on the road."

He would never be sure if he held his hand out to the girl that day with complete willingness on his part, but hold out his hand, he did.

"We have a deal," he said, and the two of them shook on it.

31

———

SAMSON

*T*his was the deal he'd made, and there was no way to run.

He hated himself for even wanting to, for even feeling the fear that was swirling through his chest, but hating it did not make it go away. He needed to focus, or he was dead before the fight even began.

Samson stood in the clearing now, along with all the other felines in the pride. Cats, large and small (small being a relative term, mind you) lounged around. Some of them lay in tree limbs that edged the clearing, others on huge flat rocks that got pleasantly warm under the day's sun.

This day's sun was sinking below the tree line, the dark blue hue of twilight descended over the earth without heed of what was to follow. Soon, every star in the endless sky would be visible, and the man in the moon would look down and witness a ceremony that only Great Cats and moons ever got to witness.

He could feel all the eyes on him, though cats had a way of seeming to be paying little attention when in fact they were rapt. There was an energy to the green, clean air of the jungle, a reverent silence.

Mila stood beside him, and Drake, King of the Beasts and his opponent on this fateful evening, stood on his other side.

As the last of the light leaked out of the sky, the King spoke to his people in the way of the Great Cats, his deep, imposing voice sounding in their heads as though it were their own.

"My children," Drake began, addressing the pride the way in which he'd been addressing them for nearly a hundred years, *"Tonight a battle for the throne will commence. Two cats will face each other with all of you as witness, and one cat will emerge your leader. If this should be the last time I stand before you, know that it has been an honor to head this pride, and that each of you has made me proud in your own ways."*

He paused, his head tilting slightly as he looked at Samson. *"That includes my opponent, my possible successor. Let us not forget what could happen should our kind go without strong leadership, and let us show the respect that is deserved to both tonight's victor and loser, no matter which cat takes which title. As always, I can promise I will fight as hard as I can."*

Drake stepped back now, and all eyes in the jungle went to Samson. Sam knew it was his turn to step forward and address the pride, and for a moment, he couldn't for the life of him think of a thing to say. Then he thought of Surah, and the words came to him easily.

Samson took a step forward and held his head high. *"Should I win, I'll do my best to do right by you,"* he said, and that was all.

That was the entirety of the ceremony. Following this, the cats spread out in a ring around the center of the clearing, leaving a large open space.

Everyone was sure to stay far enough away from where the two cats would battle, lest they find themselves at the wrong end of tooth or claw.

In all his life, Samson couldn't remember feeling quite as nervous as he felt right now.

"Take your position, son, and let us be done with this." Drake said, speaking only to Sam now.

Despite the fact that Sam wanted to be anywhere else in any of the realms right now, he had to admit he felt great respect toward the King of Beasts. Drake had always been a fair king, which could not be said of most who carried the title.

It felt as though both fire and ice were rushing through Sam's veins, and his mind cleared as his instincts kicked in, his large head lowered between his powerful shoulders, his feline eyes bright and focused. Drake's stance mirrored his own.

For the smallest of moments, it was as if time stood still, and Samson's mind was once again with the Sorceress. He sent out his love with his thoughts, telling the universe to watch over the two-leg female for whom he had flipped his life upside down, should he no longer walk this plane to do so himself. This final, stolen moment steeled him.

Then Drake roared out a growl that seemed to vibrate in Sam's own chest. His own roar and that of the other cats present followed, and Drake moved in like lightning, teeth bared in vicious glory.

Sam saw a flash of white as Drake's enormous paw swiped at his face, tearing out a good chunk of Sam's black and blue fur and drawing the first blood of the night. Then there was searing pain in Sam's left foreleg as Drake's powerful jaws tore at the flesh and fur there.

A growl of agony resounded through the jungle, and Samson realized that it had issued from his own throat. The other cats present had fallen silent, and in Sam's mind had melted away entirely.

All he could feel was the pounding of his heart, the pain caused by his opponent. All he could hear was the blood rushing in his ears, the deadly battle growls of Drake, King of the Beasts.

Time sped up to an adrenaline-filled rush. Sam slashed and

snapped back, catching Drake's hindquarters between his jaws but losing purchase before he could do any real damage.

The taste of Drake's blood touched his tongue, sending his instincts into overdrive, his large body moving of its own accord, fighting for its very life.

In reality, the entire fight only lasted three minutes, but time is a relative thing. To those watching, it seemed to go by very quickly, to pass in flashes of teeth and blood, fang and fur.

But to the two fighting felines, it lasted an eternity.

For Samson it seemed especially so. He was growing weary, starting to wear.

Drake was very obviously going for Samson's throat, for the soft place on his neck where, once ruptured, could not be repaired. Sam's smaller size worked to his advantage here, as he was able to keep low, but it was the only advantage to his smaller stature, as all he'd been able to accomplish thus far was superficial cuts and scrapes to Drake.

Thus far, he'd only been able to defend. If he didn't make a move soon, and end this thing, Sam was sure he was going to die, and it had never occurred to him until this very moment how very much he wanted to live, how very much he wanted to lay eyes upon his Sorceress before the earth reclaimed his body.

With a burst of energy, Sam slipped around to Drake's side and tried to take out his hindquarter, an injury that could prove deadly in such a fight.

But the move had the opposite effect, and Drake twisted skillfully out of the way, his large jaws clamping down with bone crushing force around the back of Sam's right leg.

Again, Sam heard a gut-clenching roar of pain. Again, he realized after the fact that it had come from his own throat. He tried to put weight on his rear leg and felt it buckle beneath him.

Using a move he'd learned from Surah, he rolled out of the

way of a death strike from Drake that just barely missed its mark.

The King of Beasts was on him again before he could take another breath. Sam saw only a flash of red-stained teeth, and moved his shoulder just in time to protect his neck.

Drake's sharp teeth sank deep into the flesh of his shoulder, sending a jolt of electricity through Sam's body. Blinding pain followed this sensation.

Weakly, Sam struck out, his paw batting at the King's face with almost comical slowness. He could feel a warm wetness seeping through his fur in various places, could smell the irony tang of his own blood.

Like so many before him, Samson was going to die on this night, die under the fangs of the great Drake. There was a moment then where time stalled, where Sam looked up and saw the disappointment in the King's eyes, for he too knew that he was going to win, that Sam simply could not defeat him.

Promise me you'll return...

These words floated through his head, spoken in the voice of his Surah. She'd whispered it in his ear on the night before he'd left, her voice as small as it had been when she'd been only a child.

Promise me you'll return, Sam. Tell me I'll see you again, even if you think it may not be so. Just lie to me, because if you don't, I'm not sure I can face what's ahead. So promise me... please.

The memory had no place in such a moment, but there it was, nonetheless. He had promised her, had promised that he would come back and see her again... and he did not want it to be a lie.

More than he'd ever wanted anything in his life, he did not want that promise to be a lie.

Energy provided by the love of a Sorceress surged through him, and the pain of his injuries melted away with a promise to return should he see through this.

Sam's mind cleared into a tunnel-vision state, his eyes focused only on the king. It was obvious Drake felt he had already won, and this was a deadly mistake.

Sam waited for his moment, watching the King's neck the way a hawk watches a mouse run through a field, though comparing Drake to a mouse was ridiculous at best.

Drake was still being run by instinct, but Sam had entered his mind's equivalent to a two-leg's. He bit down on instinct and, instead, analyzed the situation. It was another thing he'd picked up from his mistress over the years.

Drake moved in for what he was sure would be his final blow, his enormous head held low between his shoulders and his slanted eyes filled with bloodlust.

Sam rolled again, a counterintuitive move for a cat in such a situation as Sam was forced to momentarily expose his belly to do so. But it was not a move the King had been expecting, and it put Sam in just the position he needed to be in.

When he rolled over onto his feet, he did so with Drake's throat locked tightly between his jaws, and the momentum of the movement tore out a chunk of flesh that filled Sam's mouth with the king's blood.

Scarlet sprayed into the air, and surprised growls, hisses, and roars filled the night sky. Drake's bright eyes went wide, and then dark, as the body of the King of the Beasts slumped onto the ground, dead.

Sam paid no heed to the crowd, for they had not yet rematerialized in the haze of battle that had befallen him. He looked down at Drake's body, which twitched just slightly before settling for good.

It was surreal, something that could not be gripped immediately. Part of him had already accepted defeat, and now he stood over the body of a king.

When he lifted his head, the world slowly swimming back into focus, the jungle eerily silent all around him, he met the eyes of Mila, who was looking at her dead father in a way that wrenched at Sam's heart.

But he stood tall as he met the eyes of his new pride.

Then, Samson, King of the Beasts, let out a roar that shook the very earth beneath their paws.

3 2

SURAH

The Dark Lord's deep voice rang through the streets of Zadira, floated out over the fields to the north and west, echoed in the mountains to the south and east, and penetrated the thick stone walls of Surah's castle.

Every shutter, every door and window shade was shut tight, many people having fled to the mountains, or other more rural areas of the Sorcerer Territory.

A small portion of the people remained in their homes, with their shops and possessions in the capital city, and these people dare not peek out their windows for fear of what they might see.

Some of them were old enough to remember war, but many were not, many were but children, and they held their peace through confused terror, sensing the tenseness in their parents, noticing the creases above their foreheads, the tightness of their shoulders.

Surah Stormsong stood on her balcony, the hood of her thick black cloak shielding her from the wind, which had kicked up with the fall of night. There was an electricity to the air, a charge that Surah could feel thrumming through her, as if coursing through her very veins.

"Surah!" called the Dark Lord for the second time, the deep, resounding nature of his voice ringing in her ears.

She gripped the Black Stone hanging around her neck. It was a heavy object when held directly, no doubt due to the amount of dark magic it contained, but the Black Stone felt somehow weightless when it rested above her heart… which had frosted over with a chill that made the night wind seem warm in comparison.

"You call me the coward and refuse to face me, Surah Stormsong!" Dagon said. Surah watched from afar as he spun slowly in a circle, taking in her land as if surveying a new home.

"This is your leader, Sorcerers?" Dagon called out to the quiet landscape, speaking to the people hiding in whatever places they had to hide. "You deserve better than a coward!"

Behind Surah, Noelani and Lyonell stood at stiff attention, and Theo stepped up to her side. Before he could speak, Surah beat him to the chase.

"Stay here, all of you," Surah said. She glanced at the three of them only once, the look in her violet eyes as grave as the dead. "Do not follow me. That's an order from your queen. Break it, and it will be considered treason."

With that, she portaged off the balcony, materializing in an instant before the Dark Lord. Dagon had chosen a small hill just outside the city, a dramatic vantage point that he'd no doubt picked just for that purpose.

He was wearing the same black suit and mortal body he'd been wearing in the Underworld, the same crooked grin on a handsome mask that hid a devil.

His forked tongue flicked out over his lips in a way that was grotesquely serpent-like.

"Ah, dearest Surah," Dagon said, "you've come to make payment."

Surah slid her sais out of their holsters and gripped them with a wicked grin of her own. "I owe you nothing, Dark Lord," she replied with a calm some small part of her knew she should not feel. "And I told you, return to my land and I'll take your head."

Dagon quirked an eyebrow. "That wasn't a joke, then? Pity. You'd enjoy this more if you just gave in." He touched his chin, face frowning in thought. "Then again," he added, his voice lowering to a whisper, "*I'll* enjoy it more if you struggle and scream."

Anger surged through Surah that was as hot and bright as a dying star, nearly exploding from her being. Her hand flicked up and a powerful pulse of dark magic flew from her fingertips, catching the Dark Lord off guard.

The energy hit him dead center his chest, knocking his deceptively benign form into the air and onto the hard earth. Surah was unaware of it, but a bit of blackness had momentarily swirled into the violet of her eyes, like a drop of ebony ink amongst the purple.

Dagon was on his feet again within the same instant. His head tilted to the side, and some of his dark hair fell into his face.

"Well, now, that wasn't very nice," he said, the words coming out a growl.

His attack struck Surah before she was even aware it was issued. The wind knocked out of her as though an iron fist had slammed into her stomach.

She doubled over, the air rushing out of her in a painful whoosh, and lost her grip on the Black Stone. Instead, her hands gripped at her knees for balance as water filled her eyes, but it was miraculous that it did not steam up immediately with the hot rage that accompanied it.

Surah portaled forward, slashing at Dagon with both sais and drawing black blood from two separate spots on his arm.

For a moment, the façade the Dark Lord was donning blinked out of focus, and the true Demon form of the immortal was visible to all.

She couldn't be sure what look came over her face when she saw this, but whatever it was made Dagon smile widely, and apparently decide to stop with the pretense altogether. Surah watched in equal parts horror and fascination as the Dark Lord took his true form, his body mangling and morphing in a way that was both terrible and mesmerizing.

His neck elongated until it was nearly a foot long and thick like a tree trunk. His once creamy, white, and unblemished skin melted away into a scaly, rough black, the expensive suit tearing away with his body's expansion and falling to the earth in shreds.

His hands and feet grew into claws and hooves, the fingers stretching long and the toes rounding off like that of a horse.

Horns sprouted from his forehead, long and spiraling, piercing at the darkening sky. His mouth and face grew into something obscene, terrible in its animation.

Wings, black and bony, sprouted from his back and spread out to a span of nearly twelve feet. The part of his skin that she'd cut with her weapons oozed dark blood that steamed when it met the cool night air.

For a moment, Surah could do nothing but stare at the creature before her in disgust and horror. The shift had been nearly instantaneous, but each crack of bone and rearrangement of physical feature had been awfully visible.

Dagon's voice was no longer that of a mortal, but rather carried the weight and intimidation of the Dark Lord that he was.

"I tried to be reasonable with you," he said, the words vibrating in her ears. "It will hurt much worse with me in this form, and when my child is born, it will also be in true form, and thus, will rip you open from the inside out."

Surah didn't justify this with words. She flicked her wrist again, sending another wave of magic at Dagon, but was too slow this time.

The Dark Lord was much more agile in this form, and he slipped right past the strike with an ease that gave Surah pause.

Dagon saw her hesitation and gave a cackling laugh, swiping at her with his long claws. She portaled out of his grasp just in time to avoid capture, landing behind him and driving her sais deep into his scaly back, though not as deep as she'd intended. The rough skin there was harder to puncture than she'd anticipated.

Dagon spun around fast, backhanding her across the face. It felt like fire was scorching over the skin he'd struck, and Surah let out a cry.

As her head rocked back on her shoulders, the world went a blinding white. The scene began to creep back in around the edges of her vision.

She felt his claws wrap around her ankle, and again she portaled out of his hold just in the nick of time. Now she stood fifteen feet away from him, panting, the taste of her own blood filling her mouth, but the fire in her soul not close to quenched.

He roared out in rage, taking to all fours and charging at her like a bull, sharp horns aimed at her chest. Again, Surah evaded the attack, but she could not do so forever, and the both of them knew this.

She needed to take him out, and quick. Gripping the Black Stone, Surah used all her strength, sending a bolt of energy at the Dark Lord.

It struck him dead center, knocking Dagon to the ground, and knocking Surah to the ground as well. She had used so much magic in that one attack that she didn't even have enough strength left to stand up.

But Dagon did. He regained his feet and moved to stand over her, his claws clenching and unclenching, ropes of saliva hanging from his maw, where his forked tongue lolled in excitement.

Surah felt a scream bubble in her stomach as he settled himself over her, and she used what little strength she had to kick at him, but her blows were about as effective as a child's, and her struggle only seemed to excite him.

Fear threatened to overcome her. She was moments away from being raped by a Dark Lord in front of her entire kingdom (or at least those who'd dared to stay) and for a panicked moment she could think of nothing to do.

Around her neck, the Black Stone pulsed hotly, searing the skin there, snapping her back to focus. Whipping her head to the side, she bit deeply into the scaled arm that Dagon had braced beside her, slamming her jaw shut and tearing out a chunk of rancid meat, which she spat out immediately. The Dark Lord's awful blood ran down the sides of her mouth.

Dagon roared in anger and pain, and Surah used the time to scramble out from underneath him. She removed a silver dagger strapped to her upper right thigh, and thrust it as hard as she could into the Dark Lord's belly.

Where it broke skin, dozens of strange beetles emerged from the wound, pouring out the way blood would have had he been mortal.

Surah was as tough as one could come, but she hated insects. They terrified her, and had since she was a little girl. She was sure it had something to do with the time her brother Syris had put a handful of fireflies in the hood of her cloak and laughed when she pulled the hood over her head, pausing before running around in circles and screaming.

But no such panic could be had here. She may not be able to kill Dagon, but if she could evade his attacks long enough to cast a banishment spell, she could send the bastard away for a long time.

Trouble was, he hadn't given her any such opportunity. A

banishment spell was not like other magic. It could not be done with a mumbled incantation and a flick of one's wrist. It took time, patience, and enormous strength, none of which Surah had at the moment.

Suddenly, as she portaled out of Dagon's reach once more, she realized that she'd underestimated her enemy, that she had allowed her emotions—and yes, she thought now, may as well admit that the Black Stone was playing a certain role as well—to get the best of her.

These self-doubts and dark thoughts grabbed a hold of her. It was only a moment, but it was enough. She'd become distracted, and that was all it took.

Dagon was on top of her before she could take another breath, the beast pinning her body to the ground, which had not been gentle on her tailbone when she'd struck it. He held her wrists in his claws, the sharp nails there biting painfully into her skin.

His weight was enormous, crushing, allowing for only shallow, inadequate breaths. She felt his lower half shifting in the most terrible of ways, felt her cloak being ripped away, her heart beating boldly in her throat.

And then Surah Stormsong was too horrified to even scream.

3 3

—

SAMSON

The feeling slammed through his stomach, twisting it into knots and making it hard to breathe.

Mila sat across from him, had not spoken a word to him since before the fight, since before Sam had killed her father and taken his place as King of the Beasts.

Now his betrothed came forward, studying him, and spoke for the first time. *"Samson,"* she said, her sweet voice filling his head. Concern had crept into her tone, and Sam was oddly moved by this. *"Are you all right?"*

Samson's tongue felt thick in his throat, and he had to swallow twice before he responded. *"I... I don't know,"* he answered. *"Something is wrong."*

After the fight, Sam had dragged Drake's body to the river, where the Great Cats sent their dead who were too important to eat. Drake had been heavy, and the process had been long, but he'd done it because it was what was expected, and because Drake deserved the respect.

The pride had followed behind, had stood witness as Sam set the former King's body at the edge of the surging river that ran all the way through the eastern jungles for over two hundred miles.

The waters had welcomed the dead king's body, picking it up the way a mother scoops up an infant, with ease and familiarity. Mila had stood beside Sam, silent as the night as she watched the waters carry her father away. Sam was sure she must hate him.

But she was a royal cat, and she'd walked dutifully beside him while he'd led the pride home and climbed atop the king's rock in the clearing the cats occupied.

Mila had stepped up and held her head high as Samson addressed the pride as their new king, as he had claimed her as his own, just as Drake had intended in case of this turn of events.

She had done these things, but Sam could not miss the bitter resentment that had touched the corners of her slanted green eyes. And she had not spoken a word until just now, when whatever feeling he'd experienced had slammed through him.

The two cats were alone in a comfortable but cozy cavern in the heart of the jungle. They'd been alone for the past hour, and had only sat uncomfortably in silence, pretending to sleep though they both knew the day they'd had would not allow it.

Mila scooted closer, sniffing Sam with concern as he squeezed his eyes shut against the sudden sickness that had befallen him.

The answer entered his mind only seconds after the sickness slammed into his stomach: Something was wrong with Surah. He couldn't say how he knew this, but he did. He knew it as surely as he knew revealing it would only cause his new bride to hate him more.

But he wouldn't lie to her. Mila deserved so much more than Sam thought he could give her, but at the very least, she deserved the truth.

The words came before he had a chance to stop them. *"I have to go back,"* Sam said.

For several long moments that felt like lifetimes, Mila said nothing, didn't even blink as she stared at him in the darkness of the small cave.

Just when he could no longer take the silence, Mila spoke. *"You are the king,"* she said, and that was all.

She's in trouble, Mila. Really big trouble."

"You are the king," she repeated.

Samson took to his feet, his anxiety over the wellbeing of his Surah too much to even consider ignoring.

"You're right," he said, as he exited the cave. *"I am the King."*

3 4

SURAH

One moment he was on top of her, his weight crushing the air from her chest, his hot, foul breath blowing into her face, as if the fires of hell burned in his belly.

The next moment, he was gone, knocked from her as if by magic, his awful, winged form flying to the side and setting her free.

Surah scrambled to her feet, conserving her magic for the banishment spell. With a drop of her stomach, she saw who had come to her rescue.

Theo, Lyonell, Noelani and Bassil stood off to the sides, one positioned in each of the four directions, swords at the ready and the looks of warriors on their faces.

Dagon stalked over to Noelani first, breathing fire from his throat like a dragon, shooting the flames at Noelani, who rolled out of the way just in time.

In this moment, Lyonell moved in, slicing at the Dark Lord with his long Hunter's blade, drawing more steaming black ooze and beetles from the wound.

Surah charged at Dagon as well, but Bassil's voice cut

through the battle-induced haze. "Surah, the spell!" the Warlock called out. "You must banish him."

Gripping the Black Stone around her neck, blackness swirling in the violet of her eyes, Surah began the banishment spell.

Everything that happened next occurred quickly. Surah only got three words into the incantation, and then the world took on an awful clarity.

Lyonell's brave strike at the Dark Lord was a touch too slow, and Dagon gripped the Hunter's neck and snapped it to the side the way one might break a twig between their fingers.

The snap was audible, and it was this sound that seemed to freeze the world, to hold time still before letting the reality of what had just happened settle.

In the next instant there was a gut-wrenching scream, a cry so full of agony that it twisted her stomach just to hear it. Surah stood wide-eyed as Noelani charged Dagon with her blade.

Tears streamed down her cheeks, and her teeth were bared in horrible rage. She got snatched up as swiftly as her husband had, her neck snapped with just as much ease.

The Dark Lord tossed the two bodies of Surah's personal Hunters to the side as if they were nothing more than cotton-filled dolls, and Lyonell and Noelani landed in lifeless heaps upon the ground.

For these fast, frozen moments, Surah could only stare in horror, her mind refusing to process what it was seeing.

Bassil's voice cut through the haze once more.

He was approaching the Dark Lord with caution, his wooden staff clutched in his dark hand, his face as serious as an undertaker's.

"Surah! You must complete the spell!"

Again, she began the incantation, trying her best to focus despite the absolute shock that was running through her.

She would not let Lyonell's and Noelani's deaths be in vain.

She would grieve later, because now was not the time for weakness.

But she was so angry, so wracked with emotions, her eyes swirling with that unnatural black, and she reached into her cloak and threw a knife hard at Dagon, who had been approaching Theo. It stuck in the Dark Lord's back and he roared out in anger.

Yes, Surah thought. She didn't want to banish Dagon. She wanted to tear him limb from limb... and after the use of so much Black Magic, she was not even close to being in her right mind, or in control over her actions.

Dagon took to the air, apparently set on killing Surah, the heir he'd intended for her to carry be damned. His enormous wings beat at the sky, carrying him upward with a whoosh of air that lifted Surah's lavender hair off her shoulders.

Her head tipped back and she watched as he began his descent, coming down with enough force to crush her like an insect beneath his hooves. Surah didn't care in the least that she was about to die... because she was going to take this bastard with her.

She slipped a long, sharp rod from her boot, where it had been strapped to her ankle, and waited. With as much force as Dagon was descending, he would crush her, but he would also impale himself.

She had no thoughts for the consequences of this action, was not even aware of the fact that a crooked, crazed smile had found its way to her face.

Dagon moved so fast he was just a blur. He hit Surah hard in the side, knocking her off her feet and onto the ground.

For a second, she thought she must be dead, but there was an awful crushing sound, and the earth beneath her vibrated with the impact of the Dark Lord.

Surah only got a glimpse of Theo's face before his body was

crushed under Dagon's hooves, and the devotion in his gray eyes caused all the purple to leak out of hers.

She gave herself over to the dark magic of the Black Stone, and it enveloped her like a blanket, blocking out the emotions, and everything else that made her who she was.

Her hands lifted into the air, and with them, so did the Dark Lord. Dagon's glowing red eyes widened slightly as they took in the swirling, all encompassing black in Surah's.

Her grin widened as she saw the uncertainty flash over his face, and then the fear.

With a flick of her Black Magic-filled fingers, she removed the Dark Lord's head. It rolled free of his body and fell at her feet.

"You little *bitch!*" Dagon's head screamed at her, his body flapping its wings and kicking at the air where she still held it suspended.

Dark Lords could not be killed, for they were immortal, but like most physical beings, they could be dismembered, and their body parts banished to different parts of different realms.

Especially by a powerful Sorceress in the full clutches of the Black Stone.

Perhaps *only* by such a person.

Surah stooped down to Dagon's still-cursing head, meeting his eyes with a calm that belied the turmoil in her soul.

"I told you," she whispered, grabbing the chin of the severed head and wrenching the jaws open, "if you came to my land I would remove your head, and then your tongue. So I guess you know what comes next."

Gripping one of the spiral horns atop the Dark Lord's head, Surah grabbed his forked tongue with her free hand and began to saw, reveling in the agonized screams that were soon choked off with black, sticky blood.

Tongue in hand, she dismembered and banished the Dark

Lord's body to places no one would ever look, and did the same with the tongue.

The head, however, she picked up, looking down at it with swirling black eyes. A Dark Lord's head, like any other being, contained its consciousness, and now that she'd relieved Dagon of his ability to speak, Surah thought it best she keep it close.

Also, she was more than a bit out of her mind at the moment. She was on the verge of hysterical laughter when a cough broke through her thoughts, clearing some of the clouds that had formed over her mind.

She turned and saw Theo, his once-strong body crushed beyond repair, the life quickly draining from his face as he stared at her from his broken position.

"Surah," he said.

Or tried to say. His words were choked off as blood bubbled from his mouth.

Surah went to him, kneeling at his side, sadness breaking through the storm that was her soul. She touched his handsome face, the emotions coming back, if only in tiny bits.

She could almost reach the part inside her that made her who she was, but not quite. Her heart was too submerged in darkness to get the full effect of all that had taken place on this night.

But even a woman blinded by dark magic would see the devotion, the love that shined out of the Head Hunter's eyes, and Surah knew that he was dying so she could live.

Theodine Gray had sacrificed himself to save her, and Surah knew that if she survived this, his face in these final moments would haunt her for the rest of her life.

If she had doubted it before, there was no denying it now. Theodine Gray truly had loved her, and she had never done anything but shun this love.

She should feel awful over this, and yet, she felt little to nothing.

Surah held the Head Hunter's hand in his last moments, leaning down and meeting his eyes, in which the light of life was dimming.

"Your death will not be in vain, Theo," she promised. "Thank you for your service to my family… to *me*."

Before she finished saying this, Theo's final breath escaped him and his face went dull and lifeless, his limp, ruined body lying before her, as had so many she'd cared for.

The voice in which she had spoken to Theo did not sound like her own, and when her body moved over to those of Lyonell and Noelani, it did not feel like she was commanding it. The darkness in her had taken on a life of its own.

The mixture of Black Magic and trauma would not be easily undone.

Surah stood beside her two dead best friends, the Hunters who had protected her forever, since she'd been only a child. Noelani, her body crumpled, neck poised at an unnatural angle, who had read Surah bedtime stories and checked under her bed for monsters after her mother passed away.

Lyonell, who had always been a calm and comforting presence, allowing Surah her independence while putting himself in harm's way to ensure her safety. His neck was also bent in an awful way, his face and body devoid of life.

She looked down at the fallen, at her dead loved ones, the memories shared with them numbering in the thousands, and could feel nothing but rage and darkness, nothing but a primal, all-consuming need for revenge.

When a hand fell on her shoulder, Surah turned without thinking and flicked her wrist, sending whoever had touched her flying.

She saw that it was Bassil as the Warlock struck the ground, his patchwork cloak flying up over his long, dark legs in a manner that Surah found hysterical.

She was unaware of it, but the laughter that issued from her throat also did not sound like her own.

"Sorry," she told the Warlock, though the tone in which the single word was spoken indicated that she was not sorry at all. "Now's not a good time to sneak up on me, Warlock."

Bassil pulled himself to his feet with some effort, a cautious grimace on his dark face.

"Quite all right, my queen," he said. His black eyes went to the head of Dagon, which Surah still held by one of the long, spiral horns. It dangled from the end of her hand with blazing eyes and a mouth incapable of expressing its fury.

One corner of Surah's mouth pulled up as her eyes followed Bassil's. "That's one problem taken care of," she said.

The wary stance Bassil had taken was beginning to annoy her, and she felt an unreasonable amount of hostility toward the Warlock. Bassil spoke slowly, the way one does to a person holding a room of hostages.

"His denizens will come," Bassil said, nodding toward the head of Dagon. "And the Fae army will come with them."

Surah turned away from the Warlock, retrieving her cloak from the ground where the Dark Lord had tossed it after ripping it from her body.

Dusting it off, she returned it to her shoulders. Bassil stood silent, watching Surah as if she was a questionable beast that had wandered into the backyard.

Spinning in a slow circle atop the small hill overlooking Zadira, Surah surveyed her land, could feel the eyes of her people staring out at her from the shadows.

When she spoke, her voice was cold, flat, and edged with a bit of excitement that scared the Warlock more than he would ever admit.

"Let them come," the Sorceress Queen said. "Let them come so I can kill them all."

35

CHARLIE

"Going by portal would be a buttload easier, you know?" Aria said, looking sideways at Charlie as they waded through the dense trees of the New Jersey Pinelands.

Charlie swatted at what had to be the millionth greenhead fly (a name which Aria had provided) to bite him in the past hour.

"I thought you said the Halflings have entrances to the other worlds everywhere," he replied, stopping in his tracks to stare at the girl.

Aria pushed some of her red-brown hair out of her face. "We do, but that doesn't mean I wouldn't rather portal."

Charlie continued pushing through the unwelcoming vegetation. "I told you, I don't want to be disoriented when we get there. I'm not used to portals, especially not whatever Fae version of it you do… How much further?"

Rolling her eyes, Aria took the lead again, moving ahead of him. "Not much further, but if your old bones need a rest, we can take a break."

"Thanks, but my 'old bones' are just fine." He swatted at

another fly. "My skin, on the other hand, is being eaten alive by these tiny Demon-insects."

Digging into the small black backpack slung over her shoulders, Aria pulled out a spray bottle and handed it over to Charlie.

"Here, spray this on your arms. It helps keep them away."

Charlie took the bottle with narrowed eyes. "Why didn't you give this to me earlier?"

Aria looked too genuinely surprised by the question to be mad at. She shrugged. "You didn't ask for it, and you're not the only one with a lot on your mind. I guess I wasn't thinking about it."

"Did you put some on?"

"No."

"Then why aren't they biting you?"

Another shrug. "I'm half Fae. Nature's kinda my homegirl."

Charlie wasn't at all sure what a *homegirl* was, but he supposed he got the context.

"That must be nice," he commented, bathing himself in the bug spray, which smelled terrible and felt grossly sticky on his skin. But it was a price worth paying if it would cease the biting.

"Yes," Aria said. "It is."

Her tone was too even to be sure if this was serious or sarcasm. She pushed through some low hanging branches and stood at the edge of a small creek, the water bubbling peacefully through the trees, lending a moist smell to the green air.

"Here we are," she said.

Charlie stood beside her, seeing nothing but more dense forest, more green and brown, and the shallow creek.

"Okay, now what?"

Aria turned to him, her face deadly serious. "You promise to listen to everything I tell you to do before I take you in? I mean *everything*. The Fae Territory, especially the Fae Forest, is alive in a way that you can't possibly understand. Every part of it is intimately connected, is *one*. I can shield us from the Fae Queen's detection, but only if you listen to everything I say. Got it?"

Charlie nodded. He didn't have to trust the Halfling girl to know she wasn't lying about this. Those agonizing hours he'd spent wrapped in that torturous vine on the floor of the Fae Forest had shown him this truth.

It was as though the entire place was just an extension of Tristell, and she had commanded the very roots, branches, and leaves that made up the forest. She spoke, and the trees listened. Charlie would bet that vice versa was also true.

"You have my word," he said.

Aria studied him for a moment, gaging the truth in his words.

"Good," she said at last. "First, you'll need to follow my movements exactly, move right behind me, keeping a hand on me at all times. You must not break contact. Also, don't speak at all. Don't even whisper. In fact, try not to breathe too loudly. The key is to not let the forest know you're there. With my Fae blood, it'll accept me as part of it, but you, not so much."

Charlie's eyebrows rose. This was going to be harder than he'd thought, and he'd known difficult was an understatement. "That it?"

Aria grinned, her pretty face lighting up. "Just about."

"So you don't want to share with me your real reason for wanting to do this? You don't think I should know why you're really helping me?"

For a moment, Charlie was sure the girl wasn't going to answer, but then she sighed and pushed her hair out of her face, a subconscious action he recognized as a habit of hers.

"The part of me that's Fae is from my mother, who's full Faevian," Aria answered. "She's always lived in the Fae world, and a month ago, she went missing."

Charlie said nothing to this, only waited for the girl to continue.

Again, she sighed. "My superiors assure me 'the matter' will be resolved." She laughed without humor. "All these years serving them and that's what they call my mother going missing—a 'matter.'"

"What do you think happened to her?"

The look on her face was grim. "That's what I'm here to find out, but I know Tristell is behind it."

"That it?"

"That's it." She held out her hand. "You ready?"

"If we get close enough to my brother, I'm taking him out," Charlie said.

He didn't want to mislead the girl. He was well aware that his intentions could get them in trouble, could end very badly for them both.

"You gonna be able to do that?" she asked, ignoring the implications, apparently ready to risk it all as well. "Kill your own brother?"

Charlie had to swallow twice before he could answer, had to think of Surah in order to steel himself. He nodded.

"I don't really have a choice, Aria," he said, and it was the most honest thing he could have told her.

Aria took his hand, gripping it firmly with her warm fingers. She gave him a smile that was both ready and resolved.

"Then we understand each other perfectly, Charlie," she replied, and pulled him forward through an invisible curtain, an access point between worlds.

And toward whatever fate the Fae Forest had in store for them.

* * *

THE AIR in front of them shimmered, and a jolt of electric energy passed through him. It was not nearly as disorienting as portaling, but it made for a strange effect.

As they passed through whatever invisible barrier separated the Fae Territory from the human world, the Pinelands melted away and were replaced by the Fae Forest.

A shiver worked its way up Charlie's spine as he took in the smells, the sounds, the pastel-colored trees, and light pink fog hovering over the ground.

Vines very much like the ones that had tortured him here less than a day ago climbed up every surface, making a gnarled labyrinth, a sea of otherworldly vegetation.

Whereas Sorcerer Territory resembled the human world geographically, (the biggest difference being magic in place of technology) the Fae land was unique to itself. There was no place in all the realms like it, no other Territory that carried its unique forms of life.

This was no doubt thanks to the Fae that called it home, as their connection with the biosphere was deeper and more intimate than any other creature that walked the earth. It was like something out of a dream.

Or in Charlie's case, a nightmare. His heart kicked up in pace and he swallowed past a lump that had risen in his throat.

Aria turned her head, her hand still holding his, and put a finger to her lips, reminding him to stay close and silent. She crouched low, moving with an ease particular to the Fae race. Charlie mimicked her movements, half expecting the very branches of the peculiar trees to reach out and grab a hold of him.

Get your mind right, he told himself, and concentrated on the task at hand with more effort than he preferred.

Moving through the Fae Forest with Aria was a totally different experience than it had been when he'd been here before.

Before, the life that was this place had seemed to pause, to watch him the way a guard dog watches a passerby who ventures too close, with half-hooded eyes and slightly bared teeth. The Fae Forest had a *feeling* to it, and as an outsider that feeling was maleficent, threatening, imposing.

Now, with Aria by his side, shielding him with her Fae blood, or whatever it was she was doing, the experience was entirely different. The forest clearly accepted the Halfling girl, opened its arms to her without a thought.

It was pleasant, smelled of clean air that maintained a comfortable temperature. The pink fog floating along the forest floor was no longer a menacing entity, as it had been when Charlie had been held captive.

Now, it simply swirled around his boots, parted as he passed. The hair on his arms stood on end. He knew how deceiving appearances could be.

As they passed through the forest, Fae children darted among the trees, zipping past them and shaking free puffy leaves and rustling the undergrowth.

They swung from the canopies, leapt from branch to branch not unlike monkeys in the human world. They balanced above, their clawed feet clutching perches and slanted eyes blinking rapidly as they stared out from all around.

As he had been the first time he'd encountered the Fae children, he was struck with a sense of sadness for them. However this mess his brother had brokered between the Fae and the Sorcerers turned out, the ones most affected would be the children, on both sides of the battle lines.

Charlie knew this because he had been but a child when war had torn his life apart. So his heart hurt most of all for the wee ones, and a newfound rage toward his brother filled him. Michael had suffered right beside Charlie as a child. How could he be responsible for such terrible things?

Because Michael was no longer Charlie's brother. He was

Black Heart now. Charlie held tight to these thoughts as the question Aria had posed to him earlier played through his head.

You gonna be able to do that? Kill your own brother?

Aria came to a sudden halt in front of him, and he had to break free of his troubling thoughts quickly to keep from running into her.

Her small hand tightened around his, and she stooped lower to the ground, the pink fog and undergrowth swallowing her up. Charlie followed her example, his senses on high alert.

There were two voices coming from up ahead, and the hair on the back of Charlie's neck stood on end as he realized he recognized them.

One belonged to his brother, the other to Tristell the Fae Queen.

Aria sank lower still, sidling over to a nearby tree with a thick bush growing at its base. She lay flat on her belly, disappearing completely into the pink fog, waving her free hand at Charlie, who followed suit.

Cold sweat broke out over his brow. The last time he'd lain on the ground in the Fae Forest, he'd been tortured, wracked with agony for hours that had lasted lifetimes.

Suddenly, he felt foolish for coming here, for thinking he had a chance at accomplishing what he'd set out to do.

He shoved this fear away. He was here now, and his life was not the only one on the line. Charlie had to try. If he could put a stop to his brother here and now, maybe he could end this thing before entire Territories were devastated.

His brother's voice boomed loud enough for Aria and Charlie to make out his words, jerking Charlie from his thoughts once again.

"How could he have *escaped?*" Black Heart thundered, his voice was so dark and full of rage that Charlie swore he felt the earth shudder under his chest.

A high-pitched, gratingly familiar voice screeched back,

"What is Michael accusing me of? He thinks I killed his precious brother? Yes! That's what he thinks! That I killed his precious *Charlie-Boy* while he was away!"

The way she said the nickname practically dripped distain. "I told Michael, I left his brother *right here!*"

There was a grunt of anger followed by a whooshing sound, like something moving quickly through the air, and then another whoosh as something flared bright up ahead, near where the voices were coming from.

Tristell let out a screech that almost made Charlie drop hold of Aria's hand to cover his ears. Luckily, Aria held tight, shooting him a look. They needed to maintain contact so she could keep his presence hidden from the forest.

This cacophony was followed by silence. Aria crept forward slowly, pulling Charlie along with her. They were less than ten yards away now. Charlie held his breath, straining his ears to listen.

He felt very exposed in such a position, but he supposed he had no other choice now but to trust the Halfling girl. If he could get a little closer, he might be able to surprise attack his brother, take him out before he had a chance to know what hit him.

Michael was stronger with the magic, had honed his use of it over the years, but Charlie was a stronger physical fighter. The element of surprise was key here, as was making sure he didn't hesitate.

A sigh. "I'm sorry, my heart," Michael said. "But if you didn't free him from the vines, who did? One of the children?"

"The children would do no such thing… No, it had to be someone else."

"It had to be someone *Fae.*"

A moment of silence. Then: "Yes, it must've been, but none of my people would betray me."

"Oh no?" Michael asked, a playfulness in his tone now that

made Charlie's gut clench in revulsion. "You've made no enemies?"

"I've made plenty. Just not any who'd dare challenge me."

Aria's hand tightened around Charlie's, almost tight enough to hurt, and he watched as her free hand slid a small iron blade from her boot.

Black Heart said, "You sound mighty sure of yourself, dear heart, but the fact remains, someone with Fae blood set my brother free. The Forest would not have allowed it otherwise."

Aria inched closer still, and Charlie followed right beside her, the conversation growing louder with each inch, their distance decreasing while their heartbeats increased.

A third voice broke into the conversation, one unfamiliar to Charlie, and male. "Your majesty," said the unidentified speaker, "pardon my interruption."

Charlie and Aria couldn't see very well from where they were, but Charlie surmised this newcomer must be one of the Fae Warriors, one of Tristell's personal guards.

"There's been word that Dagon visited Sorcerer Territory," said the guard. "But no word of his return to the Underworld."

There was a moment of silence as this new information was absorbed.

A cold sweat broke over Charlie's brow, the air suddenly harsher in his lungs. His heart sank in his chest, which was still pressed against the floor of the forest.

Dagon had visited Sorcerer Territory. Surah had threatened to remove his head and tongue if he did so, while the Dark Lord had threatened to rape Surah.

Charlie cursed the heavens that he was away from the woman he loved. Gods only knew what the hell was happening to her right now.

His eyes narrowed and his hands clenched into fists, squeezing Aria's hand too tightly without intending to. A hot, terrible hatred swirled in him toward the Fae Queen and Black Heart, for putting all of this into play.

He had to trust that Surah could handle things without him for a little longer. He had his own affairs to settle first.

They were only twenty feet away now.

"Why would Dagon have moved ahead of us?" Black Heart snapped. "We were supposed to attack together."

"Perhaps the little Sorceress Queen provoked him," Tristell answered with a titter. "Perhaps Dagon has already killed her, and the throne waits open. This news is not necessarily bad news."

Clearly, the Fae Queen was excited by this turn of events, the intensity in her high voice picking up a touch. Charlie had not been aware a female could repulse him as much as this crazy bitch.

"Only a fool would underestimate Surah Stormsong," Black Heart said, his voice as dark as his soul. "Especially when she has possession of the Black Stone."

A cooing, birdlike sound issued from the Fae Queen. "Michael said using too much black magic could crush a soul," she trilled. "The amount of black magic to kill a Dark Lord? Do you think the little Sorceress Queen could stand that?"

There was a moment of silence as everyone listening considered this. Charlie could feel his heart beating in his throat. Up until this moment, he had not given the Fae Queen the credit due her for her cleverness.

She had set up the board so that it would take a miracle to beat her in the final matches. In order for everything to turn out all right, the love of Charlie Redmine's life not only had to defeat a dark Sorcerer and a crazy Fae with an army at her disposal, but a Dark Lord and his denizens as well.

And if Surah managed to do all that, she would still need to overcome the black magic that would have had to grip her in order for her to have even gotten that far. She would have to defeat those opposing her, and then defeat her own worst nature.

That last part alone was more than most people would be capable of.

"It's time to move," said the Fae Queen, breaking into the avalanche of thoughts tumbling through Charlie's head. "Take this and lead my guardians into battle, I will open a portal from the Underworld and unleash the Dark Lord's Demons. The plan is still intact!"

There was a rapid clapping sound and her voice reached a level of excitement usually reserved for small children.

Charlie shot to his feet, knowing if he didn't make his move and take out his brother now, he may never get another chance. His blood felt afire with adrenaline as he dropped Aria's hand and broke cover.

His brother's back was to him, and his muscles pumped, carrying him forward, breaking through Aria's attempted restraint, knife clutched tight in his hand.

Black Heart was kissing the Fae Queen, but her eyes were open, and they remained unalarmed as she watched Charlie approach his brother from behind.

Black Heart finished his kiss and portaled out of there just seconds before Charlie could reach him, none the wiser that his brother had nearly plunged a knife into his back.

Charlie howled with rage as the hand holding the blade swiped open air. Tristell used her powerful wings to flutter back from him several feet, a wicked grin on her face.

"Ah, there you are, Michael's brother," she said. "We thought we'd lost you. Do tell me how you came to be free of those vines. I'm absolutely *dying* to know."

"I came here to kill him," Charlie answered, his voice flat, blade still held tight in his fist. "But I'll settle with killing you first."

From the trees, a dozen Fae Guardians emerged, spears in

hand, surrounding Charlie and Tristell in the clearing. They began to tighten their circle, and Charlie came to the sudden realization that he'd completely botched this mission.

The Fae Queen grinned, her sharp teeth poking out over her full rep lips.

"As if you could, Sorcerer," she laughed. She took to her wings and shot up into the air, her long, flowing dress billowing out around her. "Seize him," she said, and the Fae Guardians began to move in.

Then Aria flew out of a tree like a monkey, landing on the Fae Queen's back and holding an iron blade to her throat. There was a struggle as the two hit the ground, and miraculously, Aria kept her hold of the Queen, though the fall had surely knocked the wind out of her.

"Call the Guardians off, Tristell," the Halfling girl said, her voice colder and flatter than Charlie had ever heard it, the words coming out between clenched teeth.

Aria pressed the blade against the Fae Queen's neck, where the iron sizzled the skin, making the queen grimace in pain.

To her credit, Tristell did not cry out, though the iron was clearly burning her. She nodded once, and the Fae Guardians who had been closing in on Charlie halted in their tracks.

Aria's mouth was a tight line, a look of vengeance in her green eyes.

"Good," she said. "We're gonna have us a little chat."

3 6

———

SURAH

They were coming.

She could practically see the whole thing playing out before her, could smell the storm on the wind. She looked up at the vast sky above her, stretched out endlessly in every direction.

Clouds had moved in, blotting out the sun, turning the day from a warm, golden yellow to a somber, foreboding steel. It was as if the land itself, the very atmosphere, was aware of what was coming.

Her thoughts, much like the sky, were stormy, thunderheads rolling in and dousing out the sun.

Surah Stormsong was distantly aware of the lack of light within her, but could not find it in herself to care.

In her once-violet eyes, inky black sickness continued to swirl.

Her right hand tightened around the Black Stone hanging about her neck. She could not afford to take it off during such times, and so she did not dare.

She needed the protection of the Black Stone. *Her people* needed its protection. It had aided her well thus far. Better than she'd anticipated, even. She had everything completely within her control.

"Your majesty?"

Surah's head turned in the direction of the voice, her eyes flashing darkly. She sighed with annoyance as she saw it was only the Warlock, Bassil.

"What is it?" she asked, turning back toward the city.

This hill, where Dagon had challenged her, was a perfect spot. It amazed her that she hadn't spent much time here.

Bassil's tone was wary, hesitant. "Are you all right?" he asked.

"Of course I am," she said. When he didn't leave, she turned her gaze on him once more, eyebrows raised. "What do you want? I've got work to do."

"I want to know what work that is, your majesty," he answered.

Anger surged through Surah, hot and lightning fast. Her hand rose into the air, lifting the Warlock off his feet without touching him. Her fist clenched, and he began to clutch at his throat, the air cut off from his lungs.

"That's no concern of yours," she said, but the voice coming out of her was not her own. It hummed with a dark power that vibrated in the bones.

Opening her fist, her hand dropped to her side, and the Warlock dropped to the ground along with it, hitting the hard earth with a thud.

He coughed, staring up at her with wide eyes, his hands still holding his neck.

"Is there anything else?" she asked.

The Warlock shook his head, scrambled to his feet, and retreated, nearly tripping down the hill on which they stood in an effort to return to the castle. Where she'd told him to stay.

Where she'd told Theo and Lyonell and Noelani to stay as well. And now they were dead. They were dead because they hadn't listened to her.

And now lines had been crossed that could not be retreaded. Now there was no going back, but only forward. Forward and *through,* by whatever means necessary.

She lifted her hands over her head, the Black Stone around her neck glowing darkly. Using the magic, she would address her people. The Black Stone had more than enough power for her message to be heard all throughout her Territory.

She could have settled for a written message, but she wanted her people to *see* the resolution in her eyes. She wanted them to understand what she was doing for them. They had been so quick to turn against her, so fast to condemn Charlie.

They were ungrateful, undeserving people… and that was not something that could be accepted any longer, now that she was their queen.

The image of her appeared in the air before everyone in the Sorcerer Territory. The hillside on which she stood, the capital city to her west, the country spread out beyond it.

Surah Stormsong was not aware of how she came across to the people that day, of the picture she painted by using her dark magic to reach them.

The angry sky rolled behind her, the wind picked up the edges of her fine cloak, which was darker in some spots where the Dark Lord's blood had sprayed her. Some of the black, sticky gore was smeared across the creamy skin of her forehead, a small spattering of it on the left side of her chin, which was held royally high.

Her lavender hair curled wildly around her smooth face, the insistent wind lifting the purple locks off her shoulders.

Her stained hands were clenched into tight fists. The Black Stone pulsed and glowed below her neck. Ebony swirled in the purple of her eyes, leaking out into the whites at the edges, writhing as if something alive.

"People of the Sorcerer Kingdom," she began, her voice calm and steady, eerily so, considering the circumstances. "I address you now as your queen, Surah Stormsong, daughter of our late king, Syrian Stormsong, the last of my name…

This past week has been a challenging time for our kind, and the losses we've faced have been felt by all. I stand before you now having been accused of treachery, of putting the needs of royals before those of the common Sorcerer people. These lies offend me. Those who have spread them are my enemies, and as such are yours as well. As your queen, I can assure you that those who have brought us misfortune will pay in full for what they've done."

The wind picked up around her, blowing her hair around her face, cooling her hot skin. All throughout Sorcerer Territory, royals and common people alike were watching the projection of their queen with rapt attention and alarm. They had never seen a Surah Stormsong like the one they were seeing now.

"I won't lie to you. I never have, and in this troubling time, I won't start now. We are under threat from the Fae, who have aligned themselves with both the Dark Sorcerer known as Black Heart and a Dark Lord by the name of Dagon. Dagon is no longer a threat, but I suspect a few of his Demons may find their way here in the very near future."

She paused. She could not see all the people she was addressing, but she was right in giving them time to absorb this. Had she been able to look at their faces, she might have taken note of the horror dominating their expressions. As it was, she might not even care.

Why should they not be terrorized? She'd spent the last month being so.

Surah continued on in that same calm, resounding, and deceptively cool voice. She wanted to make sure they heard every word.

"Along with the Fae army, and one of our own, these creatures will be coming for us. The magic protecting the borders will hold for sometime, but not forever. You will have noticed that I've divided the Hunters, sent them to protect you.

This means I stand here unprotected, along with the castle my family has so long called our home. I hope you feel safer knowing the Hunters are at your side."

She paused once more, feeling the truth of her words deep down in her soul. She knew speaking to them all in such a raw, bare manner was unprecedented, but honestly, what did she have left to lose?

"I've never held myself above you," Queen Surah Stormsong said. "Those of you who've met me personally know this. I can't speak to how other royals behave, but I can tell you that they are receiving the same amount of protection right now as you."

She took a deep breath, lying the last of the cards upon the table, where everyone within Sorcerer Territory could see.

"As for the matter of Charlie Redmine… It's true that he's the brother of the treasonous Sorcerer Black Heart, but the truths of the allegations against him stop there. He has done nothing to aid his brother in his plots against the crown, and he is not an enemy in the eyes of your queen, but an upstanding citizen in the Sorcerer community. This is my word, and those who would deny it are traitors to the throne.

Now… as for what's coming next. I invite you to take cover and wait out the storm, to stay close to the Hunters who've been sent to protect you… and to watch closely what happens next."

A smile came to Surah's face, and throughout her kingdom many people felt a chill sweep through their bones.

"I'm not a queen who speaks but does not show. I'm not a coward, nor someone who fears the battlefield. I invite you to use whatever magic you possess to watch what happens next, to watch your queen, the woman who stands accused of putting her needs above yours, sacrifice everything to maintain your safety."

The smile upon her face slipped away, and the look of a

warrior replaced it. "I invite you to watch as I slaughter every Fae, Demon, and Sorcerer who would stand against us… Don't worry about the magic around the borders, where many of you live. It will hold."

Surah raised her hands into the air, Dark magic sparking at her fingertips, inky black swirling in her eyes much like the thunderheads in the angry sky above.

The air above Surah's head began to turn like a vortex, the colors mixing like wet paint. The wind picked up to a near gale force. The Black Stone glowed and throbbed at her neck.

"It will hold," she said, "because I'm going to open the portal right here, so that anyone trying to force their way into our Territory will come straight to me, and I can show them what becomes of those who threaten our kind…

Please, if there are young children among you, send them to another room. It's their innocence I'm really protecting, my soul I'm trading for theirs."

All throughout Sorcerer Territory, the magic image of Queen Surah Stormsong blipped out of sight. People gathered their crystal balls, their potions, their special stones and whatever other materials they needed to tune into the show.

Mothers covered the eyes of their children, whole families trembled in their hiding places while doing whatever they had to in order to see the battle that was coming.

They were scared, many of them were more scared than they could ever remember being. Not only was their homeland under attack, but their queen was clearly in the throes of very bad magic, so no matter what came next, things were going to be messy.

Very messy, indeed.

CHARLIE

The tension in the forest was thick enough to slice, the silence heavy in the green air.

Charlie stood at the ready, his muscles coiled and prepared for attack. All around him, still maintaining their tight circle, Fae Guardians stood in much the same manner, spears and bows and arrows poised, waiting for the moment to move.

Aria was still pinning the Fae Queen to the ground, holding her wings and arms to her sides while pressing the iron blade to her throat.

It was an intimate, awkward position, but Charlie could see that it was nearly the only way to keep the bitch restrained, and a newfound respect for the Halfling girl filled him. She was a ballsy little thing.

Aria's eyes darted to the side, where a vine was slowly creeping over the ground.

"If that vine comes any closer," she said, "I'll slit your throat right now."

The creeping vegetation halted, and Tristell gritted out some birdlike chirp that was Faevian language, though one did not have to speak the strange tongue to know she'd just cursed an insult.

Whatever the Fae Queen said made Aria roll her eyes. "No need for name calling," she said. "I'll remove the blade from your neck after you answer a few questions, and since not everyone here understands our language, the common tongue will do just fine."

The skin on Tristell's throat was still sizzling where the iron was touching it, her face was pulled taut with pain. Even from where Charlie was standing, he could see the murder in her slanted eyes. He hoped Aria knew what she was doing.

"Our language?" the Fae Queen spat. "You're not one of us, Halfling. I can smell the human in your skin… and where are your wings? Oh, that's right, Halflings can't fly. Don't insult Faevian kind by including yourself within it, child."

Charlie could tell by the dark look that passed over Aria's face that these words were a serious insult, particularly the part about not having wings.

For the first time since he'd met the Halfling girl, he wondered what it must be like to be a Fae without wings. He thought now that it would be kind of like being a Sorcerer without magic, or a Vampire without fangs.

Aria ignored the barbs, her voice impressively even. "Do you know who I am?" she asked.

When Tristell didn't answer, she dug the blade a little deeper into her skin. Tristell made a small sound that was part growl, part squeal.

"One more time," Aria said. "Do you know who I am?"

"You call yourself Aria Fae in the human world. You are a Peace Broker. Though I can't imagine you're here on orders."

"If you know that," Aria replied, "then you know why I'm here. I want to know what's happened to my mother."

"Your mother?"

The blade dug deeper.

"Don't play dumb," Aria threatened.

"Fine," Tristell spat through gritted teeth, neck still sizzling. "There was an accident. Your mother was among those who got caught in it. She's dead."

Charlie thought he saw a little moisture gather in Aria's eyes before she blinked it quickly away. Her features darkened as she absorbed this, but her voice came out steady when she spoke.

"We both know it wasn't an accident, Tristell. I want the truth."

"Foolish child. What will you do when you find out?"

"I'll seek justice accordingly. Now, talk."

"Elisa meddled where she should not have," the Fae Queen said. "It cost her her life. Now release me before you really piss me off. I've got a kingdom to steal."

"I should kill you right now," Aria said.

"But that's just it, isn't it?" taunted the Fae Queen. "You can't, can you? It goes against Fae nature, and most are too weak."

"You said yourself I'm not one of you," Aria replied. "And you don't seem to struggle at all with taking life."

"Now will be your only chance," said the Fae Queen

Charlie held his breath. In his head, he was screaming at Aria to just do the deed already, and liberate them all from the Fae Queen's malevolence.

There were clearly issues with Tristell among her own kind that were deeper than Charlie was privy to, and killing her would seem to be doing everyone a favor.

But, apparently, Tristell had been right about Aria's hesitance to take her life, because in the next heartbeat, the Fae Queen sprung off the ground with animal-like agility.

Her large, feathered wings extended and knocked Aria free of her hold, sending the Halfling girl flying through the air before colliding with a tree. Her small body struck its trunk hard enough to make Charlie cringe.

Fae Guardians rushed him, and he kicked the first one hard

in the gut, sending him back onto his rear. The next he sliced with the iron blade Aria had lent him, the Fae's skin sizzling the same as Tristell's had.

Several of the others launched spears at him. He avoided most of them with a quick roll to the left, but one lodged itself in his right shoulder deep enough to send an electric shock all the way down to his fingers.

Panic swirled in him as he realized he was hopelessly outmatched. He bit down on the sensation, refusing to give into its implications.

The more of these Fae Guardians he killed, the less there was of them to attack Surah. At least his death here would not be in total vain, and he would take with him as many of them as he could.

But then Aria appeared as if from nowhere, having sprung up from the ground with the same agility the Fae Queen had exhibited only moments ago.

She ran up the side of a tree near Charlie, spinning in the air and clearing the Fae Warrior's heads who stood between her and Charlie by several feet.

Aria landed at his side with a soft thud, her balance as strong as a cat's. Her hand gripped Charlie's, and then the two of them were falling through time and space.

* * *

THE SENSATION WAS ALL ENCOMPASSING.

If Charlie had to compare it to something, he would say it was like being scooped up by an enormous, invisible hand and slingshot across the universe.

Colors, objects, and distance became nothing more than white blurs.

They hit the floor of Aria's apartment moments later, landing with heavy thuds, no grace or ease this time. Charlie tucked his head instinctively, going into a roll. This was a good thing. His shoulder struck the edge of the coffee table rather than his head.

Aria had taken the brunt of her fall through the tailbone, and she lie flat on her back now, staring up at the ceiling, panting with exhilaration and wincing in pain.

Charlie pulled himself up onto the couch, the air tearing just as rapidly in and out of his lungs. "What the hell?" he said.

Aria tensed and sat up, glaring at him with her bright green eyes. "What?" she asked.

Charlie spread his hands, his eyebrows going up, ignoring the flash of pain in his bleeding shoulder. "Why didn't you kill her? Why didn't you kill Tristell?"

Aria pulled herself up, wincing. "I think you mean, thanks for saving my life, Aria," she said. "And why didn't *you* kill her? You're the one who went there with the intentions of taking a life. I only said I was looking for answers."

Charlie supposed she was right. But, still… she'd had the Fae Queen in her clutches, and she'd just let her go.

"She all but admitted to killing your mother," he said. "She's started a war between the Sorcerers and the Fae. I guess I just thought—"

"Well, you thought wrong," she snapped. "I don't know much about Sorcerers, but Fae children are raised to take life very seriously, to respect all living things."

"You're half-human aren't you?"

"What is that supposed to mean?"

Charlie sighed, sat on the couch, and ran a hand down his face. "I'm sorry," he said, and meant it.

The girl relaxed her stance a bit, clearly sensing his earnestness. "You're right," he added. "Thank you for saving my life. Again. It's not you I'm upset with. This has all just gotten so messed up." He looked down at the knife still clutched in his hand. "If my brother had been any slower… if I'd been any faster, he'd be dead right now. I've accomplished nothing but getting you in trouble."

Aria let out a slow breath and took a seat in the armchair across from him. Whatever hostility she'd held toward him a moment ago was gone. She was clearly good at accepting apologies.

"I've never needed anyone's help getting into trouble," she said, "and don't worry about me. I'm not as stupid as my pretty face makes me out to be."

She grinned, but it was without joy. The smile of someone freshly broken. Reaching into her leather jacket, she pulled out a rectangular device Charlie was unfamiliar with. There was a screen covering the front, and Aria pressed a triangle on the surface of it.

Out of small speakers on the side, the Fae Queen's voice said, "Elisa meddled where she should not have. It cost her her life. Now release me before you really piss me off. I've got a kingdom to steal."

"You recorded her?" Charlie asked in amazement.

Aria nodded. "I needed something I could bring to my superiors. When I told them I thought Tristell was responsible for my mother's absence, they told me I was mistaken, refused to look into the matter any farther, demanded I let it go. At least now… at least now I know."

Her voice cracked on this last part, and Charlie's stomach clenched as he came to a late realization, feeling terrible about having snapped on her a moment ago.

"You didn't know your mother was dead until Tristell told you," Charlie said. It was not a question.

Voice small, she replied, "I wasn't *sure* until she told me."

"I'm sorry, Aria," he said. "I lost my parents when I was young as well. Lost everyone I loved, actually. Except for my brother." He rubbed his jaw, which was in need of a good shave. "And I guess he's as lost to me now as he ever could be."

Silence hung between them a moment. Then, Charlie said, "Will she come for you now?"

Aria seemed glad for the change in subject. "Who, Tristell?" She waved a hand. "No one knows my location outside of the Peace Brokers, and something tells me she's got bigger fish to fry."

She shrugged. "But I guess if things go her way, she'll get around to me eventually. Tristell is not known for her forgiveness, and I held an iron blade to her throat."

"I have to *make sure* things don't go her way, Aria," Charlie said, though he felt guilty. She had just found out her mother was dead, and he was asking her to risk her life again.

To his surprise, the Halfling girl only blinked at him, studying his face. After a moment, she seemed to come to some sort of conclusion, and gave a single nod.

"Where do you want to go?" she asked.

"To help Surah."

"Okay."

"Okay?"

She nodded. "Though I have a feeling she won't be happy—"

Aria was cut short when something came crashing through the large windows of the living room. Glass shattered and rained down like diamonds, catching in Aria's hair and scattering about the floor.

The something was actually a some*one*, a muscular male Fae with silver hair and eyes… and a long sword clutched in his hands.

Charlie barely had time to blink before the intruder charged forward, blade aimed straight at Aria's heart.

38

SAMSON

The sky was a steely gray, the clouds shifting above the trees of the northeastern jungle.

Rain was coming. The animals of the jungle could sense it on the wind. The cave dwellers took to their caves, the burrowers to their burrows. The green and brown trees—hundreds of miles of them, a veritable sea of green—rippled and bent in the gale. The only sound was the rustling of the leaves, the occasional snapping of branches.

Samson sat at the base of one of the older trees, an enormous conifer that had stood longer than any other living thing Sam knew of.

He watched in silence, his large head resting atop his paws, as pine needles rained down around him. He watched them but did not see them falling.

His eyes were turned inward, replaying the fight with Drake, thinking of Surah. Always Surah. Something was wrong with her, and he needed to know what.

He stood, stretching his powerful muscles, leaning forward on his forepaws and then back, bending his spine. His rear right leg still ached from the fight, but he could wait no longer.

He had to go and check on his Sorceress, because he could feel in his bones that something was very wrong.

"You're leaving," said a familiar voice, breaking into the thoughts in his head. It was not a question.

Sam turned and looked at Mila. His wife. His mate. The cat he'd sworn fealty to. He didn't want to lie to her, but how could he explain so that she could understand? He couldn't. He said nothing, only looked at her with unblinking amber eyes.

"If you go," she said, communicating in the silent way of theirs, *"the pride will follow."*

"No. The pride will stay here. I will return shortly. You have my word."

He turned to go. Sam felt guilty, but there was no time. Something told him Surah needed him *now.* He wished he'd never left her, though he knew there had been no other choice.

"It doesn't work like that anymore, Sam," Mila snapped, stopping him in his tracks.

He'd never heard her voice as commanding as it was now, and it surprised him enough to hold him captive.

"You don't get to just walk away when you want to," she continued. *"You're our king. If you're going to look for trouble, the pride has to go with you."*

Her sleek black coat caught what little light was left of the day, and her bright, feline eyes stared back at him with a defiance that was uncannily similar to the kind Surah adopted when she set her mind on something.

"Who said I'm going to look for trouble? I'll be back before the sun rises."

Mila took two steps forward, putting the two of them were nearly nose-to-nose.

"Two-legs are always trouble. I wouldn't think I'd have to tell you this. You have responsibilities here. Don't you care about that? Haven't you any honor? Or have you been living among them *so long that there's none left in you?"*

For a moment, Samson was too shocked to respond.

Some part of him knew that Mila had a point, and that it wasn't her he was truly angry with, but that part was smothered as the urgency of the situation increased.

His head lowered and his teeth bared, a sight that would have sent lesser creatures running. A low rumbling sounded from deep in his chest, and his eyes flashed in the manner of a true beast.

To her credit, Mila did not move an inch, didn't so much as blink or flinch at Sam's undoubtedly intimidating reaction. She stood her ground, met his gaze, and held it.

Ironically, this also reminded him of Surah. His wife and his mistress seemed to have many traits in common.

Except Surah loved him enough to let him go when he'd told her he had to.

"I don't expect you to understand," Mila, he told her. *"I just need to make sure she's all right. Once that's done, I'll return to you and fulfill all my duties as king."*

Her eyes narrowed. *"And when she's not 'all right'? When you find your precious two-leg needs you to pull her out of trouble, and that you can't return to fulfill 'all your duties as king'?"*

"I'm sorry, but I have to go."

"Then the pride's coming with you."

"Absolutely not."

"It's not your call."

"The hell it isn't!" He all but roared, his voice was so loud in her head that now she did cringe, if only a touch.

He released a slow breath and forced himself to calm down. *"I'm the king. You said it yourself. This is my decision. The pride has no stake in this battle."*

"You are our stake in this battle," Mila replied. *"You stupid beast. Don't you understand that if something happens to you we're lost? Without a strong leader, like my father had been before you killed him,*

we could find ourselves on the brink of extinction again. How can you not see that this isn't just about you? How can you be so selfish?"

These words were like a slap, probably because they rang with an air of truth.

For a long moment, he could think of nothing to say. When words finally did come, they sounded lame to his own ears.

"I have to go, Mila."

She said nothing for what felt like a very long time, or maybe Sam was just feeling every second as if they were hours.

Either way, the answer she gave revealed she could be as stubborn as Surah—yet another quality the two females shared. He thought under different circumstances, Mila could learn to love the Sorceress as well.

But this was the hand they'd been dealt, and the choice he made next would impact the lives of many, feline and two-legs alike.

"Then go, Samson," Mila told him, *"but know that if you do, the pride will follow. You hold our fates in your paws."*

CHARLIE

The girl was quick, obviously having inherited her agility and athletic ability from the half of her that was Fae.

Had she been any slower, any slower *at all*, the intruder's blade would have gone straight through her chest, would have killed her instantly.

As it was, Aria did an impressive forward roll, right between the male Fae's spread legs, ending up behind him.

All of this—including the impressive entrance made by the male Fae crashing through Aria's living room window—happened within a matter of seconds.

It happened so fast that it took Charlie longer than it should have to go on guard, and by the time he snapped to realization, Aria was already preparing to take the newcomer on.

"Dude!" she said, gesturing around the apartment at the broken glass. "Who the hell is going to pay for that?"

The male Fae looked surprised at this reaction, but he was clearly here to do a job.

"Aria Fae?" he asked, his silver eyes narrowed and sword still held at the ready, waiting for another opportunity to strike.

Aria adopted a fighter's stance and scooped up a wooden staff that had been resting against the wall. By the marks on it, Charlie could see the weapon had seen good use, but thought her a fool for choosing it. One didn't choose staff against blade.

"The one and only," Aria replied. "I'll assume Tristell sent you."

"You've offended the Fae Queen, and I'm here to kill you," said the male Fae. His silver gaze flicked to Charlie. "Watch it, Sorcerer," he said. "I was only sent for the girl, but I understand that you're wanted by the Queen as well."

Charlie clenched his jaw. He was pretty sure between him and Aria, they could take this guy down.

"She's no queen of mine," Charlie said.

The male Fae disregarded this as if Charlie hadn't spoken. It was clear in his stance that he was preparing to strike at Aria again.

Aria switched her staff to her right hand, holding out her left hand the way one might to an approaching beast.

"Just hold on a second there, buddy," Aria said. "You don't have to kill me. We could pull a *Snow White* and send you back to Tristell with the heart of a dear or something. What do you say?"

"You're a Halfling," replied the male Fae. It was not a question, and his silver eyes studied Aria in a way Charlie wasn't sure he liked. "And a child," the Fae added.

"I'll be eighteen in a few months," Aria said, "but whatever. If what you're trying to say is I'm too young to kill, then I totally agree."

She smiled, flashing perfect teeth, and the girl once again awed Charlie. He could see that her charm alone was giving the male Fae pause.

That was good. If she could distract him long enough, Charlie might be able to take him out.

"What could a Halfling child have done to offend the

Queen?" the Fae asked, his long silver hair spilling over his wide shoulder as he tilted his head to study her.

Charlie slipped his hand behind his back slowly, so as not to draw any attention, and removed the iron dagger he still had possession of.

"You ask that as if she's hard to offend," Aria replied. "And what does it matter? Aren't you just her assassin? Someone who does as they're told?"

This seemed to offend the Fae. "I'm paying off a debt," he said. His eyes flicked over to Charlie, who stood deceptively still.

"Does paying off that debt include killing an innocent girl?" Charlie asked.

"Mind your business, Sorcerer," the Fae snapped. "And I can smell that iron you're hiding behind your back. Make a move with it, and it'll be your last."

One side of Charlie's mouth pulled up in a smirk. "Is that what you think, fairy?"

"It's what I know."

"Oh my *God,*" Aria said, and coughed loudly into a balled fist. "I'm literally choking on the testosterone right now." She pointed the end of her staff toward the Fae. "What's your name?"

Charlie thought the Fae looked like he didn't want to answer, but did anyway.

"Arrol," he said.

Aria nodded. "Well, Arrol, are you going to kill me, or what?"

Arrol relaxed his stance a bit, but Charlie kept his guard up, aware that this could be a trick. Aria didn't appear alarmed, but Charlie noticed she still held her staff at the ready.

"Is there another option to killing you, Halfling?" Arrol asked.

Aria's smiled. "There are always options, Full-blood old man." She paused. "See how weird that sounds? So I won't call you that if you stop calling me 'Halfling' and 'child.' Sound good?"

"The Fae Queen sent me here to kill you. She said you're a traitor to the crown, and if I brought proof of your death, it finally would end my debt to her. See the problem here, Aria?"

Aria tilted her head. "All of that may be, but I don't want to die before I even get to kiss a boy, so you see *my* problem here, Arrol? Also, if you're in her debt, you messed up somewhere along the way, too."

Arrol's hand tightened around his weapon, his silver eyes narrowing. Aria held out a hand again, like a lion tamer.

"Charlie," she said, without taking her gaze off the Fae. "Don't attack him. He's going to help us. He hates Tristell almost as much as we do."

"Don't dig into my emotions, child," Arrol snapped. "It's impolite. Haven't you learned any manners living among the humans?"

"Yes, actually," Aria replied. "For one thing, I've learned that entering through the doorway rather than smashing through the window is the polite thing to do... Why do you hate Tristell?"

"I don't hate her."

"You don't like her, either, which puts us on the same side."

"I can't move against her," Arrol said, and it looked as if it pained him to do so.

Aria's head tipped back as she came to a realization Charlie wasn't privy to. "You swore to her," she said.

Arrol nodded.

"I hope whatever got you into her debt was worth it."

Arrol's gaze went distant, but returned quickly. "Depends on who you ask."

"Well, then you should be really excited," Aria said, grinning. "Charlie here has a really powerful girlfriend, and she's going to kill Tristell. So you see, you don't have to kill me. Your debt to Tristell will die when she does."

Arrol's brow arched, and he looked at Charlie as though he'd forgotten he was there. "You're putting a lot of faith in his girlfriend. Tristell is not a weak opponent."

"Neither is Surah Stormsong," Charlie said, wondering if he might not have to kill this Fae after all, which was good and well. He had a feeling there was enough death to come.

"Surah Stormsong? The royal Sorceress?" Arrol asked. "So it's true. The Fae Queen is making a move for Sorcerer Territory." Arrol eyed Aria. "I shouldn't even be talking to you."

Aria only looked at him.

"You've got the Touch real strong, don't you?" Arrol said.

Charlie had no idea what *the Touch* was, but Aria must have, because she shrugged and pushed some of her wavy, red-brown hair out of her face.

"Or maybe you're just not as comfortable with killing as you'd like to think," she said.

"Stop that," the Fae warned.

Slowly, Aria moved over to the couch, setting her wooden staff on the coffee table, eyes never leaving the Fae. She took a seat, holding both hands up.

When Arrol made no move against her, the blank expression on his face saying he wasn't fully decided on the matter, she gestured at the armchair across from her.

"Please," she said, "take a load off." She looked at Charlie, telling him with her eyes that it was okay, and added, "you too, Charlie."

Charlie was not at all sure this was a good decision, but so far the Halfling girl seemed to know how to handle tough situations. She'd saved his butt more than once in the past twenty-four hours, and he knew that he could trust her.

Not for the first time, he wondered about Aria's history,

about how she'd come to be the girl she was now. He knew there had to be a hell of a story there.

He moved over to the couch and took a seat beside Aria as Arrol sat in the armchair. Charlie noticed the envious look that came into Aria's eyes when she watched the Fae's dragonfly-like wings folding over his shoulders and back, melting into his skin to resemble nothing more than intricate tattoos.

"Wonderful," Aria said, with a bright smile. "Now, Mr. Arrol, let's discuss all the benefits of *not* killing me, shall we? First of all, you won't have to live with the death of a child on your conscience, and that alone is a pretty big thing, am I right?"

Arrol only looked at her, and Charlie was not aware of it, but the expression on his face was much the same as the Fae's. Aria had a strange way about her, even in a room full of supernaturals.

The way Aria shifted in her seat said that she was used to this. "Also," she quickly continued, "I'm a Peace Broker. I don't know if Tristell told you that, but it's true."

Aria reached into the pocket of her leather jacket and removed a gold medallion with the letters *PB* stamped into the face. Charlie leaned forward to get a look at it along with Arrol. He'd never seen one of them before, but assumed it was the equivalent of a badge for the Peace Brokers.

Aria flipped the medallion expertly over her fingers and it disappeared back into her pocket.

"Killing me would bring a world of trouble your way," she said.

Arrol gave a single nod. Apparently Aria's Peace Broker badge was legitimate enough for him.

"Reason numero tres," Aria continued, "You don't have to get beat up by my stick." She gestured down at the staff on the table between them. "If they were here, those who have been beaten up by my stick would totally testify to the fact that it sucks. Trust me."

Arrol raised an eyebrow, but he seemed more amused with the girl than angry. "You are a strange creature, Aria Fae," he said.

She sighed. "So they say."

"Aria," Charlie said, eager to end this now that it was clear Arrol wasn't going to try to kill her. He had not forgotten that Surah was likely in serious trouble, and time was of the essence. "I need to go."

Aria stood, retrieving the staff from the table with her left hand and holding out her right to Arrol.

"Right, well, it was nice to meet you, Arrol. We gotta go, but thanks for not, you know, skewering me with your sword."

Arrol stared at her hand for a moment, then took it into his own and kissed it. Charlie suppressed an eye roll at this. This guy clearly thought he was cool. But by the blush that rose into Aria's cheeks, Charlie could see that the girl obviously agreed.

"It was a pleasure," the Fae said. He looked at Charlie. "I hope you're right about Princess Stormsong. If she should fall to Tristell… Gods help us all."

"Oh, Surah isn't a princess anymore," Aria said, as if pulling the thought from Charlie's head. "She's a queen. And in this case, she's definitely the good guy, and the good guys always win, right?"

Aria's grin gave away her youth, for only those of so few years would hold to such a belief. Both Charlie and Arrol were old enough to see it.

Charlie knew well that this was not always the case. Maybe in fairytales, or the movies humans created to entertain themselves, but not in the world Charlie lived in, not in real life.

In real life, the good guys did not always win.

In real life, sometimes the good guys finished dead last.

4 0

—————

SURAH

The Black Stone glowed and pulsed at her neck, the dark magic running through her as if in her veins, leaving no part of her untouched.

Possessing her.

Having moved a mile out of Zadira, she came to a stop in a wide, open field. Tall, yellow-green grass bent heavy in the wind, lying down nearly flat, blanketing the ground, shielding it from the massacre that was going to take place here.

The thought of so much death should have sickened her, but it did not. Surah was tired of being afraid, done with playing the defensive. This mess Black Heart and the Fae Queen had dumped on her would be cleaned up today, one way or another.

They wanted blood, so she would give it to them. She would give them enough to satiate them for the rest of eternity, and they would see how much they'd underestimated her when she tore their hearts from their chests and their heads from their shoulders. They would rue the day they'd crossed her.

She was well aware that the eyes of her people were on her. Thousands of them, staring into crystal balls and magic bowls and brews and whatever else common people used for their magic. She could feel their gazes on her, and she was glad for the audience, glad that what went down today would be recorded in the memories of all.

Lifting her arms high into the air, eyes writhing with ebony, Surah pulled the dark magic around her and began to open the portal into her Territory. It was not a simple spell, but Surah was not a novice caster, and she was up to the task.

She found that the more she used the Black Stone, the more its power invigorated her. This was a side effect she had not anticipated, as the use of magic always depleted the user.

Rather than feeling depleted, she felt supercharged, ready to take on the whole damn world.

And it would be a bold-faced lie to say that she didn't like it, that it didn't feel *good.*

As if ripped by the hands of a God, a hole opened in the air before her, an impenetrable blackness filling its center, the atmosphere around its edges blurring as the light itself struggled not to be sucked in.

Power surged through Surah, heady and invigorating. She felt it shooting from her fingertips, from her toes, out the top of her head, as if magic was emerging from her very pores, rising out of her skin.

Along with this opening, she shut off any other entrance or exit in her Territory, so that if someone on the outside wanted to enter, they would have to come through this very spot... Where she would be waiting with sais in hand.

The thought made a terrible grin stretch her face, which was somehow less lovely than it had always been. All throughout the land, Sorcerer people gritted their teeth and cringed inwardly to see their ruler in such a manner, all the while unable to pull their eyes away from the scene. Hardly a word was uttered.

The portal gaped like a wound in the air, promising an outpouring of poison, disease that needed to be purged, burned away before it could taint her land.

She'd never felt as alone in her whole life as she felt in that moment, never more resolved or angry or vengeful than right then.

Reaching into her cloak, the fine material flying out like wings behind her, she removed her silver sais, clutching the weapons in her hands.

She took the stance of a fighter, her body as capable and graceful as a deadly dancer, her face set in the manner of a warrior.

Her lavender hair lifted off her shoulders, which were loose and ready. One side of her mouth pulled up in a crooked smile, and her heart settled into stone.

She waited.

41

BLACK HEART

The fires of the Underworld blazed around him, the heat only exceeded by that in his soul.

Michael had been using dark magic for years, and it had slowly eaten away at his core, until all that remained was a shell built for holding hate.

He was distantly aware of the fact that he was too far gone to save, would on occasion hear the whisper of a familiar voice, saying that this was not who he'd been meant to be, that somewhere along the way he'd taken a terrible turn, that it was all somehow…wrong.

But that whisper would be drowned out as quickly as it arose, fading into nothing, like the memory of a ghost.

All he understood now was vengeance, violence, the need to obtain more power. There was no doubt in his mind that had the royals cared more about the people they were supposed to serve, his mother and father would still be alive, and he would be a different man completely. He would be Michael.

As it was, the title Black Heart was a better fit.

The only thing that did cause a small ache in his chest was the thought of Charlie. Even after all these years, he could not shake the last sliver of regret he held over the way things had turned out between him and his little brother.

When their parents had died, the two of them had been just boys, and Michael had taken care of Charlie. He had made sure they had something to eat, somewhere to sleep, had watched over his little brother the way a parent would.

Because of the rough orphan lives they'd lived, Michael had been forced to grow up very early, to skip his childhood altogether.

He'd been shoved into adulthood, and slowly, along with his addiction to dark magic, it had turned him into this.

Had Surah Stormsong suffered the same? Or her brother, Syris? Or any of the rest of the Sorcerers who called themselves royal?

No, they hadn't. They never had to scrounge for food, to sleep freezing under the stars, to listen to the screams of their loved ones as they burned alive, trapped within the confines of their modest homes…

It had all happened so long ago, and yet the memories came flooding back as though it were yesterday.

Reaching into his cloak, he removed the small box Dagon had given him. When he opened it, he would have the power to control an army of a thousand of Dagon's Demons.

They would follow him into Sorcerer Territory and tear through anyone who stood in his way. Tristell and her Fae Warriors would follow shortly after, ensuring the win.

The presence of the box had summoned the Demons, and they circled in the starless sky above him, their shadows passing over the barren, scorched ground at his feet, the flickering light of the ceaseless flames of the Underworld the only source by which to see.

Their screeches filled the air, the creatures angrier, more agitated than Black Heart had ever seen them. Something had gone wrong with Dagon, most likely. Perhaps the Dark Lord had underestimated Surah and gone at her alone.

It didn't matter in the least. Black Heart had paid for the box he held in his hands with the blood of a king, and the Demons would do his bidding as long as he held it. If Dagon had gone and gotten himself caught or maimed by the Sorceress Queen, it was no concern of his.

He was not underestimating Surah Stormsong. He knew better than to do that. Instead, he was throwing two armies at her, and she was damned no matter what position she took.

He was sending the Demons to attack the people, so if she left them unprotected, it would only prove his point. If she chose to divide her forces to protect the people, her castle would fall to him with ease.

Either way, a usurp would take place this day, and one day, the Sorcerer people would thank him for it, would see how much better and more equal life would be under his rule. He would keep them safe in the dark days ahead. A war among the races was coming, and they needed his strong leadership if their kind was going to survive it.

People were thickheaded, set in their ways, scared. They just needed to be shown the way. Tristell and Black Heart could do that. They would unite the Fae and Sorcerer Territories and be stronger for it. A whole new world awaited them.

All that stood in his way was the current ruler. Surah Stormsong. Thanks to him, the last of her line and name. He'd killed her father, the former king, and now it was her turn.

On top of all of that, the bitch had stolen his brother from him. A terrible smile pulled up his lips, warping his once handsome face into something inhuman, like the thousand Demons still circling the hopeless sky above him. He lifted his hands into the air, holding the box the Dark Lord had given him high over his head.

Black Heart lifted the lid of the box, and the reaction of the

Demons was instant. The creatures let out ear-piercing screeches, flapping their wings more fiercely.

He could feel his will exerting itself over them, could see through their eyes and hear through their ears, could feel the wind pushing beneath their wretched wings.

Opening a portal into the Sorcerer Territory was easier than he anticipated, and he came to the realization that the magic guarding it must have been taken down.

As if she wanted him to come. As if Surah was *inviting* him in.

Well, he didn't want to be late to his own party, and he was curious to see what the Sorceress had done in preparation. He sent a hundred of his thousand Demons through the portal first, to get a feel for the situation.

His eyes glazed over as he saw the world through the eyes of his Demons, a rushing sound filling his ears as his consciousness flew through time and space. He was pleased that he got to adopt their senses. It was a perk he hadn't known was included.

Because more than anything, he wanted to hear Surah Stormsong scream.

SURAH

Faintly, from somewhere far away, she could hear them screaming.

The gaping black hole in the sky stood before her, the angry gray clouds rumbling overhead, promising a coming storm.

They were coming for her, and the first of them would break through to this realm any second now.

She was surprisingly relaxed, the dark power humming through her, filling her from the top of her head to her toes.

Let them come. Let them all come.

The land surrounding the semi-crazed Sorceress was eerily quiet save for the whisper of the wind among the grasses and trees.

It was as though the life there was holding a collective breath, afraid to exhale into the supercharged atmosphere, as if the slightest disturbance could send the whole stack toppling.

Surah stood alone in the clearing outside her city, ready to win or die for her people.

When a terrible screech rent the air, she did not cringe, only tightened her hold on her sais, her heartbeat kicking up in pace.

The first Demons flew through the portal, ear-piercing cries ripping across the sky, distorted bodies swooping low, claws reaching and jaws snapping, ropes of saliva dripping from their mouths.

The first three Surah slayed with such expert brilliance that had anyone blinked, they would have missed it. She moved with the grace of a dancer, with the power and precision of a beast, and the calculated strategy only people are capable of. The sharp points of her sais slid through their rotten forms with an ease that was sickening to witness.

And everyone in her kingdom, in fact, was standing witness.

The Demons kept coming, more and more of them, one after the other. It was only a matter of seconds before their terrifying forms were filling the sky, blotting out the gray clouds with their large black bodies. They all directed themselves at the Sorceress Queen, attacking her from all angles.

And Surah was cutting them down like weeds.

With each one she killed, she felt the power intensify within her. She was a sight to be seen, a force to be reckoned with. She moved through the fray in a sort of macabre ballet, the black, unnatural blood of the Demons accompanying the show, spraying this way and that, painting everything it touched, steaming in the cool air.

Surah was covered in the stuff. It disgusted her while also fueling her need to spill more. All she could hear was the way the evil creatures screeched and cried as she ripped the life from them. All she could see was the way they writhed at the ends of her sais.

That lively black ink that had formed in her eyes nearly blotted out all the purple now and was spreading its way into the whites. The Black Stone hung on her neck, burning the skin there, though Surah could feel no pain. She continued to kill, like a machine built just for doing so.

She portaled, sliding her sais through the chest and neck of one, and then portaled away and repeated the process before the previous Demon even hit the ground.

She moved so fast that she was a blur, hard to keep eyes on as she would appear then disappear within the space of a heartbeat. It was as though her feet were not even touching the ground.

And the ground, it was black with the blood of her enemies, just as she had promised it would be.

There was an intelligence behind the Demon's red eyes, and Surah knew that Black Heart was the puppet master behind these creatures. It could not be Dagon himself, because Dagon's head was in a secure place, and would not see the light of day anytime soon.

Surah made sure to look into the red, glowing eyes of the creatures as she killed them, her face streaked with the Demons' blood, her hands slick with it.

After what felt like both a lifetime and an eye blink, all the Demons who had entered her Territory lie dead on the ground, their bodies still warm and twitching, their cries of agony toned down to the moans of the dying.

It was like music to her ears, food to her soul. Above her head, which was thrown back in exhilaration, the pregnant gray clouds burst open and rained down upon her.

Lightning lit up the sky, striking with blinding force. Thunder followed, loud and angry, the sound so forceful as to rattle the earth.

Surah let the rain wash over her, and shed her cloak with a swift movement. It floated to the blood-soaked ground beside her.

Blades and weapons of all sorts were attached to her person, which was all muscle and curves. She pushed some of her lavender hair out of her face and looked toward the portal, her expression that of a woman with nothing at all to lose.

Which was something, because there was literally *everything* to lose, wasn't there?

This question left her mind before it could settle. She stared into the portal, and in a voice not quite her own called out, "Is that all?"

Of course, silence was the only response, though she had not gone unheard. Not in the slightest.

A laugh sounded, and it took her a minute to realize that it was she whom was laughing. The sound was off, but sure enough, she felt the sensation in her own chest.

Then she was laughing so hard that she was clutching her knees, wrapping an arm around her stomach.

The sight and sound of this was disturbing under the circumstances. Bodies of Demons lie dead all around her. Her hands and face were streaked with blood. That black presence swirled behind her eyes.

She had killed the Demons, yes, but who had truly won?

"Is that all?" Surah Stormsong called again, her laughter drying up like dead leaves in the fall. "Is that all you got?"

43

BLACK HEART

"Is that all? Is that all you got?"

The question both amused and angered him.

The Sorceress had clearly gone mad with her possession of the Black Stone, no doubt due to the fact that she'd never been cut out to wield such power in the first place.

It had taken him years to be able to master the dark arts, and much like the royal she was, Surah Stormsong just assumed that she was worthy of doing the same in a day.

What a fool she was. How arrogant. How entitled. He would see to it that he wiped that grin off her face. He would finally make her pay for all the wrong that had been done to him.

To him, and to so many others. He knew the Sorcerer people were watching, knew they were hiding in their holes and staring into their cheap crystal balls, taking a side in the match they were witnessing.

And maybe some of them were rooting for him. Some of them *had* to be, because Black Heart refused to believe that the whole lot of them were fools.

Also, that blackness in their queen's eyes had to be having

some sort of impact. In trying to prove that she could protect them, Surah was sacrificing her soul.

All in all, despite her having killed a hundred of Dagon's Demons with disconcerting ease, things were going well. He couldn't care less if the Sorceress painted every inch of the Territory with Demon blood (the same could be said about his feelings toward the Fae Guardians who would soon be joining the battle, though this was not something he would tell Tristell) as long as he took down the last of the Stormsong line.

Once she was dead, the throne to the Sorcerer Kingdom would be as open as a book, free for the taking.

And once the people saw Surah fall to him, who would dare stand in his way? Who would dare deny him the power he would clearly have earned?

No one, that was who.

She may have killed those first Demons, but that had been nothing more than a test run, a dipping of his toes in the water.

In doing so, he'd learned that she had indeed divided the Hunter forces, sending them to protect the Sorcerer people, rather than her and her castle.

Not only had she done this, but she'd sealed all the entrances into the Territory save for the portal at which she stood. Foolish girl.

He held the box out in front of him now, staring into the depthless darkness inside. In it, he saw all the things he had worked and waited so long for, the future he would build with Tristell by his side, the new world the two of them had imagined.

A world where Sorcerer and Fae intermingled, strengthening their forces by being together, and treating all as equals who lived among them.

In theory, it was not as bad of an idea as one may expect from him, but theory and practice do not always walk hand in hand, and sometimes the worst of things came from the best of intentions.

How could one rule justly when there was nothing left but hate in their heart?

Gritting his teeth, he sent the rest of the Demons through the portal. He would let them weaken her, draw out the last of her strength.

Even with the Black Stone hanging around her neck, Surah Stormsong could not fight forever. She would tire, and when she did, he would come through the portal and deliver the death that she deserved.

Before the eyes of Gods and men, he would slaughter her, and when he did, whomever should stand at her side—kin and stranger alike—would follow the same fate.

Now it was his turn to laugh. It was an ugly, cackling sound that echoed in the fiery realm of the Underworld. He threw his head back and laughed much in the same manner the Sorceress had affected moments ago, his body wracking with the power of it.

Even if she called every Sorcerer Hunter she had to her aid right now, it would not be enough to defeat what he had planned for her. The forces he had gathered were too great, the odds too heavily stacked.

Was that all he had?

No, dearest queen, he thought, the laughter still bubbling up his throat. That was not all. That was not all by a long shot.

In fact, the battle had only just begun, the blood spilled only a fraction of what was to come. Of this, he was certain.

Black Heart was all in, had every chip in the center of the table, and there was no turning back now. No retreat, and no surrender.

Today would be a day of death, and from the ashes, he would be the one to rise.

CHARLIE

*a*rrol left, bidding them farewell, opting for the door this time rather than the smashed window.

Aria sighed, looking down at the shattered glass on her living room floor. "Mr. Peters won't be happy about that," she said.

Charlie was practically jumping out of his skin to get to Surah, even though he knew Aria would have to come with him and this would likely put her in terrible danger.

Maybe it was the whole situation, but his gut was telling him something was wrong, that he needed to return to his own land post haste.

"I can fix that with a little magic when we get back," he said, nodding at the broken window, his handsome face grave, "but we need to go."

"You can fix broken glass with magic?" she asked.

"You can fix almost anything with magic, the trick is not to go breaking it further."

Aria nodded, switching her wooden staff to her left hand, holding her right out to Charlie. "Okay," she said. "Let's go then. Let's go save your world."

She smiled as she said this, and the sight of it tore at his heart. There was so much innocence behind it, so much blind faith—the kind of hope one can only find in the eyes of a child.

For a moment, Charlie wasn't sure he could do it. He wasn't sure he could let her risk everything to help him. He stared at her extended hand—it was so small, given so freely—but did not take it.

This was wrong, and the ends didn't justify the means. Then again, how could he leave his beloved to face all that she was facing alone?

There was no right answer here, no clear path, no black and white.

Aria stared at him with green eyes brighter than any he'd ever seen, and she used the hand she'd held out to him to push some of her red-brown hair out of her face. She still held her wooden staff in the other.

"Okay," she said. "I see you're having trouble with this, so I'm going to help you out again."

Charlie hardly had time to process this before Aria grabbed fast hold of his arm, and once again, he found himself falling into nothingness, as if the floor had opened up and swallowed him whole.

Just before he had fallen into the portal, he would swear he heard the Halfling girl say, "Uh, oh," before her voice was lost in the void.

* * *

As soon as they landed on the other side of the portal, the reason for Aria's utterance became clear.

They hit the hard earth with an impact that rattled his teeth, jolted up his spine. His head spun for a moment before his vision cleared and he was able to take in the scene before him.

They had landed in a field, and a look to the west told him

that it was just outside Zadira. The sky was spitting cold rain, as if trying to wash away the gore that was covering the grass at their feet.

Demons circled above their heads, screeching and screaming. Wind whipped at his face and hair, tugged at his clothes like an insistent child. Chaos stormed, thunder rumbled.

And in the midst of all this was Surah.

Her eyes were an awful swirling black. Her hands, her face, her clothes soaked in blood.

All of this Charlie Redmine took in in a matter of seconds, for a moment later Aria was tugging on his arm and screaming at him to duck.

Charlie snapped to attention just in time to avoid the talons of a swooping Demon. It came at him again out of seemingly nowhere, but Aria smacked it on the head with her wooden staff.

The Demon stumbled back, wings beating wildly at the air, dazed.

Raising her staff again, Aria shooed the creature away the way one might a fly. To Charlie's complete and utter amazement, the Demon took off, flying in the direction of the others, their focus on killing Surah.

"Pretty sure that makes three times I've saved your life, Sorcerer," Aria grinned.

Charlie didn't respond. In fact, he hadn't even heard her. He was too busy staring at the scene they'd been thrust into, the horror that was unfolding before him.

Time slowed to a crawl as he looked at Surah, at what had become of her in his absence.

He hardly recognized the woman he loved. She had the same lavender hair, the same perfect figure, the same angelic face and fine clothes, but the Sorceress slaying Demon after Demon before him was not Surah Stormsong.

Her once-violet eyes were a writhing, inky black. Her face

was set and emotionless. She moved through the air with the grace of an avenging Angel. She blinked in and out of sight—spinning, teleporting, slicing.

The black blood of the Demons sprayed and spurted. Her hair hung wet and dripping, flipping around her as if in a dance of its own.

Charlie had never seen such a thing, had only ever heard stories. It was just as the tales had said, just as recognizable as a deformity.

Surah had gone crazy with dark magic, had fallen under the full clutches of the Black Stone, which Charlie saw hung close around her neck.

Surah took no note of him, only continued on in her devastating death-dance, killing Demon after Demon, using more and more dark magic with every passing second.

The true horror of the situation struck home then. All of these realizations came to him so fast that his head all but spun on his shoulders.

Surah had opened a portal right here, had decided to take on his brother on her own, and she was doing so with an amount of black magic that could crush the strongest of warriors into nothing.

She was defending her kingdom at the cost of her own soul.

Charlie Redmine had never loved her more than he did in that moment, and his heart had never ached so terribly as well, because even if Surah could kill every Demon and Fae that came at her, she would still be lost, drowning in the darkness of the Black Stone.

He could only pray that it was not too late, that there was still a part of her that could be reached. If he had a chance at doing that, he needed to remove the Black Stone from her, to finish the killing on his own.

Just by looking at her now, he could see that this would be

nearly impossible. He'd have a better shot at stealing a steak from a tiger.

In the small moments he took to conclude this, Demons continued to pour out of the wound in the sky, rain continued to fall, and blood continued to spill.

Charlie turned to Aria, told her to get somewhere safe, and barely heard his own words for all the chaos around him and the numbness in his chest.

"I'm coming, love," he said, and moved into the fray.

45

SURAH

She did not have the time or the mind to pause and contemplate it, but she could feel herself tiring.

It was an odd sensation, not like the fatigue one may feel after a long day of physical activity, but a kind of draining at her core, as if something more than just energy was slowly being sucked away from her.

This was a very background concern at the moment, however. Her battery would run out when it ran out, but up until it did, she would continue what she'd started…

But some part of her knew that she was approaching depletion.

How many Demons had she killed already? The number was too great to know, the bits of their rotten bodies too disfigured to count.

And more just kept on coming.

Watching them spill from the portal she'd created in a seemingly endless supply should have terrified her, but there was an emptiness in her gut she'd never experienced before, as if an auto-pilot switch had flipped on inside her, but rather than driving her, it was driving her to kill.

From somewhere too close, a familiar voice cut into her battle-induced haze, and she took her eyes away from the attacking Demons for a moment to see that Charlie was here.

The sight of him stirred nothing at all within her, and she continued on in her rampage as though he were not even there.

A thought bubbled up in her mind that she was not entirely sure was her own: *Better stay out of my way, Charlie.*

46

BLACK HEART

For the first time since he could remember, the sight of his brother did nothing to stir his emotions.

Charlie appeared on the battlefield in the same fashion as the Demons (the lot of which were diminishing just a touch sooner than he'd anticipated, but this was of no concern just yet) falling out of the portal and hitting the ground with a thud.

Black Heart viewed this through the eyes of the Demons, and his physical form, which was still in the Underworld and still clutching the Demon-controlling box, was sweaty with exertion. He was ready to jump into the game.

Charlie had made his choice, and Michael had made his. He'd given his little brother ample opportunity to join him, to make the right move, and Charlie had spat in his face for it.

The Sorceress was getting tired, this he could also see through the eyes of the Demons, and the time to make the final strike was at hand.

Tucking the box into the folds of his cloak, Black Heart followed the last of his Demons through the portal, out of the Underworld, and into the Territory that he would soon call his own.

And since it had to be done, he felt he should be the one to take out Charlie.

He felt he owed his little brother that.

47

CHARLIE

*I*t became apparent very quickly that they were outmatched.

There was no way Charlie was going to get close enough to Surah to take the Black Stone from her, because he could barely move two feet in her direction without having to fight off a Demon.

There were just so many of them, hundreds, and they blotted out the gray sky, which had only grown darker. It lit up at varying intervals with tremendous strikes of lightning, as if the Gods themselves were displeased.

Charlie was no stranger to fighting, and Surah was the best warrior he'd ever personally met, but it was obvious that even she was tiring.

Even with all the power of the Black Stone—perhaps, *because* of the power of the Black Stone—she could not destroy this army on her own.

Sooner or later, her body would give into exhaustion. And then… Well, then his brother would come through the portal and try to kill her.

As if the thought had summoned him, Black Heart appeared

out of the gaping hole in the sky on the heels of what Charlie could only pray was the last of the Demons he commanded. He landed in front of Charlie with a grimace, a fireball forming between his hands.

Before Charlie could say a word, Black Heart launched the fireball at him.

He moved just quickly enough to avoid a direct hit. The ball of flame skimmed his shoulder, scorching through the fabric and burning the skin there before dying out in the driving rain.

Another Fireball was already forming in Black Heart's hands, and he met Charlie's eyes with what might have been regret, if Charlie hadn't known better.

"You always did love the fire magic best, Charlie-Boy," his brother called, yelling to be heard over the thunder and the rain, the chaos and the death cries. "It used to make you smile when we were kids. You remember that?"

He launched another fireball at Charlie, who was ready this time, moving out of the way before it could touch him.

"I remember," Charlie said. "That was back before you went insane. I can't let you hurt her, Michael."

Black Heart's eyes flicked toward Surah, who was busy taking out the Demons. He shook his head, electric blue sparks sizzling at the ends of his fingertips.

"And you can't save her, either. Even if you were able to beat me." An awful grin spread over his face. "She's too far gone now."

The words were like a fist to Charlie's gut. He'd thought of this, of course, but hearing it spoken aloud was somehow infinitely more powerful.

He wasn't aware of it, but his hand was clenched tight around the dagger Aria had given him, his teeth gritted and shoulders tense.

Win or lose, whatever happened next, things would never be the same again for either brother.

"That may be," Charlie said, "but I can kill you for what you've done."

Black Heart's responding smile was cold, and in it Charlie could see none of the brother he'd known.

"You can try, Charlie-Boy," he said. "You can sure as hell try."

As the two of them squared off, Fae Guardians made their entrance into the scene, bursting through the portal with blades blazing.

And despite the two star-crossed lovers having both faced terrible odds in their lives, Surah and Charlie had a better chance of rearranging the cosmos than they did at defeating the two armies standing against them now on their own.

SURAH

It was a dance, and the tune was fast and steady, but her movements were starting to slow, to fall behind a half step in beat.

Her muscles were straining, the air tearing in and out of her lungs like fire. Sweat rolled down her spine, tickling the hot skin there.

Surah slid her right sai through the neck of one Demon while shoving the left sai into another's wing. She portaled to a new position and stars danced behind her eyes before her vision cleared.

She swayed a bit on her feet, and had just barely regained equilibrium before a Fae Guardian swooped down from above, appearing to Surah as if out of nowhere.

When had the Fae gotten here? She had been so distracted that she had not even noticed them coming out of the portal.

Looking around for Tristell, she saw that the coward who called herself a Fae Queen had not bothered to accompany her army—

Surah was knocked to the ground just in time to avoid having her head ripped right off her shoulders by the talons of a

Demon. She hit the earth hard enough to rattle the teeth in her mouth, pain exploding through her shoulder, the breath ripped from her chest.

Blinking, she looked up into familiar emerald eyes, and saw that Charlie was the one who had tackled her. She barely let this thought process before using more magic to portal the two of them to a different, upright position.

When they reappeared a few feet away, Surah was unsteady on her feet.

Charlie gripped her forearms to steady her, concern flashing over his face. Surah saw this and shoved him away, shooting an impressive lightning bolt through the tips of her fingers and striking an oncoming Fae through the heart.

The Fae's body hardly had time to crumple to the earth before Surah did the same to two more.

She was unaware of it, but her face was drained of color, her hair plastered to her forehead, the blood of her enemies dripping from her lips. She was only aware of how tired she was feeling, of how ready she was to just end this whole thing.

And she could, couldn't she? She had enough juice left to do that. She could concentrate all of her power, and all of that borrowed from the Black Stone, to do one last blast, one last big explosion.

She could do that, and kill them all. Kill the whole lot of them the way the humans did with their bombs and missiles.

This had always been an option, though one she'd not truly considered until this moment.

Of course, this would kill her and Charlie as well, and anyone else standing too close to the battlefield, but this would keep that bastard Black Heart from the throne, and the other royals would surely pick up the torch and lead the people into a safe place…

All of this flashed through her mind in an eye blink as she took a tiny moment to absorb the scene around her. While she'd been fighting, her mind had taken on a sort of tunnel vision, but she could see now how terribly outmatched she was.

This thought should have devastated her, but instead, she felt nothing. Nothing but the undeniable need to destroy those who were standing against her, no matter what it took.

So, as the Demons circled and swooped, as the Fae Guardians struck and swiped, as the angry gray sky spat bullets of rain, Surah Stormsong continued to kill and maim.

In her head, she was moments away from completing a spell that would kill them all.

And good Gods damned riddance, she thought.

ARIA

*A*ria Fae stood beside the battlefield, her eyes as wide as saucers, her hands covering her mouth.

She had been trained since childhood by the Peace Brokers for all sorts of things, all types of tense situations, but never in her life had she stood witness to anything such as this.

Rain poured down over her, drenching her clothes and dripping from the ends of her long hair, catching in her lashes. Thunder rumbled like the hungry stomach of a God, and she shivered, though it had nothing to do with the weather.

She had retreated to the top of a small hill overlooking the clearing in which the gaping portal hung. Out of that portal, countless Demons had spilled, followed by Fae Guardians, blades blazing.

All of this was aimed at the Sorceress Queen, and despite all the insane happenings, it was Surah Stormsong that Aria could not pull her eyes from.

She killed so expertly it seemed as though it was what she'd been born to do. This was a conundrum, because when Aria had met Surah earlier she had sensed so much good in the Sorceress Queen.

And Aria was pretty much as good as one could be at reading people. Arrol had not been wrong in saying that Aria had the Touch real strong.

But as she looked at Surah Stormsong now, it was as though a dark entity had possessed her, had ripped free Surah's spirit and replaced it with its own. Her eyes were a terrible, writhing black, her blood-streaked face pulled into a tight grimace.

All throughout Sorcerer Territory, the reactions of those watching were much the same as the Halfling girl's. It was obvious that this thing was going badly no matter who was left standing in the end.

If *anyone* was left standing in the end.

Aria had to do something. Fae Guardians were still spilling out of the portal, joining the many who had already arrived. The body count of Demons and Fae alike was growing by the second.

Everything that crossed through that portal was going to die.

Hands trembling slightly but legs steady, Aria Fae began moving toward the black hole in the sky.

She was going to close that portal, or die trying.

SURAH

She tripped.

She could not believe it, but she tripped.

Her right knee simply buckled without warning, and she stumbled forward, narrowly avoiding the business end of a Fae Guardian's blade.

This small misstep was all it took. There were too many attackers to make any false moves, and in the half heartbeat it took for her to realize this, a Demon was bearing down on her from above. Her brain did not even have the time to consider portaling.

She resumed casting the spell in her head, the spell that would put an end to all of this. As long as her death wasn't immediate, she would be able to finish it in time.

Then a flash of black and blue snapped her thoughts in half.

The Demon that had been bearing down on her was tackled out of the air by Samson, who had not arrived a second too soon.

Surah had thought she was beyond feeling, but her heart swelled briefly at the sight of her tiger, who was tearing apart the Demon he'd taken down with beastly ferocity.

"Miss me, darling?" Sam's voice asked in her head.

Surah found that she couldn't answer. She was too busy staring at all the Great Cats that had seemingly appeared out of thin air, and were now aiding her in killing the Fae and Demons.

Their powerful jaws snapped bone and spine, their growls and hisses adding to the warlike cacophony that was the moment.

Seeing this renewed her strength, but she was still moving too slowly. As if sensing this, Samson moved beside her and crouched. Surah climbed atop her tiger and used more magic to blast at the opposing army.

She was grateful for Sam's arrival, but there was a part of her that wished he had not come, because even with the help of the Great Cats, she wasn't sure it would be enough, and now, if she ended up having to detonate the black magic bomb, Samson and his pride would be blown toward the heavens right along with her and Charlie.

And anyone else standing too close.

51

CHARLIE

His brother's fist smashed into his face hard enough to make his vision go black for several seconds.

Charlie stumbled backward, shaking his head and swiping out blindly with his blade.

Black Heart laughed as he looked at Charlie with the same expression he'd been giving him since they were boys; a cocky sense of superiority that was particular to older brothers.

But a moment later, his laughter dried up, and anger and surprise came over Black Heart's face. Charlie looked around at what had caused the reaction and saw that at some point during the scuffle with his brother, Samson had arrived, and he'd brought with him dozens of Great Cats.

A bit of hope swirled in Charlie at this, and at the same time, despair. They were still terribly outnumbered, and Samson would likely get himself and his kind killed.

This was almost more tragic than the loss of people, because the Great Beasts were already endangered, a dying breed.

Love, Charlie thought, the word piercing through the haze of the battle. *Love can make you do some crazy shit.*

With this on his mind, Charlie flipped the dagger in his hand so that he was gripping the hilt, and before he could second-guess himself, he threw it at his distracted brother's black heart.

And in doing so, broke part of his own.

5 2

ARIA

So many things happened in the handful of moments that came next that it was impossible to take all of it in.

It was like trying to look at a picture that pulled the eye in every direction, a kaleidoscope of chaos that stunned and shocked.

Aria had no time to be distracted. She moved through the fray with the determination of someone privy to all that was at stake. The sheer amount of death that had taken place already was enough to twist her stomach, to bring salty tears to her eyes, which were squinting in the driving rain.

She knew only that she had to reach the portal. If she could reach it, she might be able to use her Fae magic to close it, and keep the rest of the Fae Guardians from being slaughtered in this field, staunching the already high death toll.

The Demons she couldn't care less about, for they were soulless creatures, powered and controlled by only darkness and hate. But every Fae that died here today would only have been following the orders of their crazed queen.

Aria made her way closer, batting away the occasional

Demon that ventured too close with her staff. Her hair whipped around her face as she approached the hole in the sky, from which Fae Guardians were still arriving in twos and threes.

Her heart sank as she realized she was going to do it, to cut off access and in doing so flip her own world upside down.

Because even if Surah did defeat Tristell and Black Heart today, there would be Aria's superiors to answer to, and it was this she feared most of all.

What would the Peace Brokers do when they found out her actions here today? How would they react to her evidence of Tristell's treachery? What would they do with someone who stepped so far beyond their boundaries?

Aria could not even begin to guess at the answer to this, and her mind was made up, anyway.

And there was the chance that her organization would understand. Halflings were known to be Empaths in the strongest sense. As a Fae Halfling and a Peace Broker, she'd been taught that every single life has value, that every life is sacred.

This was why her weapon of choice was a wooden staff rather than a blade. Why she'd been trained to incapacitate and disable, not to kill. Never to kill.

Maybe her people would understand that she was only trying to save lives in closing the portal; Fae, Sorcerer, and Great Cat alike.

Or maybe not.

As she finally reached the portal, she supposed it didn't really matter, anyway.

CHARLIE

Black Heart cried out in rage, and for a moment, Charlie thought that the dagger he'd thrown at his brother's chest had hit home.

Instead, Black Heart batted away the blade as though it were nothing, not even having to touch it, just flicking it away with magic.

The cry of anger Black Heart gave was due to the fact that the portal in the sky letting in the Fae Guardians was closing, cutting off a good percentage of his force.

Charlie did not waste the moment of distraction, he charged his brother and made contact, tackling him to the ground, landing a hard right to Black Heart's jaw that Charlie felt in his own gut.

It terribly wrong to be directing such force at his kin, but there was no way around it. Only one of them would leave this fight alive.

Charlie was knocked back several feet by an invisible blow to his solar plexus, the air whooshing out of his lungs painfully as his brother regained his feet and used more magic to lock Charlie's arms to his sides.

Panic filled him as Charlie found he couldn't lift his arms, couldn't move. Black Heart was holding him magically in place.

"You never could take me without magic," Charlie spat, his heart aching a bit at the thought that these would likely be the last words he spoke to his brother.

Black Heart pushed his dark hair out of his face and swiped at the blood on his lips, his green eyes—the same emerald as Charlie's—as pitiless as a Demon's. He stopped when he reached Charlie and placed a hand on his shoulder.

Charlie tried to shake off the touch, but could not get his muscles to obey, so he only stared at his brother with all the fire he could muster.

Looking down, Charlie saw that Black Heart was holding a sharp knife in his hand, the tip of it resting against the fabric covering Charlie's chest.

"I never wanted it to end like this, Charlie-Boy," he whispered, and as he did so, the hand holding the knife reared up, preparing to drive itself deep into Charlie's chest.

But something struck Black Heart from behind, hard enough to make his eyes widen and his head hunch down between his shoulders. Out of what Charlie was sure had to be pure reflex, his brother turned to see what had struck him.

Black Heart's attention was only diverted for the smallest of moments, but it was enough. Charlie found that he could move again, and before he could change his mind or think about the consequences, he jammed his dagger into his brother's neck, driving it in all the way to the hilt.

There was a moment then when the entire world froze for Charlie Redmine, a moment before the body of his older brother trembled and went limp, a moment before life as he'd known it forever melted away.

Just a heartbeat, really. A heartbeat before he became the murderer of someone who shared his blood.

The *last* someone who shared his blood.

Michael's eyes rolled and met Charlie's, surprise and realization clouding over his face.

In this moment, the noise of all the happenings around them faded away, the cries of those fighting and dying, the howling of the wind, the spattering of the rain.

And for a small slice of time, it was just Michael and him. Just Charlie and his big brother.

Then blood bubbled out of Black Heart's mouth, carrying with it his final words. They were but a whisper, but the sound of them would haunt Charlie's dreams in the days to come.

"Didn't think you had it in you, Charlie-Boy," his brother said.

And then he was gone.

5 4

ARIA

$\mathcal{A}$ ria Fae stood in utter awe as she watched Charlie Redmine drive the dagger she'd given him deep into his brother's neck.

The Sorcerer's scarlet blood sprayed into the open air in a way that Aria found oddly cinematic.

But when some of it splattered over her face, she could only stand where she was and gape. She had saved Charlie's life for a fourth time, if she had counted right, but who could say?

She was frozen to the spot, her mind at a standstill. All the craziness surrounding her melted away, and all she could see was Charlie. The look on his face just then would never really leave her mind.

Watching him kill his brother had been much like watching someone drown a part of their own soul. And her heart hurt for him.

As Aria Fae slipped out of the moment, the world swimming back to her attention, and she looked around the battlefield on which she stood, the bodies of Fae Guardians scattered everywhere, the scorched spots where the Demon's bodies had finally turned to dust, her heart hurt for them all.

Words her mother used to be fond of saying came to her then: *In war, there is no victor.*

Aria could see the truth of this now. She could *feel* the truth of this in her bones.

The thought of her mother brought tears to her eyes, and she blinked to clear them. As she did this, one of the last remaining Demons swooped down on her, and she only had time for her eyes to widen before it reached her.

Then there was a flash of black, and just before the creature could touch her, it was tackled out of the air by one of the largest cats Aria had ever seen. The cat tore at the Demon with razor sharp teeth and claws, flinging bits of it this way and that with a ferocity that was somehow spectacular for the pure nature of it.

The cat was an enormous panther, easily three times the size of any Aria had seen in the human world. Her jaw hung open as she watched the beast tear the Demon to shreds.

As she looked around at the Sorcerer Territory, she realized there was so much about the supernatural world that she knew nothing about having lived with humans most of her life.

In the time it took for this to happen, Aria turned and saw that there were hardly any Demons or Fae left alive, and those that were still alive were either being torn apart by a big cat or skewered by Surah's sais.

Bodies.

Bodies were everywhere.

After a while, as the deaths of all those who'd stood against the Sorceress Queen were ensured, a silence fell.

It was so deep, so complete, that it seemed to Aria as if the earth and the heavens were pausing, and she found that she was having trouble breathing steadily.

Such devastation had a way of wearing at one's soul.

At least it's over, Aria thought.

But then the crazed Sorceress Queen let out a scream of rage that scorched the sky, and Aria realized she'd called it too soon.

271

CHARLIE

Surah's scream of rage was so intense that Charlie looked up from the body of his dead brother.

It pulled him out of the trance that had befallen him, away from the cliff of despair that he had been standing out on.

The battle, it seemed, was over. The portal had been closed. His brother was dead. The Demons he'd been controlling were also dead.

Charlie had crushed the small wooden box that had fallen out of his brother's cloak under his boot, not liking the looks of the thing, and like magic, the remaining Demons had turned to dust that was then washed away by the rain still falling and falling.

That left only the Fae Warriors who had made it through the portal before it closed, and Surah and the Great Cats made short work of them, though Charlie had been too engulfed in his own deeds to notice.

But he noticed now.

The sound that came from Surah was too full of darkness not to capture him, and as he looked into the eyes of the woman he loved, he couldn't seem to find the Surah Stormsong he knew anywhere.

"Who closed the portal?!" Surah screamed, and it was as if the voice had come from an angry goddess, shaking the ground with its force.

Magic flew from her fingers in sputtering sparks, and her face was free of all color, her eyes a swirling black. The Black Stone around her neck throbbed and glowed, its power blanketing her in a darkness through which it was hard to see.

Charlie's heart jumped when Surah approached Aria, stalking over to the Halfling girl with a menace that made Charlie jump between the two.

He held his hands up to the queen, his tongue thick in his throat. "Surah," he said, wary. "Your fight isn't with her."

Without blinking, Surah flicked her wrist, and Charlie was thrown into the air, knocked aside with her magic. He scrambled to his feet as Surah bore down on the girl, his heart sinking in his chest.

To his surprise, now it was Samson who came between Surah and Aria. Charlie couldn't hear what the tiger was saying, but he knew the two of them were communicating in the telepathic way they had.

Whatever Samson told her made her eyes narrow and her hands clench into fists.

For a split second, Charlie thought Surah was going to strike out at Samson, which was so unthinkable it scared him more than he cared to admit.

But then Surah snapped her fingers, blinking out of the battlefield upon which so many of her slain foe lie, portaling out of sight to only Gods knew where, murder clearly on her mind.

SURAH

Charlie was in front of her.

Standing between her and the Halfling girl who had likely closed the portal Surah had opened.

Taking Aria's side. Had he fallen in love with the Halfling while she'd been away, trying to save the kingdom so that they could be together?

It would be just like a man to do so. She flicked her wrist, knocking him out of the way.

If Charlie chose the other side now, that was his folly. Surah was the Sorceress Queen, and she was done playing games. She could not allow traitors to be amongst her, be they Halfling, Sorcerer, or even a man she'd thought she loved.

At this, a small voice within her whispered that she still loved Charlie Redmine, but the ringing in her ears, the anger in her veins, the darkness in her heart, easily drowned it out.

Then, Samson was standing in front of her, his amber cat eyes locked on hers, his familiar voice sounding in her head.

"Leave the girl, my love. You're in the throes of bad magic. You should take off that stone."

Surah's voice was colder than Sam had ever heard it, though she was not aware of this.

"She closed the portal. I could've ended this right here, could have killed them all, but she closed the Gods damned portal."

"You did end it, love... No more death needs to come on this day. Look around, Surah. Enough have died. The girl didn't mean you any harm... You need to take off that stone."

Surah felt a bitterness toward the beast that surprised her, even in her crazed state. Maybe he was right about the Halfling girl, but he was wrong about something else.

More death did need to come on this day.

She told him as much and then blinked out of sight. Black Heart was dead, but there was a certain fairy bitch that still needed dealing with.

And if Surah had to burn the entire Fae Forest to the ground to get to her, then so be it.

This shit would end today.

CHARLIE

"She went to the Fae Forest," Aria said.

She gripped Charlie's arm when he gave no response, and said, "Charlie, we have to go after her. Surah went to the Fae Forest, and she's going to kill everyone in it. We have to stop her."

Charlie heard the words the girl was saying, but he couldn't make sense of them. His mind was too wrapped up in all that had transpired, his body numb in the aftermath.

Aria slapped him across the face hard enough to make his jaw clench. She watched him for a moment, ready to jump out of the way should he retaliate, (which, of course, he would not) and when she saw he wasn't going to, held out her hand.

"We gotta go after your girlfriend, dude," she said.

Charlie saw now that her pretty face was drained of color, and she looked like she might be sick.

"Just open a portal for me," he said. "I'll go."

Aria continued holding out her hand, shook her head, rain-water flicking off the tips of her hair.

"I know there are casualties in war," she said, "but there are children in that forest, Charlie, and if Surah goes on a rampage, they'll be the first to die. I'm coming with you. We have to stop her."

Charlie closed his eyes for the smallest of stolen moments. He cleared his mind, pushing away his doubt and horror and grief at all the things that had happened this day. He wasn't entirely sure how he'd gotten here.

It seemed to him that just yesterday he'd been keeping bar in the countryside, minding his own business.

Now he was here; outside the capital city on a battlefield of dead Fae and more Great Beasts than he'd even known still existed. The woman he loved was insane with dark magic, a danger to all she came near.

He opened his eyes, met the gaze of the Halfling girl. "Just send me, Aria. I'm gonna stop her."

Aria stared at him as if she didn't want to say what she was going to say next, but had to.

"Thousands of Fae children, Charlie," the Halfling girl whispered. "What if you *can't* stop her? What if there's only one way to stop her?"

"I won't let her hurt the children, Aria. I promise," he said, though he knew in his heart that this was not a promise he could make, and the look that came to Aria's face said that she knew this, too.

The truth was, if Charlie couldn't stop Surah, if Charlie couldn't bring her back from the darkness she'd become lost in, then no one in all the realms could do so, and she was lost forever.

He could only hope that his love for her could break the hold black magic had on her, could free her from the chains its hate and vengeance had wrapped around her, as he had done once before in a cave in the jungle.

That day seemed like a million years ago now, as if it had happened in some other lifetime.

And if he could not bring her back, Gods help them all.

Aria opened up a portal, and Charlie was about to step through when a deep voice sounded in his head.

"Bring her back, or don't return at all."

Charlie looked into the amber eyes of Samson, the fur around his mouth covered in gore, his long tail held low.

He nodded at the Great Beast and went after the woman he loved.

5 8

SURAH

Surah moved through the Fae Forest with complete abandon, cutting down the trees, burning down the smaller vegetation with a swirl of her wrist, the fire catching and spreading, smoke filling the warm air.

Searching.

Destroying.

She would burn every bit of this place to the ground if she had to.

"Tristell!" she called, her voice echoing through the trees. "Tristeeeeellll!"

She was met with silence. The only sound that of small creatures scurrying deeper into the woods, the occasional squeal or squawk as the growing flames came too close.

The Fae Queen was a coward. Surah formed a fireball in her hands and launched it at a really tall, really old tree for which she did not know the name, but the puffy leaves that covered its branches went up in flames instantly.

"Tristell!"

Moving forward, she saw them coming through the trees,

and retrieved her sais from their holsters. She eyed the Fae Guardians encircling her, and shook her head in disgust.

"You coward!" Surah called. "You would have me kill the last of your soldiers rather than face me yourself?"

Surah launched her left sai into the chest of one of the Fae Guardians, who dropped dead on the spot. With a flick of her wrist, the weapon was back in her hand.

"That's another one," Surah said, the flames in the trees growing more intense by the moment.

Rather than attacking her now, some of the Fae Guardians were trying to put out the spreading fire.

Surah sheathed her sais and formed another fireball between her hands, launching it at a large tree and staunching any progress the Fae had made at containing the flames.

"I'll burn this entire Territory to the ground, Tristell, and everything and everyone in it!" Surah called out. "You wanted a fight? Now you've got one. Come out and face me, you coward!"

There was a rustle in the trees, and Surah looked up to see the Fae Queen perched on a branch high above her head. Her slanted eyes were burning as brightly as the growing flames around them.

"You foolish Sorceress *bitch*!" the Fae Queen screeched, and as she did so, her enormous feathered wings unfurled on her back. She swooped down at Surah the way a hawk might descend upon a mouse.

Surah rolled out of the way of Tristell's strike, preparing to impale her with her sais from behind.

But the Fae Queen was faster than expected, and she took to her wings again and struck out with the sharp nails on her hands, raking Surah across the eyebrow, drawing blood.

Surah swiped it away with her sleeve as it began to drip into her eye.

Tristell landed on her feet again, standing opposite Surah. The two queens squared off.

"Weak without your magic," Tristell spat. "And even weaker with it. What a worthless species you are. You can't control yourself."

Surah's head was spinning with exhaustion, and her vision went blurry for a moment. She reached up and touched the spot where Tristell had scratched her, and realized that she must have had some sort of poison on her fingertips, because it was getting harder to concentrate, harder to stand.

A moment later, Surah fell to the hard floor of the forest. As she did so, Tristell stood over her, lifting her clawed foot and setting it atop Surah's throat, crushing out the air.

The Fae Queen grinned, her sharp teeth flashing behind red lips. She opened her mouth to say something, but what that something was, Surah would never know.

Because she wasn't completely paralyzed just yet, and Surah used every ounce of strength she could muster to drive her sais into the Fae Queen's stomach, effectively killing Tristell and the unborn child within.

The last thing Surah felt was the warm gush of blood that washed over her hands. The last thing she saw was the shocked looked on Tristell's face.

And the last thing she heard was someone calling her name, but it must've only been in her mind, because it was spoken in the voice of Charlie Redmine.

Then the darkness swallowed her whole.

5 9

CHARLIE

The night dragged on for an eternity, and by the time the sun finally rose over the horizon, Charlie had been convinced a new day would never come.

It was as if time had stood still, drawing out the horrible happenings. It had seemed to him that the rain would never stop, the sky would never lighten, as he sat at Surah's bedside and waited for her to open her eyes. *Prayed to the Gods* that she would open her eyes.

But time was a funny thing, a construct of the mind, not existing outside of consciousness, and it was the part of us that kept going, no matter the circumstances under which we physically and emotionally stood.

The new day had come, the sun beginning to rise with utter accountability, as if all the events of the previous day equated to nothing. Lost in the fabrication of time.

All of these thoughts were just to keep him off the real things he was avoiding pondering. Like the fact that Surah might never wake up. Or how he had stabbed his own brother to death.

The last time Charlie had cried had been as a child. On the day after his parents had died. He remembered because he had promised himself he would not do so ever again, could not take the vulnerability it made him feel. And so he had not shed a tear since, not in over a decade.

And, yet, as he sat here staring at Surah's face, at her still, unresponsive body, thinking about how everything had gone so wrong and could never, ever be put right again, he felt like he could cry. He felt like he could cry until the sun refused to shine.

Someone behind him cleared their throat, and Charlie was jerked out of his thoughts. Turning his head, his body slack in the chair, exhausted by emotion, he saw Bassil, the Warlock, standing in the doorway. He was holding a guitar in his hands.

Charlie turned back the way he'd been facing, didn't respond.

Bassil entered the room and shut the door behind him. He took a seat in the chair beside Charlie's and set the guitar down next to him.

Silence hung while both of them sat looking at the unconscious Sorceress Queen laid out before them. There was a heaviness in the room that one could feel on their shoulders.

Samson was lying at the foot of Surah's large bed, and Charlie had the distinct feeling that the tiger was contemplating eating him, and that maybe that wouldn't be any more painful than what he was feeling now.

"You are not helping her condition, Charlie," said the Warlock, in that deep, calm voice of his. The words were not spoken with any malice, only stated as fact.

Anger boiled up in Charlie with a haste unusual to him. But then, these were not normal circumstances.

"You've already told me that," he snapped. "I don't get what I'm supposed to do."

"Try again," Bassil replied.

"I tried all night!" Charlie yelled.

Samson lifted his head off his paws. Charlie took a deep

breath, trying to calm himself and failing. He managed to lower his voice to a reasonable level.

"I played the song. I played it a thousand fucking times. I poured my heart out, professed my love in a million different ways." His shoulders sank and his voice lowered to a whisper. "And she hasn't woken up. She hasn't batted an eye."

Bassil's face remained relaxed, a small crease in his dark brow the only indication of his worry. "There's someone who's offered to help," he said.

Charlie looked up now as Aria entered the room. Her face was somber, lacking its usual light, and she looked as scared as a mouse entering a cat's lair. With the way Samson was looking at everyone, he supposed this wasn't too far from the truth.

"How can you help, Aria?" Charlie asked, and hated himself for the desperation that rode his words.

He'd already allowed the Halfling girl to give so much, and here she was again.

Aria slowly approached the bed where Surah lie, as if Surah might jump up and bite her at any moment. She rubbed Sam between the ears, and the fact that he let her surprised everyone in the room.

A pained look came over Aria's face as she looked down at Surah. She bit her lower lip so hard Charlie thought it might bleed.

"I'm an Empath," Aria said, her eyes locked on the sleeping Sorceress. "Most Halflings are to some extent, but my ability is stronger than most. We call it *the Touch.*"

She paused, and Charlie stared at her as if she'd spoken some alien language. Like most others, Charlie didn't know much about Halflings, and he'd never heard of an Empath.

"It means I feel what others feel… directly," Aria continued. "I feel the emotions of those near me as strongly as if they were my own." A tear rolled down her cheek and she swiped it away quickly, her gaze still stuck on the Sorceress queen. "And, I can absorb emotions."

Charlie opened his mouth, closed it, and opened it again. He didn't know what to say to this.

Finally, he managed, "Are you saying you can pull the darkness out of her?" he asked, and again hated himself for the hope that filled his voice.

Aria shook her head, and Charlie was simultaneously relieved and despaired.

"Not out of her," she said. "She's under a blanket of magic so thick I can't get through." She looked up now for the first time, her green eyes meeting Charlie's.

"But you," Aria continued, "I can pull some from *you*. I can take away the dark emotions you're feeling right now. They'll come back after a day or so, but I can take them for now."

"Why would I let you do that, Aria?" Charlie said. "Why would I want to subject you to this? You've already done so much. I can't ever repay you."

Aria smiled sadly, more tears spilling down her face, but her shoulders squared and set. She gestured at Bassil.

"Because the Warlock tells me that love is the only thing that's powerful enough to fight black magic," she said, "and you can't produce the amount of love needed to save her with all the guilt and heartache you're feeling over your brother."

She paused, took a deep breath, wiped the tears from her face, and held out her hand to him. "So let me take it, and then you can play a song for us."

Charlie looked at the girl, thinking that if he ever had a daughter, he hoped she was just like this generous, kind-hearted Halfling girl.

"I don't know if you understand what you're offering," he told her. "I've never felt pain like I'm feeling now."

Aria let out a slow breath. "I'm an Empath, Charlie, and even though I've only lived for seventeen years, trust me when I say that being an Empath comes with its own special kind of torture. I'm no stranger to emotional pain. We've actually become something like old friends."

The way in which Aria said this left no room for question. A deep voice filled Charlie's head, the first words from the tiger since Charlie had jumped into the portal to get Surah out of the Fae Forest.

"Do it," Samson told him, also leaving no room for question. There seemed to be an unspoken *or I'll eat you* attached to the words.

Charlie looked at Surah, then back at Aria, and took her outstretched hand.

"I owe you one," he told her.

Aria grinned, that glow that was so natural to her appearing for a moment before dying back out. "Actually, you owe me five, but who's counting?"

6 0

SURAH

She was floating, surrounded by nothing, lost in the darkness.

There was no sound, no light, no smells.

She was aware of only the pain, the anger, the terrible monster that was eating at her mind. She was bodiless, just a consciousness with no way of healing itself.

Screaming silently. Crying without tears.

And she would be here forever. Wherever *here* was. There was no escape, no entrance or exit. There was only the void. The void and the agony. An eternity of it.

There was no way to calculate how much time passed, no such thing as time in this place that was not a place. Her soul was dispersed in the ether, broken down to the raw thoughts that had made her who she was. Who she'd been…

When the music came to her. It came slowly, note by note. At first, she was not sure at all it was even there, or if her mind was so far gone that every experience was a construct of it.

But it kept playing, and eventually grew louder. A melody she felt she'd heard somewhere before, in some distant lifetime on some distant plane.

Then it was all she could hear, and she latched onto the sound of it, afraid to let it go. More afraid than she'd ever been.

A voice accompanied the melody. A deep, soft, *familiar* voice. Just a humming, really. A humming that sounded like home.

But she had no home. She was nothing. Just a consciousness floating free in the vast universe, a dying star shooting across a black sky.

Charlie, she thought, and held tight to the name that reached her through the darkness, surfacing in this galaxy of despair like a life raft in an angry sea.

* * *

SURAH'S EYELIDS FLUTTERED, and the first thing that registered was the soreness of every single muscle in her body.

A familiar voice filled her head, and it sounded more relieved than she had ever heard it.

"Oh, thank the Gods," Samson said. *"I was getting ready to eat your boyfriend."*

"Sam," Surah said, but her voice came out a rough whisper. Her throat felt like it was on fire.

Sam's black and blue head appeared over her, his amber eyes staring at her as if he'd feared he'd never see her again. *"Don't ever scare me like that again."*

Surah replied silently, the method easier than speech at the moment. *"You came back."*

"Did you ever doubt I would?"

She pulled herself up to a seated position, wrapping her arms around her tiger and noticing for the first time that they were not alone in her room.

The music she'd heard had stopped, and Charlie sat beside the bed with a guitar across his lap and a stunned look on his handsome face.

Bassil and Aria were also here, and they too looked slightly shocked, if a touch wary.

Surah felt as though she had not seen any of them in ages, and her heart settled slowly down to her feet as the memories of the past day came flooding back to her.

Then she was crying, the tears falling from her eyes in rivers, all the things she'd stored up for when it was all over bursting free and wracking her body. The others sat with their heads down, tears filling their eyes as well.

She supposed they had won, but at what cost? Was there ever really a victor in war? Surah was sure now that there was not.

Aria broke the silence first, and Surah noticed that the girl was not glowing in the way she usually did. Her face was drawn with grief.

Aria wandered over to the doors of the balcony, and as she looked out, her breath caught in her throat. When she turned back to face Surah, some of the light had returned to her pretty face.

"You should come see this, your majesty," said the Halfling girl, to whom Surah would later learn she owed her life.

Aria turned back to the glass doors, holding her hand up as if touching something only she could see. "It's beautiful," she whispered.

Charlie helped Surah out of bed, and Bassil held the door open as they all stepped out onto the balcony.

Below, thousands of Sorcerer people stood holding candles. They lined the streets of the city, overflowed into the fields beyond, so many of them that it seemed nearly everyone in the entire Territory had come.

When they caught sight of their queen, they erupted into cheers.

6 1

SURAH

Surah hated goodbyes, but at the same time, understood the importance of them.

She was grateful for them, because she had lost so many loved ones in her life without ever getting a chance to say good-bye, and knew from experience that this hurt even worse.

Still, she wouldn't be able to hold back her tears much longer, and she didn't want Sam to see her cry. She knew he had to go, and didn't want to make it any harder for him.

"Will I get to see you?" she asked. *"Will you visit?"*

"Whenever I can," he promised.

The two of them sat in a private courtyard atop the roof of one of the castle's turrets. Night had fallen, and to the east, she could see the glow of dozens of amber eyes in the darkness, knew they were waiting for their king to return with them to the jungle.

"What's it like, being King of the Beasts?" she asked. "I didn't know there was such a thing."

Sam was silent for a moment, regarding the stars. *"I suppose it's similar to being a Sorceress Queen. Lots of cats depending on me. Dealing with threats to my authority, making decisions. I've watched you rule for so long, I can only hope some of your ways have rubbed off on me."*

Surah had to breathe deeply to keep the tears at bay. She didn't want him to go. She wished so badly he could stay.

"They followed you into battle… How did you get them to do that?"

Sam licked her hand, his tongue warm and rough, and nuzzled his head against her neck.

"They would've followed me, anyway. I'm their king, but since our jungle is in Sorcerer Territory, I explained to them what it could mean if the Fae invaded. Your family has always been respectful of the jungles and the Great Beasts. Other two-legs would have long since destroyed our habitat, and our kind would likely be extinct. I told them it was also our Territory we were fighting for. And that wasn't a lie."

"Thank you, Sam," she whispered, running her fingers through his fur for what felt like the last time.

He said he would visit, but the truth was, he was leaving her. When she awoke in the morning, he would not be by her side. When she shut her eyes tonight, Sam would shut his elsewhere.

They were parting ways, and though she'd always known this day would eventually come, she never could have prepared for it.

When he left, Samson would take a part of Surah with him, and she would hold a part of him.

"Thank you for loving me despite it making no sense at all," she told him.

If a tiger could smile, Sam would have been doing so just then. *"As if I had a choice in the matter,"* he replied.

Surah took another deep breath, the air shuddering in her chest. "You need to go now, don't you?"

Sam didn't answer. They both knew he did. She grabbed his large head in her hands and kissed his furry face. His amber eyes closed as she did so and a low chuffing sounded in his chest.

When he pulled away from her, she could see the reluctance on his face, and she nodded so that he would know he could go. The sooner, the better. She really didn't want him to see her cry.

Surah watched as the Great Tiger slipped gracefully off the turret top, onto a stone ledge below, and in through a window. Moments later, he emerged on the edge of the field, his tail swishing as he took his leave.

She waited until she saw his amber eyes glowing in the distance toward the east.

The other cats slipped away silently into the night, but Sam stood staring back at her for a long time, as if he could sense her tears all the way from there.

And then he, too, slipped away.

A sob shook her chest and she let the tears come, seeing no reason to fight them.

"You okay?" said a deep voice behind her, a slight country lilt riding the words.

Surah turned her head and looked at Charlie, whose handsome face was more than lovely in the moonlight. It had been a terribly long day for both of them. There had been funerals, council meetings, and addresses to the public; all the stuff that went into ruling a kingdom.

And the two of them had lost so much.

"Of course I am," Surah said, though they both knew it to be a lie. She looked back out over her Territory, so quiet and peaceful, the clear night allowing every star in the sky to be seen.

His arms slipped around her from behind, and the warmth of him sparked a fire in her stomach, a heat in her chest that only he could ignite. He held her close to him, his strong body a perfect match to her own.

"Will *you* be okay, Charlie?" she asked him.

Charlie took her hands and spun her around to face him. His

fingers rested against her cheek, as if he almost didn't believe she was real.

Without saying a word, his eyes told her so much, his feelings for her radiating out of them. They had risked everything to be together, had defeated all the odds, for this moment right here.

Surah's heart, though battered, felt fuller than it had ever felt, as if it may just burst right out of her chest. There was sadness over all that had transpired, yes, but there was also love.

And when Charlie leaned down and kissed her, the whole world melted away, leaving only the two lovers who had managed to rearrange the stars.

When they were able to separate, Surah asked, "Do we get to live happily ever after now, Charlie?"

He pulled her close, and she rested her head against his strong chest, listening to the steady beating of his heart.

He said, "Yes, Surah Stormsong. I think we get to try."

And this, as it turned out, was good enough for her.

ABOUT THE AUTHOR

H. D. Gordon is the author of several fantasy series with strong female leads. She is the mother of two amazing daughters, and a lover of nature.

She believes our actions have ripple effects, and in the interconnectedness of all things.

H. D. spends her time with family, eating desserts, and taking strolls through the forests of New Jersey.

For more information visit:
www.hdgordonbooks.com

ALSO BY H. D. GORDON

The Alexa Montgomery Series

Blood Warrior

Half Black Soul

The Rise

Redemption

Heiress of Magic Trilogy

Born of Magic

Thief of Magic

Throne of Magic

The Aria Fae Series

The Halfling

The Masked Maiden

The Blue Beast

The Haunted Hero

The Demon's Deal

The Wolf Wars Series

Moon Burned

Moon Broken

Moon Born

Moon Battle

The Blood Pack Trilogy

Moon of Fire

Moon of Shadows

Moon of Curses

Academy of Witchcraft

The Awakening

The Summoning

9 798742 082675